Best (
Niki B

The Keys
to Love

A Florida Keys Novel

MIKI BENNETT

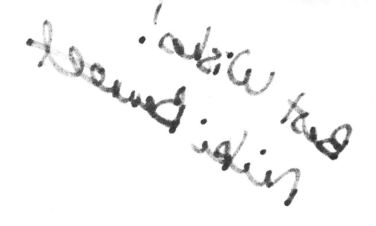

First Edition

ISBN: 0998848107
ISBN 13: 9780998848105
Library of Congress Control Number: 2017902588
WannaDo Concepts Publishing
Charleston, South Carolina

Dedicated with love to
my parents, Sonny and Irene

* * *

"Hi there, sweetie. Me and...what was your name, again? Oh, that's right—Maddy. We were just having a little girl talk. Now you've ruined the mood." She put on a ridiculous pouting face. Maddy had never before beheld a woman with such evil intent. She could read between the lines of everything Andrea was doing, and she knew Jason could see it too.

"Andrea, this little issue is between you and me. Maddy has nothing to do with it, and you will not bother her anymore. Do I make myself perfectly clear?" Jason's voice was as hard as stone. To Maddy, he sounded like a different man.

"But darling, that is where you're wrong. Just like I was telling your girlfriend here before you walked in the door, she's dating *my* husband, and she just went on a trip with *my* husband. Don't you think that will sound just lovely in a court of law?" Andrea stood there, facing him with a sickening smile.

"Andrea, you will leave now before I call the police for trespassing. I will not put Maddy through this, and you will not bother her again. Do you understand?" Jason sounded menacing now.

Maddy was still standing there as if watching a scene out of a movie. It was so surreal. Even worse, though—everything suddenly went black.

* * *

1

The train's rocking motion had almost put her to sleep. Maddy had caught the 5:00 a.m. train out of Charleston, South Carolina, and for someone who seemed to be tired all the time, getting up early enough to get to the station on time was a huge accomplishment. But her excitement kept her awake the entire morning from the moment she'd stepped aboard the Amtrak Silver Service train headed south to Florida. She was on her way, by herself, to the Florida Keys for a month! As she swayed back and forth with the movement of the train, she suddenly realized that what had seemed an impossible dream only a few months ago was now becoming a reality. There was nothing to be done now but relax and watch the sunny Florida scenery pass by.

Spending some time away alone was something she had been contemplating for a while. Because of the many changes in her life recently, the thought of running away from it all had a certain appeal. She needed a break, especially now, from the overwhelming circumstances she had faced over the years. A twenty-five-year marriage that had failed two years ago. And all of her efforts to help her lovely daughter, Hope, who'd had type 1 diabetes since she was an infant.

Next in the flow of stressful circumstances had been her recent diagnosis of a rare chronic disorder, Mastocytosis. This illness left her at times with allergic type reactions that would land her in the emergency room requiring immediate medications to keep it from escalating to a life or death situation. Luckily she'd found a caring, smart doctor who took the time to listen to the list of Maddy's nearly lifelong symptoms, and she finally had some answers that would help her start to feel better and heal.

After Hope married and moved into a home of her own, Maddy no longer needed the large house that had become hers alone in the divorce settlement, so she'd sold it six months ago. Maddy had felt a little empty and displaced when she'd walked out of her former home and all of its memories that last time, but she knew it was the right thing to do. She was going to live with her parents temporarily. All of these changes, from long ago, down through the years, to just recently, played havoc with her emotions, making her feel like she was on a never-ending roller coaster. Intuition told Maddy it was time for a break from reality. She needed time to rest. Time to sort out what had happened over the years. Time to deal with the feelings that had accompanied everything that had occurred.

Yet it was also time to make a new plan for her future. Maddy had always been a planner, but right now she felt as if she were being tossed to and fro like a leaf on a windy day, directionless. Then one morning two months ago, she awoke with an inspiration. She'd go away on a trip for a month or so, to one of her favorite places: the Florida Keys.

She had loved the Keys from the moment she had crossed the bridge from the Florida mainland over to Key Largo on that very first trip all those years ago when she was still married and Hope had just turned fourteen. They had taken a vacation and traveled down to visit Riley, who'd been Maddy's best friend since kindergarten. Just two years before that summer vacation, Riley and her husband, Carter, had moved to Islamorada in the Keys with their three children. Maddy and her family had stayed with them for five glorious days, and she remembered how much she'd loved everything about the islands: the water, the ocean breeze, and all the little beaches dotting the edges of the Keys as well as the laid-back atmosphere that seemed to be the way of island life. She especially remembered the wonderful day they'd spent in the city of Key West. When Maddy got back home after the trip, she couldn't help being secretly envious of Riley and her idyllic life in Florida. Then, after the divorce, Maddy's sweet parents realized that Maddy and Hope were in dire need of some relaxation and took them back to the Keys as a surprise. They left Maddy at Riley's door and took Hope with them to explore the islands, leaving Maddy and Riley to spend some quality time together. It was exactly what she'd needed—the trust and familiarity of a best friend for encouragement and also a shoulder to cry on. So when she hatched this escape plan of hers, the first and only destination she thought of was the Keys.

To make sure her family, especially her parents, didn't worry, Maddy decided to get her trip completely arranged first and only then let them know about it. If she already had the answers to the million questions that were sure to come up, she hoped the resistance to her idea would be minimal. As a first step, she found a small rental cottage on the water, complete with a dock, located on Riley and Carter's street. This would negate the objection that she wouldn't know anyone if she needed help. Also, it was close to a medical center should she need assistance, and a Walgreens drugstore for her prescription medications was just around the corner. So the questions that would most likely come from her mom could be checked off the list. Since she was staying in a house instead of a hotel, she could prepare her own meals and eat the foods that were safe for her and wouldn't trigger a reaction. She knew from her previous trips that her favorite grocery store, Publix, the same grocery chain where she bought most of her safe foods at home, was right down the road from the cottage. Traveling to her destination would have to be by train—being cooped up in an airplane with recirculated air and potential chemical triggers was not an option, and her neck and back would not be very happy with a twelve- to fourteen-hour driving trip. On the train, she could relax and stretch out, even though the close quarters meant situations that could set off a reaction were possible. It would be a lot easier, though, to get medical attention if needed when on the ground than while flying through the air.

Riley would be meeting Maddy at the train station in Miami and would drive Maddy's rental car down to

Islamorada, allowing her an additional hour of rest. As for paying for her little retreat, that would come out of the savings account she had established after the sale of the house. Thankfully, her parents had instilled in her at a young age the value of being debt-free whenever possible, and now that lesson was serving her well. She had no debt; the income from her investments and her disability check were sufficient for her to live on and would now allow her to take some time away from the stress and the current reality of her life. She hoped this would be the start of a healing process for her, both physically and mentally.

She decided to spring the idea of her trip about two weeks before her scheduled departure during one of the regular family dinners they had every couple of weeks or so. Since their family was large, with many aunts, uncles and cousins along with their friends, these mealtime get-togethers were special and allowed everyone to share their latest news. Rather than compete with the raucous conversation at the table, Maddy waited until after they had finished eating to pull her parents and her daughter aside and tell them about her planned trip to the Keys. And she'd been right. Every question she'd anticipated came flying at her like bees to honey. But she was prepared, and by the end of the conversation, while they weren't as excited as she was about it, they accepted the fact that she was going. Truth be known, Maddy suspected they were a little happy for her. However, her mom had asked one question that continued to occupy her mind even after she had left the family gathering.

"Madison, are sure you want to do this? There are so many places much closer to home where you can get away to be by yourself, and I promise we won't bother you." There was concern in her voice as she sat next to Maddy on the family couch, holding her hand. She always used Maddy's full name when she was worried or upset.

"I do, Mom. I can't say that I'm not a little apprehensive. My whole life I've always traveled with someone: you and dad, then Greg and Hope. I've never just been away by myself—making my own decisions without worrying whether I'm pleasing someone or everyone. As selfish as this may seem, I want to put myself *first* for just a little while. I made sure that I did all the planning and research so you guys would know I didn't just make a rash decision. By choosing the Keys and staying so close to Riley and Carter, I wanted to make you especially feel better about my trip." Maddy could tell that her mother was worried already, but she could also see from her eyes that she, out of everyone, would be her biggest supporter on this adventure of hers.

Her mother's question was still bouncing around in her head when she went to bed that night. As she'd already admitted to her mother, she was concerned about going somewhere alone. It seemed as if she'd always been with someone, especially now after being diagnosed with this illness. Maddy had been through several reactive events with her illness having to call 911, something that had unnerved her. But she wanted to find a way to live and embrace her new "normal." She wasn't going to let this disease take over her life. Nor was she going to let the other stressful issues she had experienced keep her from the life she desired. She felt that going away to the Keys was a step in the right direction—it would give her time to seek clarity, to take the next healing steps toward reclaiming the life she wanted, to give her a break from the realities of the world at home.

But the burning question in her mind now was: What kind of life do I *really* want? She knew that coming to accept the circumstances and the life changes that had troubled her over the years was crucial. The first of these had been navigating a stressful marriage to a man who was so self-centered it felt like they were roommates instead of husband and wife. Next was becoming a mom to a beautiful baby girl who would need her constant, vigilant attention because of her diabetes. But now Hope was married to a wonderful man named Shawn who adored her, and helped her manage her disease. This had at least put Maddy's mind at ease on this front. But then had come her own long, drawn-out divorce and all the hurt associated with the fact that her husband had no desire to try to make the relationship work after twenty-five years of being together. He just wanted out, and nothing she did or said, none of her efforts to make things better, made any difference. Topping everything off was the rare condition she suffered with, misdiagnosed for so many years until finally she received her true diagnosis. Now she at least had a starting place on her healing journey. The mystery of what was causing her to feel so bad physically, what was bringing on weird, sometimes serious reactions out of nowhere and leaving her ill for days, had been solved. All these challenges and changes were part of her past. Now that she was single again, Maddy knew that it was time to figure out the next stage of her life. She finally had a chance to take care of herself, to put herself first on her calendar. She was starting from scratch, and it felt like she was discovering herself all over again.

Maddy wanted to find out what excited her most in life, what made her eager and enthusiastic about getting up each morning—the activities, places, and things that made her heart sing. What truly made her happy. She had been doing some soul-searching and had started thinking about what had captivated her as a child, and her love for art and the ocean were the first things that came to mind. When it came time to pack for her trip, she made sure to include a journal so that she could record her thoughts and ideas about all the deep questions that lived inside of her. She also made sure to include a blank watercolor book, paints, and brushes, the means of once again giving expression to her love of art. A camera was also a must-have for the journey; the pictures she took would both inspire her paintings and record this little getaway of hers. This time spent alone would help her figure out what she wanted in her life now. And that was worth some of the uncomfortable feelings she might have had that night after talking to her family. As she fell asleep, her confidence returned because she knew deep in her heart that this trip was the right next step for her.

2

Riley was doing her best to wait patiently for Maddy's train to arrive. The prospect of having her best friend with her for a *whole month* was beyond exciting! They had been practically joined at the hip since they were four years old in kindergarten. All through their school years, from elementary to high school, everyone would joke that if Riley was around, Maddy was sure to be close by, and vice versa. They had been there for each other through bad gossip, lost boyfriends, and even attendance at separate colleges, and none of these events had dampened their friendship. Riley had been Maddy's maid of honor at her wedding, and Maddy had been Riley's matron of honor just two years later. Even their children were only a few years apart in age. Then Riley's husband had been offered a position at a firm in Islamorada, and the thought of ending their closeness was the hardest thing in the world for both of them. Vowing this separation would not change their friendship, they made a pact to always give it priority, even if they could only talk on the phone or write letters. And they'd never faltered. When texting became available, they both burned through their messaging limits very quickly. The advent of FaceTime was a real boon—they had standing dates twice a week for a virtual face-to-face chat, and everyone in both families knew not to violate the figurative Do Not Disturb sign on the door during these times—unless someone was bleeding, of course! Maddy had only been to visit Riley twice since her move, but Riley, who was able to travel more frequently, would come to Charleston as often as she could. Riley had been there when Maddy received the news about Hope's diabetes and the meticulous care she would need. She had also supported her through her divorce, and now she was helping Maddy navigate the choppy waters of this rare disease. Riley truly counted her blessings that she hadn't had to go through what Maddy'd had to, but she was very glad that she had been able to offer support to her best friend through these difficult times.

To say she was thrilled about Maddy's trip and month-long stay was an understatement. She'd been beside herself when Maddy called to tell her of her planned vacation in the Keys and had started making a list of all the things they could do while she was here. Then Carter gently reminded her of two things: First, Maddy was coming for rest and relaxation, something she desperately needed, and sightseeing all over the Keys from sunrise to sunset might not be Maddy's intention for this trip. Second, even though she worked from home, Riley did have a job. So, as reluctant as she was to admit it, she knew Carter was right on both counts. But it was hard to imagine not spending every moment she could with her best friend, because it had been so very long since they'd had some girl time together. Now that their children were grown, she felt this trip of Maddy's could be turned into a grown-up version of a sleepover! But she had to keep in mind the reasons Maddy was coming to South Florida: to leave the stress behind for just a little while and give herself some space to make decisions about the next phase of her life. Riley had offered Maddy the spare room at their house, but she had insisted on renting her own place. Riley knew just the house. It was at the end of her street, and she was glad she'd been able to help Maddy secure the rental. It was a beautiful little cottage right on the water, with a dock and everything! She and Carter were actually friends with the owners, a really sweet couple who owned several rental properties in the area. They often came to the parties that the neighborhood had about once a month. When Riley told them about Maddy and what she had been through, they'd offered to rent the house to her for the entire month at a price that couldn't be beat. Thrilled, Maddy had sent the money via FedEx the very next day. Only four houses would separate the two best friends.

Another reason she was glad Maddy would be spending her vacation in this particular house was that Riley knew just about everyone in the neighborhood. Because of the laid-back manner of living in the Keys, neighbors got to know each other very well, and they were always cooking up something to do together—from boat cruises and shopping excursion to relaxed get-togethers by the water. Riley loved her little neighborhood family and couldn't wait to show it off to Maddy—and for everyone to meet the best friend she always talked about. Every one of Riley's childhood tales included Maddy in some form.

But there was one person Riley wasn't too familiar with: the gentleman who lived in the house at the end of the street, right across from where Maddy would be staying. He seemed to keep to himself and had only been a resident in the neighborhood for about nine months. She did know, though, that he was renting the house, and she always made sure he was invited to the neighborhood social events. In fact, that's how she'd first met this very handsome man. His name was Jason Burnett; he was tall and tanned, and he had dark brown hair and the manners of a gentleman even if he had come across as distant. If pressed to guess his age, she probably would have said he was in his forties, but he certainly didn't look it. Riley had by chance seen him in the front yard one day without his shirt, and she couldn't help but stare. To say he was well built was putting it mildly—his toned muscles rippled with every move. She was glad nobody had been around to catch her staring at him! From that point on, she'd found it hard to talk to Jason without remembering that day. Their conversations were always short but very polite. Riley almost felt at times that he didn't want to be bothered but she wanted him to know that he was always welcome to the neighborhood get-togethers, yet he never attended. She couldn't wait to tell Maddy about her sexy neighbor across the street. This juicy piece of news made her feel like she was in high school all over again. Even though this man could make every woman take a second look, she had her Carter, and he'd made her one of the happiest women alive.

She certainly didn't have any interest in this man for herself, but she couldn't help but admit that he sure was nice to look at.

Maddy could feel the train slowing down as it approached Miami, its final stop. As the conductor made the arrival announcement, the excitement she'd felt that morning bubbled back up to the surface. She was here! Well, she wasn't quite at her little getaway house, but she knew who would be waiting for her on the train platform: Riley! Despite some people's warnings that once they were "grown up," their friendship would fade, it hadn't—not a bit. It was just as strong now as it had been when they'd met in school, even stronger, actually, now that they had been through some of life's ups and downs. Maddy had told Riley that she could make the trip from Miami to their house by herself, but both Carter and Riley had insisted that they meet her at the train station. They could help her with her luggage, and Riley would do the driving back to the house since Maddy would already have had a long travel day. Maddy knew that was Riley just being herself, and she couldn't help but love her for it. So she had agreed to the arrangement and now was secretly glad they would have that ride to the Keys together so they could talk, just the two of them.

Maddy picked up her handbag and carry-on tote, and as she stepped off the train she began looking for her personal greeting party. She saw no one she recognized. Just as she turned around one more time to look for her friend, Riley ran into her so hard that their foreheads smacked together.

"Ow! Thanks for my Florida greeting!" Maddy said with a huge smile as she rubbed the sore spot on her head. But

Riley just hugged her up and said, "I'm so glad you're finally here. I was beginning to think the train got lost or something because it seems like we've been waiting here *forever*! How was the ride?"

"A little bumpy, but I think I did pretty good. Can tell it's gonna take me a few minutes to get my land legs back," she remarked as she started walking with Riley toward the luggage pick-up area with Carter falling in behind them. Her legs *were* a little wobbly, and she seemed to have just a slight bit of vertigo, but she was confident it would quickly pass.

"Hi Carter," Maddy said, looking back at him over her shoulder with a happy smile. "I would give you a hug, but someone has such a grip on my arm that I can't turn around. Consider yourself hugged!" and she blew him a little kiss.

Carter smiled. "I expected as much, so I just stayed out of harm's way." Maddy laughed and Riley just rolled her eyes. She'd certainly hit the jackpot with Carter, Maddy thought. He was sweet and caring, and he loved her best friend. Their relationship confirmed to Maddy that real love did still exist. Even though her own marriage had ended in divorce, she had a beautiful daughter, testimony that there had been love at one time. And as she watched Riley and Carter together, she hoped that one day she would find her own true soul mate just as they had found each other.

"So how many pieces of luggage are we looking for, and did you mark them with a ribbon like I suggested?" Riley asked as she surveyed all the suitcases being lined up for pickup.

"Let's see, *Mom*, I brought three. They are all large—chocolate brown with teal fabric handles. I decorated them myself using Mod Podge and this great tropical fabric I had stashed away. They should be very easy to spot." Riley rolled her eyes again, but this time the look was directed right at Maddy.

"You decorated the handles?"

"I was just trying to help—and look, it worked!" she exclaimed, pointing to the first bag she'd easily spotted. The other two were close by, so they each grabbed a colorfully handled case and headed to the Miami airport to pick up Maddy's rental car. It wasn't long before the silver compact with Riley at the wheel and Maddy happily ensconced in the passenger seat followed Carter's sedan out of the parking lot and headed south toward the Keys. It was already dark; Maddy wished she had arrived during the day, because she loved the feeling that came over her when she saw the aqua-blue highway dividers on the bridges crossing over into the Keys. It was like stepping into another world.

"Well, this is a record for you," Riley laughed as they traveled down Highway 1.

"What do you mean?" Maddy looked puzzled. She had no clue what Riley was referring to.

"Your luggage! Only three bags? Hell, I remember our trips in high school and college. Four suitcases minimum, and that was on a short trip!"

Maddy started laughing, because Riley was so right. "We were a tiny bit excessive back then, weren't we? I remember I felt like I had to bring my entire closet, so afraid that I would leave the perfect shirt or pair of shorts at home. My dad would get so frustrated that I thought he was going to strangle us! That all seems so long ago. Well, now that I'm a big girl, I figured that if I forgot anything, I'd just buy what I need or come borrow it from you. The main thing was bringing my medications, camera, and sketchbook with pens and pencils. Those items are on my 'must have' list nowadays."

"So, tell me and don't hold back. How are you feeling?"

"Right now I'm pretty tired. The trip was long, but I tried to rest as much as I could on a swaying train. But the excitement of coming here made that a wee bit difficult. Did have to take some Benadryl for the trip, but I expected that. The best thing is that I didn't have to wear a mask, because I had a small little area all to myself." Maddy hated wearing a breathing mask, which was necessary for her if she were going to be close to chemicals or the occasional person who'd decided to bathe in cologne. Her mask was with her arsenal of medications just in case she needed something in a hurry.

"I'm not talking about the trip here. I mean *how are you really doing*?" Riley emphasized.

"Glad to be here. So much has happened within the last few years, and suddenly I feel like everything has caught up with me. I thought I was handling it all very well, you know? In a way I guess I am, but something just feels off inside. Good Lord, I sound like I'm a crazy or something."

"You are sounding kinda deep, but certainly not crazy. You *have* been through a lot. But you know you can always talk to me. What are best friends for?" Riley looked over at Maddy and smiled.

"You're right, and that's why I thought of you when I decided to get away for a while. That and I just love it down here. Two trips to the Keys were never enough, but I could never find a good time to come back. Something always seemed to get in the way. Money, illness, work—you name it. But things have settled down a bit now, and that's why I decided this was the perfect time for a month away. To just figure out what I want to do with my life now. Plus, I know exploring these islands is just what I need to relax and unwind. To give me some time to just think. The times I've been here before, the trips were so quick I barely had time to do that."

"As long you don't overdo it."

"Now you sound like my mom again! And I did make her a promise this morning before I boarded the train that I would take it easy and not overdo it. She in turn promised not to bug me with daily phone calls, which is pretty unusual for her. Then she tucked some money into my hand and told me to have fun," Maddy said, smiling at the memory.

"I've always loved your mom, and still do. She loves and cares for everyone, no matter what. Not many people like her anymore," Riley said thoughtfully, and Maddy knew what she was thinking about. Riley's childhood had been a tangled web of divorced parents who detested each other, shuffling her and her little brother back and forth between homes every other weekend. When Carter got the job in the Keys, she'd told Maddy she was glad to be moving away, because even though she loved both of her parents, the impact on her of their hatred for each other was stress she could do without. Maddy could tell through their phone calls then FaceTime chats over the years that since her move here to the islands, Riley had finally healed from her past. Maddy hoped that this trip would be the start of a new healing journey for herself as well.

The hour-long ride to Islamorada went by quickly. They chatted nonstop as though they were on one of their daily Internet calls, sometimes laughing so hard they'd have tears in their eyes. Even though Maddy was so tired, she felt wonderful. To laugh and to be with her best friend was a type of medicine that money couldn't buy.

"Tomorrow night it is dinner at my house. I already have food you can eat, so no need to bring your own. I know that must be a pain in the ass sometimes. And this weekend we're hoping to put together a neighborhood barbecue, where you'll be able to meet most of the neighbors. As of right now, everyone is coming except your neighbor across the street. He seems nice, but he pretty much keeps to himself. Not sure if he has moved in for good or just staying temporarily, because he's renting that house month to month," Riley said. "But this I do know. That man is hot! Good looking and built! I got lucky enough to see him once shirtless and in shorts. Wow—just wow!" Even though it was quite dark in the car, Maddy could see the huge grin on Riley's face.

"Um, you do remember you're a married gal, right?" Maddy peered over at her with both eyebrows arched high.

"Just because I have a ring on my finger doesn't mean I can't appreciate Mr. Burnett's almost perfect physique."

"I thought you just said he was a mystery man. How do you know his name?"

"Remember—Neighborhood Watch president here. Had to introduce myself when he moved in. Too cute! And I've seen no women at his house."

Maddy rolled her eyes. "Well, at least I know the neighborhood is safe with you at the helm. You seem to know *everyone* in your little Keys town."

"That's what makes it fun and relaxing. I just love living here!" Riley said with a contented sigh.

3

Before she knew it, Riley was turning onto her street—and Maddy's for the next month, for that matter. Though Maddy was by now very tired and hungry, she felt revived excitement at nearing the end of her long journey. Because Maddy was a friend of hers, the owners of the house had left the keys with Riley instead of the special place at the front door usually reserved for late-night arrivals. The cottage was fully supplied with everything Maddy would need, except food, but because of her unusual condition, Maddy had brought her own linens and towels. She had already planned a shopping trip to the local Publix tomorrow to get her fridge and kitchen cupboards stocked up, but tonight would be a minimum amount of work: just change the sheets, take a shower, eat a snack, swallow two of her necessary pills, and climb into bed.

As they pulled up to the house that was to be her home for the next month, pure joy swept through Maddy. She had done it! She was here, about to enter the little house she had looked at daily on the Internet for the last two months. Though the details of the little sea cottage were mostly obscured by the darkness, Maddy felt a sense of accomplishment that she had come this far on her planned journey. She had taken that all-important first step and had followed through on her plan.

A little porch light illuminated the way to the front door, which was on the second level of the home. She had been somewhat concerned about this—she would need to climb at least eighteen steps to get into the house. But she had ultimately overcome her uneasiness, telling herself it would not be a problem, that she would take it slow. But then she thought of the three heavy suitcases and her tote bag. Ugh! But Maddy knew that between herself and Riley, they could do this. Had her best friend not been with her, that would have been another situation altogether, one she didn't even want to think about.

"We are officially here at your home away from home!" Riley announced in a regal voice. "I'll take the bags up, so you go ahead and check out the house," she said, handing the keys to Maddy.

"I can help carry the bags up, too."

"You're already breaking your promise to me. You've had an extra long day, and the last thing you need is to haul these big-ass suitcases up those steps," Riley said, pointing at the front of the house.

"Riley, I'm not a China doll made of glass. I won't break. I might have to go slow, but I can do things. I promise!"

"I know that, but please be careful, ok? I just got you here, and I want you to have a good time, not spend it inside the house ill because you were too stubborn and refused help. I know you're tired, so let me do most of the heavy lifting, ok? And while you're here, please let me know if you need help. You don't have anything to prove to anyone by trying to do everything all by yourself."

Maddy couldn't be upset with Riley, because she knew the intentions were sincere and from the heart. But sometimes Maddy felt that her independence was slipping away, which was another reason this trip was so important to her. She was essentially taking her first trip alone, and she needed to prove to herself that she was still capable of living a somewhat normal life.

"I'll be careful. I'll take my tote bag, my purse, and one suitcase, the lightest one. Is that ok?" She stuck her tongue out playfully at Riley and turned to get the bags.

"At least we've reached a compromise. I'll do my best not to be such a mother hen while you're here, but I just can't help it sometimes," Riley declared as she grabbed the handles of the two remaining bags.

Once she'd reached the top of the stairs, Maddy realized it wasn't as bad as she'd thought it might be—that or she was still running on adrenaline from all the excitement of the day. As she opened the door of the cottage, Maddy instantly felt at home. In both the kitchen and the big family room, the owners had left on a soft light, reminding her of the glow of candles. There was also a sweet note on the foyer table welcoming her to the neighborhood and providing her with their phone numbers should she need anything during her stay. As she looked around, a feeling of relaxation enveloped her. She couldn't wait till tomorrow when she would be able to more fully explore the house and the grounds outside.

"I told you this was a nice house," Riley said as she deposited Maddy's other two suitcases in the foyer. "Kerry and Jen really take care of their rental properties, and they are a great couple. Can't wait for you to meet them!"

"I love it," Maddy said softly as she continued to look around the house, amazed. The pictures on the Internet did not do it justice.

"Want me to help you get unpacked?"

"Riley," she said, taking her friend by the hand and sitting her on the large sofa. "I love that you want to take care of me. Believe me, I truly do. But I have to do what I can on my own. You can't be with me every minute of the day. Like I promised, though, if I need something, you will be the first person I call. And you don't have to worry. I will not try to be Wonder Woman." Maddy said, raising her right hand as if she were swearing an oath.

"I know I can be a bit overbearing. Carter has gently reminded me that I need to rein it in, but I'm just worried about you. Especially with this illness and everything you've been through. I can't help it, but I'll do my best to stay out of your way so that you can have a relaxing time. But I will warn you—there are some things around here we just have to do…but let's save that discussion till later, because you look like you're about to fall asleep." And actually, Maddy really was. Now that they'd reached the house, the day of travel had finally caught up with her, and the extreme exhaustion was something that Maddy was unfortunately too familiar with. It was one of the symptoms of her illness that she had just come to accept.

"I am, and all I'm doing tonight is going to bed. Tomorrow is for unpacking." Maddy hugged her friend good night and watched as Riley walked down the short street to her own house. The next moment, her phone's text tone beeped, and Riley's message appeared on the screen, letting Maddy know she was home safe and saying good night.

Maddy quickly located her linens, pillow, and blanket, and then got her bed ready for sleep. She chose the room overlooking the water, although as she gazed out the window now, all she could see was inky blackness. A few lights twinkled on the small docks lining the inlet, but she couldn't make out any details. She only knew that the water, a beautiful clear turquoise, was right outside her window, and that thought alone made her whole body relax. The ocean soothed her both mind and body. Even though at home she lived within thirty minutes of three beaches, there was something different about the Florida Keys. The atmosphere, the relaxed beach vibe, the friendly people—she loved it all and couldn't wait to start her exploring tomorrow, keeping her fingers crossed that she would feel up to sightseeing.

As she dried off from her quick, warm shower, the rumbling of her stomach reminded her that she hadn't eaten anything since her small dinner on the train, a meal she'd packed for herself early that morning. She had to take her own food with her practically everywhere she went, so now she dove into her tote, pulling out just enough organic crackers with natural almond butter to quiet down her noisy stomach. Thankfully these were two of the foods her body seemed to tolerate fairly well, so she quickly finished her snack and slipped into bed. The cool, soft sheets on the cozy pillow-top bed felt like a giant marshmallow. She fell asleep almost instantly.

4

Maddy woke the following morning to faint orange and yellow streaks of light streaming in between the slats of the window blinds. Wow! This was the first time in a long while that she hadn't been up before sunrise. Broken sleep had become such a routine for her—the irregular sleep pattern of rising too early and then having to take afternoon naps was normal for her. She was hoping to change that cycle while she was here, though, and she could say she had accomplished it for at least one night! Embracing a healthier routine overall was a major goal of this retreat. She hoped to change her "normal" to a new, healthier lifestyle in all areas of her life, physically and mentally, to help her deal with a disease for which the doctors told her there was no cure. Deep inside, she felt she could do things differently and stabilize her health without taking so many medications or dealing with physical restrictions, thus allowing her more freedom and independence. This morning, as she stared at the sunbeams shining through the window, Maddy's soul told her she was on the right path.

As she sat up in the comfy, king-sized bed, she could tell that her journey yesterday had taken a bit of a toll on her. Every muscle in Maddy's body, from her head to the tips of her toes, felt sore. The lingering fatigue was begging her to snuggle back down under the silky covers. Without a doubt, today would have to be one of rest, but she needed to unpack first and then make a quick trip to the grocery store to stock up on food. But once these chores were done, she planned to sit outside by the water and rest, either painting or drawing until it was time for dinner at Riley's house this evening.

As Maddy slowly got out of bed, she noticed for the first time more of the details of her surroundings. Last night had been a blur of activity, and she had not taken any time to look over her new getaway. Now she saw that the bedroom was painted a soft ivory, and splashes of coral and turquoise in the form of lamps and small decorative items accented the surfaces of the bamboo furniture. The weathered wooden planks of the floor gave the room just the right touch for an island house. Pictures of sunsets, beaches, and boats adorned the walls. Maddy stood up and on shaky legs walked over toward the windows, noticing as she drew near that they were actually a set of doors leading to her own bedroom balcony. Delighted, she opened them and found herself overlooking the water of Florida Bay. She stood mesmerized by the beautiful scene. The sun was already high in the sky. Maddy took in a deep breath, and as she looked around from the outside and then back into the large master bedroom, all she could think was, "This is perfect."

She made her way to the huge master bath that was connected to her room and eyed with pleasure the large tub perfect for soaking and relaxing and the beautiful shower stall beside it with its large, see-through glass tiles to keep the water in. The painted walls were a perfect pale aqua color that complemented the bedroom beautifully. And instead of a plank floor, large, cool ceramic tiles in white met her bare feet. This room was triple the size of her bathroom back home, and she loved the spaciousness.

On her way to get the suitcases she had left in the family room the night before, she took a quick peek at the rest of the house. The kitchen was spacious with beautiful light tan marble countertops, stainless steel appliances, and the same ceramic-tile floor as in the bathroom, only here it was a light shade of brown. Storing her food would be no problem in the many cabinets that lined the walls, and a huge window over the sink looked out over the street and the surrounding neighborhood. From the kitchen, she wandered into the large family room. It was painted in the same ivory color as her bedroom, maybe a shade darker. Again, Maddy was met with bamboo furniture that gave the room—the entire house, for that matter—the feel of the tropics. A large, chocolate-brown ceiling fan whirled away in the middle of the room, its huge, palm-leaf-shaped paddles keeping the temperature nice and cool. The floor was the same as the bedroom's, and the entire look was exactly like she'd imagined it would be. Like in the bedroom, coral and aqua lamps, rugs, and artwork accents dotted the room, and on one wall hung a huge, flat-screen TV. The foyer area was cute with its umbrella stand shaped like a banana tree and the little entry table where she had found the welcome note the night before. On the wall above it was a beautiful mirror framed in seashells, beside which were hooks to hang keys. The other two bedrooms and second bathroom were smaller than hers, but all the rooms had that tropical flavor that so appealed to Maddy. The whole place had the look and feel that she had been craving when she'd decided to make this trip.

The last thing she checked out were the sliding glass doors leading from the family room onto a back porch. As she opened the doors and stepped outside, she was once again greeted by the Florida sunshine and some chirping seagulls as they flew by. Essentially the same view of the water as from her bedroom, here she couldn't see the Florida Bay as much but was able to see farther down the water canal, which was lined with docks and boats. These were probably the lights she'd seen last night when she'd peered out what she'd thought was a window in her bedroom. The view was beautiful from both balconies—either one was fine with her!

Her next stop for house exploration would have been the first floor below, but Maddy decided to save that for later, after she came back from her much-needed shopping trip. She got dressed and snacked on some of the goodies left from yesterday's train trip. When she looked at the clock and saw that it was already ten o'clock, she realized it was way past time for her medication.

"No," she said to herself, "I will not stress about my routine." She knew she had to be careful, but she reassured herself calmly that a minor timing issue with her meds was ok. After checking out the forecast for the day on her iPhone—partly cloudy with a high of eighty-three degrees—she went through her still-folded clothes and picked out a bright coral T-shirt, denim capris, and a pair of multicolored flip-flops. Most of the clothing she had brought consisted of casual beachwear because she wasn't planning on going anywhere fancy. This trip was downtime for her, not like a cruise where one had to plan for every type of occasion. This had made packing much easier. But with her stomach growling once again, it was time to get some groceries.

She texted Riley that she was going to the store, that she would be back soon, and that she didn't need any help, since she knew that would be the first thing Riley would ask. She didn't want to bother Riley for help, because even though she was at home, she was at work. One of the reasons Riley and Carter had been able to make the move to the Keys was that Riley could perform her job entirely by telecommuting. Carter, too, although he made the occasional trip to his head office in Miami, communicating with his colleagues there mostly via the Internet. Maddy had wondered if while she was down here she might be able to find something on the World Wide Web that would help her rebuild her life, maybe share her artistic talents. At the moment, she wasn't sure, but that was why she'd brought her laptop with her: to investigate the possibilities. Another of the items on her list of things to do while she was here.

Even though she was still tired from yesterday's trip, inside her was also a feeling of exhilaration that gave her a bit more energy this morning. She was really here. This was the little place she had dreamed about for the last few months. Even though Maddy really wanted to stay at the house, unpack, and *then* head outside, food was a necessity. So she grabbed her keys off the hook near the front door, made sure she had her purse with wallet, and headed out the door.

It was bright and beautiful outside but already starting to heat up. As she walked down the front stairs, Maddy noticed that the lawn had no grass—the front of the property on either side of the walkway that led to her car was full of shells and rock. It was so unique, very much the look of the islands. Under the house, in a space usually reserved for parking, instead sat a beautiful picnic table with a built-in gas grill over to the right side. She glanced toward the dock and the water behind the house and was just able to glimpse what seemed to be one of the famous Indian tiki huts that were specially built in the Keys. She knew she needed to get shopping, but her curiosity got the best of her—she just had to check out the downstairs area.

As she walked toward the inlet, she could see the clear sky between the tiki hut's leafy top and the surrounding palm trees. Using her keys, she entered the downstairs area of the cottage, which included a laundry room complete with washer and dryer, another bathroom, and the fourth bedroom. This area would be perfect for teenagers on vacation, she thought. Maddy then headed back outdoors to check out the tiki hut. Underneath its grass roof, a huge double hammock swayed ever so gently back and forth with the breeze coming off the water. She knew immediately that this would be her ideal spot for relaxation! She could just picture herself lying in the hammock, drink in hand and snack waiting on the nearby table. Maybe her journal or sketch pad in her lap. A walk around the tiki hut revealed the water inlet and Florida Bay beyond. It was stunning, and Maddy could feel her whole being release and unwind as she looked at the view before her.

Something about the aqua-green water just called to her—she couldn't explain it, nor did she want to. When she reached the water's edge, she could see just about to the very bottom. The water was clear, unlike the cloudy ocean water back home. She could see fish, big and small, darting in and out of the plants that undulated back and forth with the motion of the currents; they seemed to be waving at her. As much as she wanted to simply plop down in the hammock and laze the day away, she knew she needed to get her shopping done and to haul her groceries up those stairs, something she wasn't looking forward to but was determined to accomplish by herself. Reluctantly she turned from the beautiful scene before her and headed toward her car. She would be able to enjoy this seaside haven later during one of many enjoyable interludes she hoped for in the coming days.

As she sat in the driver's seat with the air conditioner on full blast, it wasn't long before she located the nearby shopping center with her GPS app. Maddy had never used this feature on her phone before but silently thanked Hope, who had made her practice using the feature over and over before she left home. Now she realized that this little phone app would be a big help in finding all those places she wanted to visit over the next month.

Finding the store wasn't hard at all, thank goodness. On the way there, she also found most of the other places she might need to visit over the coming weeks: a Walgreens drugstore, several gas stations, and lots of local restaurants. Even though her food choices were limited to about twelve items, she was determined to go out to eat even if she had to bring her own. Maddy wanted to watch the local people, meet them, maybe make some new friends. She also discovered that the hospital was closer to her than she'd thought, so at some point when she talked to her mom, she could reassure her that help was indeed nearby if it were needed.

Her cell phone rang just as she was grabbing a bag of potatoes to put in the shopping cart. Fumbling quickly, she fished out her device and looked at the screen. "Hey, Riley! Did you get my text?" Maddy asked as she continued through the produce section, picking up squash, apples, and other vegetables and fruits that were on her "safe to eat" list.

"Hell, no! I forgot to look. Where are you? I went to the house and saw that the car was gone. Scared me!" she cried. Riley sounded like a mom speaking to a child who had just been found.

"If you had read my text, you would know that I've gone shopping. There is no food in the house, and my snack bag from the train trip is just about empty. And I'm not sponging off you guys while I'm here," Maddy said, laughing. "Next time, check your messages. I didn't call because I didn't want to interrupt what you were working on today."

"First of all, if I want to worry, that is my prerogative, so deal with it! Second, I promise I will check my phone next time before I go into panic mode. I forgot I'd turned the ringer off during my meeting. And third, you are welcome to anything at my house at any time. I mean that—anything. I wish I'd known you were going so I could have helped you. Are you sure you'll be able to get your groceries up those stairs when you get home?"

Maddy smiled to herself. This was Riley being Riley again. Sweet and caring, like she'd always been ever since they were young. "Yes, I can. Even if I'm slow as a snail, I'll be ok. If I do have any issues, I know you're only four houses away, but thanks for checking on me," said Maddy.

"I know. I'm being overprotective again, but I can't help it. You'll just have to deal with it," Riley said in her most sullen voice.

"I'll be fine. Besides, I know you're working. In the car last night, you told me about the project you had to finish today, along with that meeting. Plus, I know you've got to be tired after our long night yesterday. Quit worrying about me, and I'll see you for dinner. Six thirty, right?" Maddy replied as she continued her circuit around the grocery store. "Tonight maybe we can start planning our trip to Key West."

"Sounds good for dinner. As far as a Key West trip—most definitely! But do me a favor and call when you get home? I'll come and help you get your stuff upstairs. Maybe Carter will even be back by then. Ok?" Riley asked.

"Riley, please stop. You're going to make yourself sick with worry while I'm here, and I don't want to be the cause of it,"

Maddy said into the phone, knowing it would probably be this way for at least her first week here. After that, when Riley saw that she really *was* ok, then she wouldn't be so vigilant. Maddy had to keep reminding herself that her best friend was only being so watchful over her because she knew the details about Maddy's illness and what she'd been through. Riley had even done a lot of research, helping her when she'd first received her diagnosis. So Maddy would just have to wait and see.

She picked up the food staples she would need for about the next week or two. The heaviest things she bought were the cases of water. One of the stock boys at the store loaded them into the cart and then took them out to the car for her, but she would have to ask Carter for help with those. For her, cases of water and a long flight of stairs was not a good combination, and she didn't want to take any chances. They would just have to sit in the trunk for a bit. Maddy was just happy to be getting some real food she could cook instead of having to rely on the snacks that had been her meals yesterday. Even better was that the grocery store had everything she needed this morning and no other stop was necessary, which meant she could head straight home. She was already picturing herself swinging in the hammock under the tiki hut.

The trip to the store was so freeing that Maddy was already beginning to feel more of her independence again. The sky was now a brilliant blue, the palm trees along the highway were swaying in the gentle breeze, and the temperature was warm but felt good. When she pulled onto her street, it hit her again like a bolt of lightning—she was really here on her own in the Keys. She had taken that leap of faith and made her dream a reality. Suddenly she wanted to just put up her groceries as quickly as possible and head to Anne's Beach, the place she had been dreaming about since the day the idea for this trip had come to her. She had to remind herself that she had a whole month to visit her favorite spot, and she could go as many times as she wanted. Pushing herself too hard would result in a pushback of symptoms severe enough to put a wrench into her trip plans, so she promised herself that she would settle for sitting on the dock with her sketchbook. Maybe a manatee or dolphin would pay her a visit.

The thought of sitting outside in the shade with art book, pencils, and maybe watercolors actually sounded relaxing. Maddy had started rediscovering her passion for art and drawing during the stress of her rocky marriage. Also, while caring for Hope through the tough times of controlling her diabetes, Maddy looked to her art for stress relief. One particularly rough day, she'd pulled out an old sketchbook and started drawing and doodling. It relaxed her so much that drawing and painting became her drug of choice to relieve the weight of the problems all around her. Then, when she started having mysterious symptoms of her own a few years later, it was her creativity that helped her escape from it all. Painting, drawing, and doodling were her favorites, but she also liked crocheting, a craft she had taught herself when she was twelve years old. Maddy's creative side helped her deal with not only her physical issues but all the changes that she was facing: Being newly single at forty-eight. Hope starting her new life with Shawn in their own home. Moving back in with her parents, even though the room she occupied was almost like her own little apartment. But that creativity also distracted her from decisions she knew needed serious consideration, like what she wanted to do with her life now, and how she could regain as much of her health as possible.

As she parked in front of the pale yellow house, she glanced at the numerous bags in the backseat that needed to be transported into the house and sighed. She could do this, she thought, giving herself the pep talk she needed. She could feel that her limbs were already a little weak, having not yet fully recovered from yesterday's voyage, and she was also getting a bit thirsty and felt a heart palpitation every so often. These were the effects of Mastocytosis for her when she was tired but if she could just get the groceries inside, she would most certainly ask Carter for help tonight with the water. She got out and opened the trunk first, unsealing the case of water and taking out four of the small bottles to drink this afternoon. That would hold her over till this evening.

With a tote bag in one hand and three small plastic bags from the backseat in the other, she made her first trip up the stairs, moving slowly. When she reached the top, she was hot and slightly dizzy, but it was nothing she hadn't experienced before. She would just take it slow, she reminded herself as she sat the first load on the kitchen counter and headed outside and down the steps again.

5

When Jason Burnett finally looked up from his computer, he realized that it was daylight outside. Not just a sunrise but a completely bright sky, with the sun higher than it should be. He was shocked when he looked at the clock and saw that it was already ten thirty in the morning. He stared out the front window of the house he had rented during his stay for his current project. Usually he would find a place on the job site for his motorhome, but this time he'd wanted to try renting a house in the Keys as a treat to himself, and so far his decision had been a good one. The house that his assistant, Maria, had found for him was right on the water and close to his work. He could get used to this kind of view, he thought, as he looked out the back window at the waters of beautiful Florida Bay.

He had been working for seven hours already after waking very early this morning, ideas for his current remodeling project coming to him almost like a dream during the night. The job was coming together nicely and should be completed on time, maybe even a few days earlier than expected, within the next four to six weeks pending any weather delays. His early morning planning session had helped him finalize some more last-minute details and clarify what still needed to be done to complete the renovations of the beautiful turn-of-the-century home located on Key Largo.

When he'd originally come to work in the Keys almost nine months ago, it had been to restore an older hotel located on the water into the grand resort it had once been. When word circulated of the quality of Jason's work, Thomas Martin, the owner of the home he was now restoring had persuaded him to accept the renovation job once the resort was finished. Jason hadn't planned on staying here this long, but after talking to his assistant, he was able to fit the restoration of the grand house into his schedule. The resort had taken only seven months to complete, a feat he was proud of, but accepting the house renovation had added at least three to four more months to his stay. Not that it was a sacrifice to have to remain in the Florida Keys—if he admitted it to himself, he actually loved it here. The weather, the relaxed lifestyle, the great food—everything about these tiny Florida islands was so different from the many other places around the country he had worked. He'd even thought fleetingly that it might be hard to leave here when the job was finished. But the nature of his business was that another house or building somewhere else was always waiting, so he was almost constantly traveling.

He had worked in many places around the United States, restoring buildings and homes to their original grandeur or completely remodeling them according to their owner's wishes. He was very good at what he did and had built an excellent reputation along with his very profitable business, all since his painful divorce from his ex-wife, Andrea, almost ten years ago. Moving from city to city with a different project each time had helped him heal by keeping him busy doing something that he was good at and that he thoroughly loved. He'd promised his mom that he wasn't just running away from what had happened, but maybe he was. After going through such a painful breakup, he'd had no desire to put down roots in any one place. Traveling and living out of suitcases had become his life, and it suited him just fine.

He also had no desire to commit to another relationship. He had met and dated a few women along the way during his travels but once the job was complete the relationship ended also. He didn't want to go through that pain again so even though he was nice and a gentleman, he made sure that they knew he was just passing through town.

When he and Andrea had married, they'd had so many plans for their future. He was an up-and-coming architect who loved working with his brother to restore old homes. He thought his ex-wife was supportive of his passion because she always seemed so interested, constantly asking questions about his work. In hindsight, the purpose of her seemingly genuine interest was just to gather information for her own secret plans, ones that involved other men and not her husband. The memories of that time in his life still made him feel like a fool and brought feelings of anger and frustration, even though over ten years had passed. He had trusted her so completely that when he found out about the multiple affairs she'd indulged in during the four years of their marriage, the shock of the discovery took days to sink in. But when it did, the fury he'd felt inside was hard to contain, especially when she tried to place all the blame on him.

She claimed it was his fault that she'd had to seek comfort and companionship elsewhere—he was always working. He didn't spend enough time with her, she'd said. But when they had talked, she'd encouraged him to make enough money so that she wouldn't have to work. She wanted to stay home with the two children they both said they wanted to have, and he'd done everything he could to reach those goals, thinking that she was doing the same, even though the job she had didn't pay as well as his. He worked every chance he could, saved his money, learned about investing, and stayed out of debt. They had tried to have children, but Andrea never conceived. Then, when he learned about the multiple men she had been seeing, he instantly knew why she'd never gotten pregnant. She had been on the pill the whole time, even when she claimed they were "trying." It disgusted and embarrassed him to think that he had put all of his trust into this woman he thought he knew and loved. Once everything was out in the open, he immediately asked her to leave and never come back.

Their divorce was quick and relatively simple. They didn't have much to divide, and since Andrea was capable of working, there was no alimony to pay. The day the divorce was final was the day Jason decided to travel, working on odd remodeling jobs here and there. He just wanted out of Las Vegas and away from the memories. He sold or gave away everything he didn't absolutely need or that wouldn't fit in his truck and then hit the road. He had some small savings from the sale of the house, and he decided that working as a contractor would help him get away from the madness that had been his life those past few years. People loved his work, so he started a portfolio of the restoration work he'd done as well as his architecture drawings for new homes. Now, almost nine years later, he didn't have to look for work—it found him, just like the house project he was working on now. Andrea had tracked him down on several occasions, trying to convince him that she had changed, wanting to be a part of his life again, but he saw through her charade each time. It wasn't a coincidence that she suddenly started showing up after word of his work and popularity had spread around the social circles she aspired to be part of. He knew she did not want him for himself—she was after the prestige and money he had worked so hard for, so each time she contacted him, he would either ignore her entirely or insist that she leave him alone. It had been three years since he'd last heard from her, and the rumor was that she had remarried. He doubted it was true. But if it was, he was just glad it wasn't to him.

As Jason walked out of the room he'd dubbed "The Office," he glanced out the front window and could tell the day was going to be another beautiful one. These days of no rain or crazy weather made his job so much easier. Working around weather conditions had always been part of this career he had chosen, so it seemed he was always checking the weather app on his phone or looking up at the sky. Just then he saw a car pull up in front of the rental house across the street. Great—another weekly renter.

Since he'd been here, he'd seen that place taken by many pleasant couples and families, but he had seen his share of crazies, too. Just two weeks ago, the owners had had to kick out a group of college kids. They had been very rowdy every night, to the point that he'd finally had to call the cops. One night their partying got completely out of hand—drunk kids everywhere and music so loud that he could barely hear his own TV. He found out later that the house had been rented to four Harvard seniors and that they had told Kerry and Jen Russell, the owners, that they were going to use their spring break here to finish their senior theses in a relaxing atmosphere. The kids were so convincing that the owners didn't bat an eyelash when they were handed a certified check for the entire week's rental. If he'd heard right, those kids had received no deposit or money back even though they'd only spent three days there. He had also watched as various contracting outfits went in and out of the little house over the following week, making repairs, he assumed. He could only imagine how bad the damage had been. Hopefully, he thought as he watched the car come to a stop, this wasn't going to be a repeat.

Jason couldn't help but watch as the beautiful, blond woman stepped out of the car. Dressed in her bright T-shirt and the jeans cut off below the knee, she definitely looked like she was here for a vacation. He looked around, expecting to see other people with her, maybe a husband, children, or friends, but saw no activity around the house. When she started unloading plastic bags filled with groceries and proceeded to slowly climb the steps to the front door, he knew she must be alone. Maybe she had come early to get the little rental ready for her family, he thought. He continued to watch her as she came down a second time and grabbed some more bags, but as she started back up the stairs, she seemed to be moving very slowly, maybe even having trouble, taking only one step at a time with only one bag in each hand. Maybe she was hurt? Jason saw no bandages or anything else to indicate a problem, but he kept watching. When she emerged from the front door for the third time, she stood at the top for just a minute before coming back down the staircase very slowly and grabbing two more bags. Jason could feel in his gut that something was amiss, but he told himself he wasn't going to get involved. That was the motto he'd adopted everywhere he'd lived. Especially here in the Keys. This was time just for him. Maybe some beers with people at work but he had kept mostly to himself during this project. He had needed a break. No women. No making friends. Just some alone time. But in the end, he just couldn't stand there and watch her struggle, so he pushed himself out the front door reluctantly and walked across the street.

"Now this is a workout," Maddy said to herself as she picked up only two bags again. Either they were heavier than she'd thought, or her arms had already had enough for the day. She had been up and down the stairs only three times, yet she already felt like she had run a marathon. She knew her body was telling her she'd done too much, but the bags had to come in, so she promised herself a prolonged rest time under the tiki hut outside or maybe in the lounge chair on the upstairs balcony. As she made her way down the steps for her fourth trip, she saw him coming from the house across the street.

She wasn't sure by the way he walked toward her if he was friendly or not—his body language was hard to read. But Riley had been right—this man was what her daughter would call "hot." He was at least six feet tall, probably more, and his physique told her this man was in shape. Maddy noticed the toned muscles of his arms emerging from the sleeves of the plain white T-shirt he wore with a pair of blue jeans that fit him perfectly. As he drew closer, she could see that his dark brown hair was streaked ever so lightly as if it had been bleached by the sun. The closer he came, the quicker her pulse raced. Was it from exhaustion or the effect of this extremely nice-looking man walking toward her? All she knew was that she needed to get a grip on this male sensory overload, and she reminded herself to tell Riley she hadn't done a very good job describing her neighbor.

"Hi," Jason said in a monotone voice as he walked around the car to where Maddy stood reaching for more grocery bags. Now she could see his light blue eyes, and before she knew it, she felt jittery all over.

"Hello," Maddy said as she stared at him. When she realized she was standing like a frozen statue, she quickly tried to hide her embarrassment.

Jason wasn't sure what he wanted to say next, because the woman standing in front of him had him a little tongue-tied. He usually had no trouble talking to anyone, so this made him feel awkward. She was more stunning up close than he'd imagined when he saw her through his kitchen window. Her blond hair and hazel eyes had him staring and acting like a shy schoolboy. Remember this was a solo trip-no involvement. Help her with the groceries and go home, he told himself.

"My name is Jason Burnett. I guess I'm your neighbor from across the street for the next week." He reached out his hand to shake hers and immediately noticed how soft and delicate she seemed to be. "I saw you unloading your car, and I don't mean to pry, but you looked like you could use some help." Aside from the police fiasco a couple of weeks ago, this was the longest conversation he'd had with anyone outside of work since moving to the neighborhood.

"Hi, I'm Maddy Sumner. To be honest, even though I usually don't let strangers into my house, I really could use some help. Those steps are just about to get the best of me. I guess I'm a bit out of shape." She smiled up at him, not wanting to give him the real reason for her step-climbing problem but the look on his face was cool, not as friendly as she had hoped. She was secretly glad he had come to her rescue, not just because he would assist her with the bags but because she had now met the mystery man Riley had told her about. A weird but wonderful feeling came over her, as if she were a teenager meeting the new cute boy at school for the first time. But if she read his body language correctly, it was completely different than how she was feeling.

"I can't thank you enough. And by the way, I'll be your neighbor for the next month. I ran away from home, so to speak. My friends, Riley and Carter Mason, live four houses down the street. Riley mentioned she'd talked to you when you first moved into the neighborhood and that even though they didn't know you very well, you seemed to be nice. I will definitely tell her that her assessment was right. But she also told me that you never attend any of the local neighborhood parties they put together here. You must be extremely busy, or maybe you're an introvert." The words came out before she could stop them. She couldn't believe what she had just said. Great, Maddy, she thought to herself. Her nervousness at being around Jason was causing her to ramble like an idiot. Now she had insulted the man who'd just offered to save her from maybe crawling up those steps with her shopping bags.

"I'm sorry! I didn't mean anything by that. Just Riley is very social and prides herself on knowing everyone and their business, but in a nice way. She is protective of her little neighborhood." Maddy wanted to crawl under a rock but instead did her best just to keep her mouth shut.

Jason wasn't sure whether to be offended or to laugh. This woman had spunk, and he smiled as he watched her try to correct what she thought was a gaffe. She was right, though. He hadn't been very social with anyone, and he had indeed declined all the neighborhood invites because, as always, he would be leaving soon and didn't want any entanglements. It was harder to leave a place when he had become close to the people around him.

"No need to apologize. Well, Maddy, let me help you take your groceries inside. Is this all, or do you have more in the trunk?" At this, she opened the lid of the trunk, and when he looked down at the two cases of water, he grabbed them first, hoisting one onto each shoulder and proceeding up the stairs with Maddy close behind with a few more bags. She certainly couldn't keep up with him, but since she felt embarrassed, she tried as hard as she could, not wanting to appear weak and needy. This turned out to be a mistake, though, because by the time she reached the second floor, she could feel the familiar tingling sensations going through her body and a slight dizziness. In her world, this was called "brain fog," and it was setting in, making it hard for her to think and talk. "Not now, *please*," she said to her brain and body, "especially with this man here with me!"

"I'll go grab the rest of the bags, and you can start putting your things away. That will save you another trip down the stairs." Maddy nodded and silently thanked Jason who had come to her rescue. She started putting the groceries away, slowly filling the empty cabinets and bare refrigerator, watching Jason each time he deposited bags of food on the kitchen counter. She wanted to say something each time he came through the door but felt a little tongue-tied whenever she saw him.

When all the groceries were finally in the house, she turned to see Jason standing somewhat awkwardly in the doorway.

"It was nice meeting you, and I hope you enjoy your vacation. It's beautiful here right now. You picked a great house with a wonderful view. Good thing you are here for more than a week because that's not nearly enough time to explore the Keys."

Maddy smiled as she walked toward the attractive man standing in her door. "Then a month should give me plenty of time to see the sights, do some relaxing, and maybe enjoy some time in Key West. Once again, thank you so much for your help."

"You are more than welcome." Jason hesitated a moment but went ahead with his next question anyway. "I know it's none of my business, but you're here by yourself for a month? I just figured you were renting the house like most people I've seen since I've been here, usually families or college kids spending mom and dad's money," Jason said, wondering if she were married. Wait, where had that come from? No involvement—he had to keep reminding himself. And his current project was wrapping up shortly. But this was the first time in as long as he could remember that he'd felt an attraction to a woman that was beyond the physical. No he told himself. No strings this time.

"No, it's just me. The rest of my family is at home, and by "family" I mean it's just me and my daughter. She got married recently and I'm here by myself for some time away. My friends I mentioned a minute ago, Riley and Carter, know the owner of this house, so I was lucky to be able to rent it for the whole month so that I could get away for a while." So, now she'd basically told a complete stranger that she was single and staying by herself. Why, oh why, had she done that? Something about this man prevented her from editing her words before they came out of her mouth. But she had to admit that Jason seemed different, and she really couldn't explain the draw she felt toward him. There was just something about him that made her wish he would stay and talk.

"So, you're basically running away from home?"

"I guess you could say that. My family would certainly agree with you. They didn't believe I would go off on my own for a month, but here I am. Day one...well, I guess I should say day two of my sabbatical, if you count my extra long travel day yesterday by train." She looked at the groceries still in bags on the counter, not caring if they got put into the cabinets and refrigerator. She hadn't had a real conversation with anyone other than family, a few close friends, and doctors in so long that this was quite refreshing. But she was still feeling the effects of the stair climbing and needed to take some medication and water, but she didn't want to do or say anything about how she was feeling with him present. Right now, those things seemed less important. She would love to keep talking to the man who had her weak in the knees.

"Well, it was nice to meet you, Maddy.

"Thanks Jason. Again, I appreciate the help more than you know. Maybe I'll see you around." She was hoping that he would respond with a positive remark like "That would be nice" but he went out the front door and down the steps quietly. She shut the door and then stood at the kitchen window, watching him walk back across the street, smiling the whole time but wondering about his cool demeanor. He most definitely had the gentleman manners that Riley had mentioned but Maddy knew that she had not impressed him. Maybe she could share a few friendly "hello's" during the week if she saw him outside to see if he might open up more. But why was she thinking of this? A vacation romance wasn't part of the idea for her retreat. It would just complicate things even more in her life. But she had to admit that he was stunning and was very glad she accepted his offer of help for more reasons than one.

But now it was time for medicine. She felt weak and shaky as if from a minor reaction, but could it have something to do with meeting Jason? Most likely it was a combination of lingering fatigue from yesterday, the exertion of shopping this morning, the unaccustomed heat, climbing the steps, *and* meeting the handsome man. She fumbled through her bag, grabbed her pillbox, and quickly took a dose, drinking as much water as she could. She knew this would settle down the symptoms she was having, or at least it usually did.

As she sat down to wait for her medicine to work its magic, she began to think about Jason again, but this time her thoughts were different. "Why does he have to live across the street?" she wondered. She'd planned on a no-makeup, pony-tail kind of vacation. But not now! Quite the attractive man lived across the street from her little place in the Keys, and if she was honest with herself, Maddy had to admit it excited her. He brought to life a part of her that she hadn't felt for a very long time.

6

She went to dinner over at Riley's house around six thirty, bringing her own food that she'd fixed just before leaving the house even though Riley had insisted it wasn't necessary. After Jason had left and her symptoms had calmed down, she was able to put the groceries up and take a much-needed nap, not outside as she had earlier planned but rather curled up on the comfortable couch in the family room. She hadn't realized how tired she was until she woke up in the late afternoon, just in time to fix her food, freshen up a bit, and walk quickly to her friend's house.

"I met my neighbor across the street today," Maddy said casually as she scooped up some potatoes as everyone began passing the food around the table. She wanted to take a serving of the roasted asparagus and grilled fish, but those were not on her safe food list. Anyway, right now she was more interested in how Riley would react to her statement. Maddy's intuition was right. Her friend immediately stopped focusing on putting food on her plate and looked at Maddy with a stunned expression and the beginnings of a sly grin.

"Wasn't I right? A cutie for sure!" Both Carter and their son Kenneth looked up from their plates with surprised looks on their faces at Riley's description of Jason.

"I'm just telling it like I see it. He is very cute, just seems to be a bit on the quiet side. So, tell us the scoop—what happened?" The look on Riley's face indicated she couldn't wait to hear some juicy details. Carter shook his head laughing, and Kenneth rolled his eyes.

Maddy looked around the table. "So that we don't bore the guys during dinner, let's talk outside after we eat while we enjoy the sunset." Riley gave her a pouting look and agreed. But Maddy knew Riley was probably just about to burst! They continued on enjoying their delicious dinner, the conversation light and friendly, and after a quick clean up, Maddy and Riley stepped outside together.

"Ok, spare no details, please. I want to hear everything!" Riley said as she and Maddy settled into the big, comfy lounge chairs on the back porch of the house, close to the water. The sun was setting, creating a beautiful canopy of colors, as Maddy leaned back in the chaise, taking her time and watching Riley squirm.

"To begin with, you were right on the money. He is one *very* nice-looking man. I had just returned from the store with groceries and was having a terrible time getting them up the steps. Next thing I know, Jason is walking across the street and asking if he could help. I must have looked like a deer in headlights. I got so tongue-tied! But in my defense, my symptoms were acting up just a bit, because I'm still tired from yesterday's trip. If he noticed anything, though, he was polite enough not to say. He was a godsend, because I don't think I could have taken all the bags up those stairs."

"You were supposed to call me if you needed help! But I'm sure glad I didn't have to under the circumstances. You're probably the only person around here he's had anything to do with or really even talked to. Might this be a little romance brewing on the islands?" Riley asked playfully, kidding with Maddy. "If so, I give you my approval to go for it."

"I can answer that with a big 'no'. He was friendly and nice but that was it. He helped me with my groceries, told me I had rented a nice place and basically went back to his house. But I did watch him from my kitchen window. It's been so long since any man caught my eye." Maddy looked over to see Riley hanging on to every word she said.

"That's it? Nothing more? Damn. He must definitely be a loner. I was hoping he would be your Florida Keys fling," Riley said playfully.

Maddy sat up and looked at her friend. "Have you completely lost your mind? A relationship is off the table this month. But at least I have something nice to look at across the street." They both started laughing as they continued to relax in the loungers outside.

"Well, you need—and deserve—to have some fun. Do something crazy. If that includes an island fling, then you should go for it," Riley said.

"Like I already told you, romance is on the shelf for now. If it should magically happen, it won't be with Mr. Burnett. He just carried my groceries in and left. And that was a good thing, because my symptoms were coming on really fast, and I had to take meds the minute his butt was out the door."

"So, you *did* notice his butt! I did too when I first saw him." Riley lay back in her chair, eyes closed, wearing that same smile she'd had on since Maddy had made her announcement at the dinner table.

Maddy gave up and shook her head. She knew it was hopeless to have a conversation about anything right now, because Riley's head was stuck in a "Jason across the street" loop. So she sat back and enjoyed watching the orange and purple sky turn into a dark midnight blue dotted with twinkling stars.

"Anyway, I'm here for only a month. I'm content just to have my extended family right here in this house. Remember, I came to the Keys to get away and be a little selfish. Reduce stress and get some much-needed time away. A man would just complicate things," Maddy said softly.

"But what if a man is supposed to be part of your 'selfish' vacation? Who knows?" Riley was now watching the stars too in the dark sky above. "I do know that you need to be careful. You don't know much about this man, and he has already been in your house. Not saying he's a crazy idiot or anything. Everyone down here is friendly, and we watch after each other. But he has kept to himself since he moved in months ago, never accepting any invites or getting to know anyone. In my book, that is kinda weird...but damn if he doesn't look fine," Riley said smiling once again.

"I understand you're concerned, but if you meet someone and they aren't inviting you to their next party within the first thirty minutes, you think they're running from the police. That's what makes you so special, Riley! But I will be careful—and besides, he was just helping today, and I probably won't see him anymore." With that, she said her good-byes and walked back to her little house, Riley watching just to make sure she got in safely. Maddy waved to her and decided that a talk was in order. As sweet as Riley's intentions were, Maddy didn't need a mother hen while she was staying here. But she would have to choose her words carefully—she didn't want to hurt her best friend's feelings. Riley might act tough and cheerful, but she had a soft, sweet heart. Right now, though, a nice, warm shower and a soft, comfy bed were calling Maddy's name. Tomorrow, she would relax by the water in the hammock under the tiki hut. Something to look forward to.

Maddy had to admit it: the mornings were beautiful here in the Keys no matter what the weather. Just enough of a breeze always seemed to be blowing to make it feel comfortable outside. She had only been here a week so far, and she was loving every minute of it. After the first eventful two days, she did need to take a break and indulged in a "do-nothing" day that turned out to be splendid. She spent practically the whole of it lounging in the hammock under the tiki hut. She watched the water, felt the breeze on her skin, and every now and then sat on the dock dipping her feet in the warm, clear ocean water.

She loved watching the silver streaks of all the little fish darting in and out of the shifting shadows. But the highlight of the day occurred in the afternoon, when ocean visitors in the form of a manatee and her calf suddenly came up out of the water not ten feet from where she sat! She was over the moon that she had her phone with her and was able to capture images of mother and baby as they seem to float lazily through the water. Maddy watched them till they swam away, back out into the bay, and then she resumed her cozy position in the hammock. Only then did she realize how quickly the day had flown by and how genuinely relaxed she was feeling.

As the week progressed, she started marking off a few of the things on her Must Do in the Keys list. She promised herself it wasn't a to-do list because she wanted to be as spontaneous as possible, but there were some definite things she wanted to see and do before she headed back home. One of these was an excursion to Anne's Beach, one of the first places she'd wanted to visit as soon as she arrived. In her two previous trips, she had loved spending time at the lovely little park with its beautiful beaches, but unfortunately on both occasions their time had been limited. She'd made the decision before she even left Charleston that she would come here as often as she could during her stay. It was beautiful, peaceful, and quiet for the most part, even though there were other tourists or locals around. The water was a clear aqua blue that stayed quite shallow for a long way out into the ocean, so her first visit to the beach involved a thirty-minute soak in the soothing warm water. Maddy walked out into the ocean till it was a little above her knees and plopped down into its sun-kissed warmth. Again, she was amazed at the little fish that dared to come right up to her and then darted away. Just as long as they were little fish, she laughed to herself.

These waters were healing for her. She could feel it through her entire body as she lay back and floated in the shallow water. Maddy had told several of her doctors that for some reason she was drawn to seawater, especially when she wasn't feeling well, and most of them dismissed her observation. Two of them, though, agreed that ocean water could be healing, its warm-but-not-hot temperature relaxing the muscles, the natural minerals absorbing through the skin, and the sea breezes bringing in clean ocean air. At least she had a few doctors on her side as she tried to tackle her chronic illness as naturally as possible. And soaking in the water of the Florida Keys was part of her homemade prescription.

Maddy also found a few restaurants offering beachside dining where she could go, eat, and watch the water. The best places were the small, out-of-the-way diners and restaurants that didn't mind if she brought along her own food. Even though her illness was more serious than simple allergies, she would explain it that way to the wait staff, and as long as she was able to order something off the menu, usually a baked potato or maybe some steamed veggies, she could stay and enjoy the scenery, read, or write in her journal. In the evenings, Riley and Carter would usually join her, and they would have a blast. They were being so gracious, and although Maddy told them more than once that they didn't have to go everywhere with her, she was beginning to think that her vacation was becoming a "staycation" for them. She could tell their evenings out were giving them a much-needed break from their work-at-home routine.

And this week, she also saw Jason almost every day, sometimes more than once. They would exchange a polite "Hello" but that was about it. Secretly she wanted more of a conversation with this handsome man, even though she tried to convince herself otherwise. But she felt like he wanted to keep to himself so she settled on the fact that they would be no more than neighbors. That was what she wanted right? Honestly, no. She wanted to know more about him: Where was he from? What did he do for a living? How did he pick the Keys as a place to live? And so much more. She could have come up with a ton of questions every time she saw him, but he practically ignored her after each of their friendly greetings. She found herself looking out for him each day, even peering out the front kitchen window at the sound of a car outside just in case it was him. She was acting like a schoolgirl with a terrible crush, and she couldn't tell anyone, especially Riley. If she confided her feelings to her best friend, knowing Riley the way she did, she would probably march right over to his house and ask, "Why aren't you talking to my best friend? She likes you." Riley was just that outspoken.

7

Maddy's first weekend in Islamorada brought with it a small get-together of neighbors at Riley's house. There were about twenty-five people in total, all neighbors living on the same street. Maddy met so many people that she couldn't remember all their names, but she instantly liked each and every one. They were all so friendly and welcoming! As she watched the group of people around her, she now understood Riley's description of her "neighborhood family." Listening to the various conversations, she realized these people genuinely cared for each other, helping when needed and celebrating every chance they could. She even met the Russells, the owners of the beautiful house she was staying in.

It was pretty late when everyone started on their way home, leaving just Maddy, Riley, and Carter to clean up, even though there really wasn't much to do.

"This was wonderful, guys. I can see now why you love it here so much. Maybe next time you can try to invite Jason again," Maddy said softly.

Riley was instantly at attention. "Ok, so what's the scoop? I know you. You wouldn't have said that if something wasn't up. Do tell," Riley insisted, grabbing Maddy by the arm and sitting her down on the couch like a child that was about to be scolded.

"Nothing, really. It's just that every day this week, since helping me with the groceries that time, I've seen him outside, and he always makes a point to say hello but that's all. Then he totally ignores me."

"You like him! Have you thought of asking him over for a drink? Maybe sit out back on the dock?"

"No way!" Maddy quickly responded, although the thought made her pulse quicken. She felt a bit of excitement at the possibility.

"It wouldn't be a date or anything. Just a neighborly chat," Riley was quick to point out.

"It just feels funny to ask him. Isn't that being a bit forward?" It had been so long since Maddy had navigated the waters of dating that she wasn't sure what was appropriate and what wasn't. But then this wasn't dating, she scolded herself.

"Yeah, but you have one hell of a view from that dock, and those nice lounge chairs. Plus, maybe he doesn't want to intrude on your vacation. Most people renting a house in the Keys are only here for a few days or a week. By now he's used to people coming and going pretty frequently. You, on the other hand, are altogether different. A month away by your-self, and you are single and pretty." Riley stretched a little and then got up to take some more glasses to the kitchen.

"It would be nice to get to know him. He seems nice, and it was sweet of him to carry all those groceries into the house for me the other day. But this getaway was for some selfish mental and physical healing. I didn't plan on developing some kind of schoolgirl crush on the neighbor across the street," Maddy said, sighing and smiling at the same time.

Riley laughed. "Oh, so it's a schoolgirl crush?"

Now she'd done it. Now Riley would never leave this alone.

"Ok, I'll admit I do find myself looking for him. Ugh, this is so weird. This is how you feel when you're thirteen and you know for sure you're going to marry Guy Tarren when you grow up," Maddy said, exaggerating.

"Eww, gross! You had that big of a crush on that boy with all the zits?"

"He wasn't that bad. I certainly felt like I was in love. Oh, I don't know. I can't deny that I'd like to know Jason better. This all just feels so strange. It's been a long time since I've been excited about a good-looking guy. I haven't allowed myself that luxury…and it feels kinda good." Maddy felt embarrassed expressing these feelings to Riley.

Soon, though, they both started laughing and reminiscing about their teenage loves. There had been many, and they went over each and every one, smiling, laughing so hard at times that they had tears in their eyes. Before they knew it, the clock was striking midnight, and Maddy could feel her body signaling to her that she had done just a bit too much that evening.

"I've got to go home now, especially if we're still going to that picnic at the Seven Mile Bridge tomorrow. What time do you want to leave?" Maddy asked.

"Let's plan on ten o'clock. That will give us time to do some exploring or just sit and relax at the park, depending on what you want to do."

"That sounds great." She yawned as she gave Riley a big hug, said good night, and headed out the door.

The night was beautiful. Even though a few street lamps dotted the roadside, Maddy could see the gorgeously clear night sky, once again full of stars. And there was that subtle breeze that she loved. She enjoyed her walks home from Riley's house. The little neighborhood felt safe and secure with everyone watching out for each other. And though she was feeling a bit unusually tired, she was happy.

8

Jason's sleeplessness was proving very frustrating. He had spent the evening at the local bar and grill watching a beautiful sunset with a few of the guys from the work site. Sitting and relaxing with his coworkers was nice, but Jason kept reminding himself that this was only temporary—if all went as planned on the job site, he would be leaving the Keys in six weeks or so. But for the first time in as long as he could remember, he knew he was going to miss this place. The Keys had affected him like nowhere else he had been in the past ten years of moving from one project to the next. He felt relaxed here, and—dare he think it—he felt *at home*. But that wasn't his plan, and he knew it was only a matter of time before he'd be back on the road. Maybe that was why sleep had been more elusive lately. He wished he knew the reason, because he could really use some rest.

Since reading in bed wasn't helping his insomnia, he went to grab a snack from the kitchen, and as he glanced out the window, he saw Maddy walking down the street toward her house. She must have spent the evening with her friends—he had noticed quite a few cars lined up in front of their house earlier. He hated to admit it but he had a strong attraction to her. He had done everything to basically avoid her this past week and he would find himself thinking about her off and on during the day. He still remembered what he had promised himself when he arrived here of just time for himself-no personal connections. When it came to relationships, his past still haunted him, plus he was always on the move, going somewhere new. What was it about her that was so different from the other women he had met over the years? He wasn't sure, but she seemed to be always on his mind.

As Maddy approached the gate to her house, she suddenly had "that feeling," and it was hitting her like a freight train. "No, please, not now!" she thought frantically as she pushed open the gate and headed for the steps as quickly as she could. Her legs and arms were becoming weaker with each movement she made, and her balance was becoming precarious. She could tell that her blood pressure was dropping while her heart started racing; her head felt fuzzy, and the itching on her chest and back began working its way down her body. She desperately wanted to get into the house and take the Benadryl she kept in her little tote bag and she wouldn't have to resort to her Epi-Pen.

But now her thoughts were starting to get jumbled, and she felt like she was in another world. She knew where she was, but nothing felt real to her. She needed her rescue medicines *now*. With each step she climbed, her condition worsened, and by the time she reached the fourth step to the front door of the house, she'd collapsed. She tried to go through her tote, but her numb fingers fumbled around through the contents without locating the Epi-Pen, her water bottle, or her phone to call Riley or 911. Everything seemed so far away. She tried to crawl up another step, but by now she couldn't make a move and panic started to set in. Her breathing was becoming more difficult, but thankfully she could still draw in air. She lay on the steps and simply couldn't go any further. She didn't know what to do; her mind was suddenly a blank.

From his kitchen, Jason watched the scene unfold before him. He'd observed her walking toward her cottage until she was finally opening the small gate, but then she seemed to slow down suddenly, even stumbling a bit when she tried to take a few more steps. Maybe a little too much to drink? He had been there and done that just a few times himself. But from his vantage point, he saw that she'd gone from walking fine to suddenly trying to steady herself and finding nothing but air to hold onto. This caused her to weave forward until she finally reached her front steps. It wasn't until he saw her try to crawl and then seem to collapse that he became more concerned and decided he should make sure she was ok. He wanted so much to run across the street, because his gut told him this was not a drunk woman trying to make it home—but, then again, if she were indeed inebriated, he didn't want to embarrass her, either. Now, though, as he looked across the street, he saw that she was slumped on the staircase and not moving. Drunk or not, he decided to see if he could help.

"Maddy, can you hear me? Maddy, answer me. What's wrong?" She looked up at him with glassy eyes, but she seemed to be having a hard time comprehending what he was saying. Just then, she did her best to point to something, but he wasn't sure what she was doing. Then he saw the medical ID bracelet.

"Medicine," was all she said, her slurred words sounding scared. Knowing he could get her to the hospital faster than if he called 911, he scooped her up in his arms and walked quickly to his SUV. Once he had her secured in the vehicle, he ran for his keys.

"Maddy, I'm going to take you to the hospital. It's just around the corner. Ok?" Jason said nervously as her breathing became increasingly ragged.

"Medicine. Bag. Phone." Maddy knew what she wanted to say, but she couldn't put whole sentences together. She had been through this before, but each time the anxiety it produced made it feel like the first time.

"Just hang in there. We're almost there!"

9

When she opened her eyes, Maddy wondered why her whole body felt like a giant piece of lead. She felt very heavy and extremely tired. Her surroundings seemed familiar...and then she realized she was in the hospital. She felt the blood pressure cuff around her upper right arm and the pulse oximeter on the index finger of her left hand. The IV in the crook of her left arm was hooked to a bag of fluids hanging from a hook behind her. What had happened now started coming back to her: Her walk home. The sudden reaction. Jason taking her to the hospital...

How long ago had that been? Maddy's memory seemed so foggy. When she looked to her right, she saw Riley leaning back in a chair, eyes closed and sleeping. To her left she saw Jason. He was still here! More and more details started flooding back to her, and she closed her eyes as tears she couldn't control came rolling down her face. She'd been so sure this wouldn't happen here, but it had. She had done everything right, hadn't she? She had avoided her triggers, but something had gone wrong.

"Hey there," Jason said, having seen her eyes open back up. "How are you feeling? And why the tears? Everything is fine, and the doc says you're doing good. You can probably go home shortly. They just wanted to make sure you were stable and hydrated. It seems you haven't been drinking enough water," he said with a smile. She couldn't help but smile back at his attempt to make her feel better.

"I'm so sorry, but thank you for helping me once again. I'm starting to remember everything now, and it's so embarrassing. How did you know I needed help?"

"Couldn't sleep. When I went to the kitchen, I saw you out the window having trouble walking, and then you seemed to collapse on the steps. Wanted to make sure you were ok, and you couldn't even talk. Then I saw the bracelet and brought you here."

He grinned at her. "I will admit that at first I thought you had indulged in the liquor bottle a bit too much, but between the doctor and Riley, they told me a little about what's going on. Sorry you're having such a hard time."

He thought she had been drunk! That actually made her laugh. "I probably would have thought the same thing if I had been in your shoes," Maddy remarked. Just then, Riley awoke and saw them talking. She jumped up so fast that the chair almost turned over on its side.

"I knew I should have walked you home!" Riley stated, startling both of them. "You were so busy all week, and then we were up late a few nights too. I know better, and so do you. And why haven't you been drinking enough water? You're on your second bag of fluids, and the doctor said you might need to come in tomorrow for more depending on how you're feeling. Anyway, why didn't you tell me you were having a reaction before you left to go home?" The blur of words spilled out so fast that at first all Maddy could do was just stare at her friend.

"Well, I felt fine before I left your place, really I did. Just tired, but it was after midnight, for goodness' sake. My bedtime is definitely earlier than that. I just wanted to get home, take a shower, and crawl into bed. But you're right. I did do a lot this week. It's just hard to sit and rest when there is so much to do down here." She had done more than she had planned in her first week. But it was just so invigorating to be in the Keys that it seemed a crime not to be out exploring every day, even though she knew she was spending the whole month here. She just wanted to soak in everything so that when she did head back to Charleston, a piece of the Keys would remain with her. Admittedly, a few times during the past week, she'd heard that little voice in her head reminding her to take things a bit slower, but she'd been feeling fine. She definitely had no idea she would end up in the ER. This was certainly not a place she wanted to be.

"Thank goodness Jason saw you through his window. There's no telling what would have happened." Now Riley sounded worried and like a scolding mother.

"I was trying to get to my tote bag with my EpiPen and then call you, but things just spiraled a bit faster than usual.

I can tell they must have given me the meds as soon as I got here. That's why I feel so exhausted."

Maddy turned to look at Jason, who looked tired himself but still very sexy with his disheveled hair and dark stubble across his jaw. "Thank you so much, again. That these little episodes can pop up so suddenly concerns my family a bit when I say I want to go somewhere by myself. This month is really a big deal for me because of my illness...and a few other things." Maddy wasn't about to discuss her personal life and the reasons why she had rented a house in the Keys while lying in this hospital bed.

"Just glad everything worked out," he said softly as he gazed at Maddy. So, she had an illness, and from the looks of things, it was a rare one that could be limiting. But he would never have known she was sick just by looking at her. She looked healthy, and she certainly was beautiful. She seemed strong willed and very determined not to let her condition slow her down, though, and he certainly had to admire her for that.

"When they let you go, I'm staying with you tonight. Tomorrow we will just chill out and watch old movies all day," Riley said authoritatively.

"What about the picnic?"

"We'll have to reschedule that. You aren't going anywhere tomorrow." Riley was being a bit bossy, but Maddy knew it was just her way of caring, so she said nothing to contradict her.

"No, I don't want you to change your plans because of me. Too many people are going. Besides, I'll be fine. I have your number on speed dial, and if I need anything, I promise to call. I just did a bit too much this week, I see that now. Usually when

I get to travel, it's only for a few days or a week at best, so I'm used to trying to do as much as I can in that short amount of time. I forgot that I came down here for a month on purpose to relax—and definitely not to end up here." With each minute that passed, Maddy already started feeling more like herself. The IV medications and fluids always seemed to work wonders for her during a reaction, as did the occasional oxygen if needed. At least she had no tubes wrapped around her ears with a nasal cannula in her nose to aid her breathing, so that was a good sign. At times like this, she was thankful her doctor had written an emergency-room protocol that she carried with her everywhere. Maddy was also glad of the medical bracelet that adorned her wrist. The doctors could get specific information about her illness and treatment by calling a number inscribed on it.

"Well, I'll be working from home tomorrow, so if you need anything, here is my number so you can reach me anytime, day or night." Jason took a small notebook and pen out of his back pocket, wrote the number on a piece of paper, and handed it to Maddy. "Really, if you need anything, let me know. Glad you're feeling better."

Maddy couldn't tell if it was pity in his eyes or a genuine concern for her. They'd had only brief encounters over the past week, plus that day when he helped her with her groceries. But the look her gave her before he walked out of the hospital room gave her goosebumps. He lingered just a second, gave her a beautiful grin, and then he was gone.

Riley was looking at her with the biggest smile on her face.

"What?" Maddy asked as she saw Riley's face light up like a Christmas tree. "What has you so happy?"

"I definitely feel like I'm back in high school. He is into you," she said, continuing to smile and leaning back in her chair.

"Why? Because he helped me tonight? Gave me his phone number in case I needed help again? Sounds to me like he's just being a nice neighbor. Remember, he has practically ignored me all week. I'm just glad he was there tonight," Maddy said coolly, secretly hoping that Riley was right.

"No, there's some chemistry there—I can see it. He watched you like a hawk the whole time he was here. He found my number as your emergency contact in your purse, and he called me and told me what happened. By the time Carter and I got here, they said you were stable and let us come back here to your room. Jason stayed right here too. Yes, there is definitely something brewing!"

"I honestly don't remember much till now. It was all kind of a blur. I hope I didn't do anything stupid," was all Maddy could say.

"If you did, he didn't say anything." Riley continued, "He asked some questions about what your illness was, but I gave him only a vague description, no details. But then the doctor came in asking all kinds of questions, so he probably knows more than you wanted him to. Sorry, but I sure am glad he was awake last night and saw that you needed help!"

"Me too." Realizing suddenly that she was wearing nothing but a hospital gown, Maddy blushed and asked, "Who took my clothes off and put me in this gown?"

"That I don't know, but I'm pretty sure it was the nurses. I seriously doubt that Jason took advantage of a sick woman in the ER. Doesn't seem like the type." Riley laughed, and Maddy rolled her eyes. Riley certainly knew how to lighten up the mood.

"Maddy, according to the doctor, this was a minor reaction. You've got to take it easy for a couple of days," Riley said in a more serious tone.

Just then the doctor came in to see how she was doing, and he gave her some instructions. "I know you are here on vacation, but resting and staying hydrated should be your main focus for a couple of days. The nurse will be in shortly with your discharge papers, but should you have any other problems, come back. When you arrived, you were semiconscious and your blood pressure was too low. Your breathing was shallow and slightly labored, and you had minor hives around the chest area. You were progressing to a full anaphylactic reaction. I know you are aware of what to do in these situations, but just be careful so that you can enjoy your time here in the Keys. And thank you for having all the information ready for us. Mastocytosis is rare, and having your ER instructions available helped us treat you quickly."

Maddy thanked the doctor before he walked out of the room. She could already see what she would be doing for the next couple of days: resting. At least she had the hammock and the ocean water as part of her backyard. Not a bad place to recuperate, but she would rather be going to the picnic at the bridge that they had planned for today. She would just have to reschedule it for another day. Maybe she could use this downtime for some of the journaling she had planned to do while she was here, hopefully to give her some clarity about what she wanted to do with her life now. Getting healthier was one of her main priorities, because she hated these trips to the hospital. But in this case, one good thing that had come from this mishap was that she'd gotten to see Jason again. "At least I know for sure that he has more than ten words in his vocabulary," she thought to herself, smiling. And that he was sweet and caring. He had come to her rescue this evening like a knight in shining armor.

By the time they arrived back at Maddy's house, it was five in the morning. Though completely exhausted, she felt a lot better than she had just a few hours ago trying to climb these same steps. Riley helped her into the house and stayed while she took a quick shower and put on her pajamas. Before she left, she also made sure Maddy had everything she could possibly need on her bedside table: phone, water, medication, and snacks. But Maddy was fast asleep even before Riley shut and locked the door to her little house.

10

Jason had been up for several hours, working on redrawing new plans for his current home remodeling project. But he was having a hard time concentrating on his work. He was wondering about Maddy and how she was doing. He found himself getting up and wandering past the front window every so often to check on any activity in the little house across the street. Last night wasn't the first time he'd seen someone collapse, but it had really worried him. He had witnessed a man have a heart attack, but people nearby had been quick to administer CPR, which he later learned had saved the man's life. He had encountered cuts, broken bones, and such assorted injuries on various job sites, but last night had truly thrown him a curveball because he'd felt so helpless not knowing what was happening to her. Then, discovering that she had a rare illness even the doctors were baffled by was even more perplexing. His brain was telling him to stay away, to forget about the woman across the street except for helping her if the need arose. But his gut was sending him another signal. He wanted to learn more about this woman, so headstrong and determined as she dealt with a chronic illness. And he also couldn't deny his physical attraction to her.

Jason hadn't stopped thinking about her all week, and now, after last night's event, it was even worse. This was all so foreign to him, having feelings for someone who was a complete stranger. All he knew was her name, that she was on vacation, and that she had an illness. He asked himself again: What makes her so different from the other women I've met over the years?

As he did another window check, he finally saw Maddy standing in her kitchen window, just opening the curtains, probably hoping for some sunshine. Today's forecast was calling for showers and thunderstorms, the kind of forecast he hated, so he was glad it was Sunday and not a workday. With the beautiful Florida sunshine so elusive today, he hoped Maddy would get the rest she needed. He really wanted to go see her, but he hesitated each time he stepped to his front door.

As he paced the floor between his little workspace and the door, he kept trying to convince himself that visiting her was the right thing to do. "I was the one who helped her last night, so it won't be weird for me to go over to her house, right? I'm not breaking my 'no connections" rule by seeing if she was on the mend. Oh, what the hell," he thought. "I'm going to go check on her." He answered his own question by walking out the door and heading across the street.

When she woke up, she knew it would be later than her normal time because of her unscheduled hospital visit hours earlier but also because the sun wasn't streaming through the window blinds as usual. She checked her cell phone, first seeing that it was already one o'clock in the afternoon, and then, according to her Weather Channel app, that they were in for a cloudy day with a chance of rain. Thus oriented, she lay back on the bed and thought about the previous night's events. Her whole body seemed to ache, from the top of her head to the very ends of her toes, and everywhere in between. It was almost as if she'd had a very bad case of the flu, but Maddy knew from experience that this was just how her body recovered after having what other people would describe as a severe allergic reaction. In reality, though, she wasn't truly allergic to anything. "Ah, the joys of this little illness," she thought to herself.

A "no-sun day" was confirmed when she glanced out the kitchen window. Then her eyes shifted to the house across the street. Maddy thought she'd seen movement through the windows and was secretly hoping to catch a glimpse of him. Jason had been there for her last night, no questions asked. He'd also stayed at the hospital till she woke and was sure she was going to be ok. And if Riley was right, he seemed really interested in her. She had to admit she'd found herself thinking about him each day, and now he had been part of her rescue the previous evening. She hoped that he might be more willing to talk, maybe even getting to know him better now that he had helped her two times. But she also knew that some people didn't handle illnesses very well, choosing to ignore the issue or avoiding altogether those who were chronically ill. She had friends and family members that chose not to see her or even acknowledge that she was living with this invisible disease. Even her ex-husband hadn't been able to stand the pressure of it, and although he claimed her condition wasn't the reason for the collapse of their marriage, she knew in her heart that it had been a big part of it. She had promised herself that after he walked out and as soon as Hope was out of college and making it on her own, she would just start again. No relationships. Just take care of herself, maybe get a dog. But this man across the street had put a chip in the wall she had built to protect herself from the pain of her past and the daily stress of dealing with her symptoms. She was trying to stay positive, but the thought of getting close to someone again with the inherent possibility of getting hurt was always in the back of her mind. As she walked away from the window, she concluded that maybe it was best for them to remain just neighbors.

Though she was still weak from last night's episode, she was feeling ok. The doctor's orders for resting would be no problem. Even though the sky was cloudy, the air was still warm, so she decided to go outside and set up a little area for herself under the tiki hut where she could relax in the hammock by the water. If it started raining, she could be inside quickly, except for climbing those steps, which she knew she could do this time—she'd just take them a bit slower. And since it was going to be a stay-at-home day, she stayed in her favorite pajamas. She gathered together everything she'd need: her water, snacks, medicine, journal, and sketchbook along with a couple of beach towels and a pillow for the hammock. Her iPhone would provide some background music if the mood hit her, and she would just unwind and relax while absorbing the atmosphere around her. She really wanted to paint with her watercolors, but if she kept adding more items to her tote bag, she wouldn't be able to carry it. Drawing and sketching was the next best thing, and the alluring scenery off the dock gave her lots to work with.

Maddy had just settled into the hammock and closed her eyes when she heard footsteps in the gravel rock that surrounded the house. She'd forgotten about Riley's text telling her she would be over in a little bit.

"Hey, Riley, I'm out back in the hammock," she called out. "Decided to stay in my PJs since I was under orders to rest. I didn't think any of the neighbors would mind," she said, laughing.

"I think you look rather cute, and as one of your neighbors, I certainly don't mind," Jason said as he came around the corner and found her lounging under the tiki hut. She was indeed dressed in a bright, coral-flowered T-shirt with matching pants. Damn, he was glad he'd come over.

When Maddy saw it was Jason instead of her best friend, she was so startled she could feel her face turn at least five shades of red. "Oh...hi!" she said, quickly looking around for something to cover up with. Even though her attire wasn't that bad, she still felt embarrassed. But really, he'd surely seen her at her worst last night. "Have a seat," she said sheepishly, gesturing to the chaise lounge opposite the hammock.

He looked so sweet as he stood there with three little flowers in his hand while trying to move the chair under the little hut closer to her. She was grinning on the outside, but her insides were doing flip-flops. He had come to see her, exactly what she had secretly hoped for!

"Wanted to check on you to see how you were doing. Oh, and these are for you," he said, handing her the already-wilting flowers. "Figured you might sleep in a bit with such a late night. Is this a bad time?"

"No, not at all." There is never a bad time for you to come over, Maddy thought, but this she kept to herself.

"How are you feeling after last night? You look so much better. I mean, not that you looked terrible last night, just that you were sick. Hell, I better stop before I make a bigger fool of myself." He laughed and just shook his head.

Maddy laughed too. "Yes, I'm feeling much better, thanks to you. And you're right. I know that I must have looked a bit rough last night. Stumbling around and almost passing out on the steps? If I remember correctly, last night you told me you thought I was drunk."

"It did look that way when I saw you out the window. But you just didn't strike me as the type of woman who would drink to the point of passing out. I can usually read people pretty good," Jason said, a sly grin on his face.

"Glad you had your personal 'people radar' working over-time last night. I would have probably still been on those steps this morning, or worse. Sorry I kept you out so late last night… or this morning, I should say."

"Well, maybe next time we could be out a little late for something fun instead of an ER visit," he said softly.

Did he just kind of ask her out? That's what it sounded like to her. Her insides started to flutter again. "I could agree to that," she said, feeling flushed all over. "Right now I'm obeying the doctor's orders and resting. I don't feel like going through a repeat of last night, especially on vacation. So I'm being a good girl and doing as I'm told."

"That's one of the reasons I came by—to make sure you didn't decide to go off and play tourist. But if you don't mind my asking, Maddy, what is really wrong? What kind of illness do you have? The doctors last night sounded like they thought you were crazy, and I even heard one of them say that he had to look it up on Google. But then they got your...what did they call it? 'Protocol,' and they were able to help you. I'm sorry if I'm being too nosy." Jason peered at her, wondering if he had gone too far with the questions.

Before she had a chance to answer him, a soft rain started to fall, and they heard a rumble of thunder in the distance. "Let's go into the house, and I'll fill you in on all the wonderful details."

Jason helped her pack up all her stuff, and they headed for the steps. Jason had a very interesting but certainly a great view, in his opinion, of this unique woman as he followed her up the stairs to the house.

But Maddy was very conscious of the fact that he'd had a very complete look of her, pajamas and all. She suddenly remembered that the garments she had on were particularly thin and cringed because the rain was making them even more transparent. But there was nothing she could do about it now, so she tried to push it out of her mind even though she knew her cheeks were probably turning red once more. They got into the house just before the rain started coming down heavily.

"We timed that just right. Would you like something to drink? I guess what I should say is would you like some water. That's all I have in the house right now, except for some almond milk. I need to go grocery shopping." Maddy made a mental note to include soda on her next shopping list.

"Water is fine." Jason sat on the sofa, and Maddy could tell he was nervous as she handed him a bottle of water. She went and sat in the oversized plush chair across from him, taking the thin blanket from its arm and draping it around her to cover up her pajamas. Now *she* was nervous, and suddenly, she knew why. She liked him. Even though they hadn't yet had a full, decent conversation, she felt a strong attraction to this man.

"So, what's the scoop?" Jason looked at her as he leaned back into the sofa and began sipping his water.

"Yes, about last night. I have an illness called Mastocytosis. It's a bit complicated, but to simplify the explanation, I have too many Mast Cells in my body and they can cause allergic-type reactions to just about anything: food, water, heat, cold, the sun, sound, chemicals, fragrances—really anything. The reactions can be mild or serious. Last night was what I would call a moderate to severe reaction. I know most of the things that can cause my body to trigger, but sometimes one of them sneaks by me and I'll have what the doctors call a flare-up or reaction. The one last night really hit me out of the blue, because I had been feeling great all week, except for being just a bit tired. The problem was that I did too much because I was so excited to be here. I stressed my system, so my body slowed me down. There is no cure for it. Medications and eating healthy help keep my body stable. There is always a possibility it could turn into something worse, but I choose to think that it won't. Lately I've been having more reactions than normal, but that's because stress at home has been a little on the high side thus the reason why I decided to come here for a month. To get away and take some time for myself. I want to get my health back as much as I can, and I also have a few other things going on in my life. Getting away to take some time for myself sounded like exactly what I needed. So, here I am. That's my little story in a nutshell." Maddy looked at him carefully, and then took a sip of her water, waiting for his reaction.

Jason sat quietly for a moment, mulling over her story. "Sounds similar to my cousin who has a peanut allergy, but this is maybe a bit worse."

"Not worse, just different, even though both illnesses are treated similarly if the reaction is severe like last night."

"I'm surprised you're here by yourself," Jason said tentatively. "I can see why your family would be concerned."

"My family wasn't overly enthusiastic about my plan. I made sure I had all the bases covered before I told them. Plus, staying so close to Riley helped my case for coming here alone. They—my parents and daughter—also understood that it might be good for me to get away. My ex-husband couldn't care less and probably doesn't even know I'm not in Charleston. This vacation was to be a treat for myself, a month to relax in one of my favorite places. Except for last night, so far I'm having a pretty good time." Especially when you are sitting across from me, she thought to herself. Maddy hoped she had answered his big questions, because now she wanted to know more about him.

Jason wasn't quite sure what to say. She had a serious illness, but to look at her you would never know it. She looked healthy and beautiful. Her eyes were bright, and her smile made him melt just a little. He would never have known if he hadn't actually witnessed her symptoms.

"You certainly don't look sick. I would have never guessed you had a chronic illness. You look so healthy. How do you manage it?" Jason asked, still trying to come to grips with her situation.

"At first it was hard," Maddy said in a hushed tone. "I was bounced around from doctor to doctor like a beach ball. They misdiagnosed me with so many things that I can't even remember them all, and this was over a twenty-year span. And medications!" she said, laughing and shaking her head. "I have one shelf in my closet back home that resembles a small pharmacy.

"Those medications that were supposed to be helping me were actually causing more problems, and in a weird way they helped me finally get the right diagnosis. My breakthrough happened when I met another woman whose symptoms were similar to mine. That's when I first heard about mast cell diseases. They are still considered rare with only a few specialists scattered around the country. And like you saw last night, the majority of medical personnel have no clue, so that's why I keep a bracelet on my wrist and papers in my tote or handbag. It's been two years since I was officially diagnosed, and I'm still trying to find a good plan of medicine, food, and more so that I can live a somewhat normal life. That was part of the reason I hopped on a train here. But I've discovered there's no such thing as 'normal,' because everyone is so different. Sorry...I've been rattling on and on."

Maddy looked over and caught Jason looking at her with what seemed like compassion in his eyes, not the stoic look of someone that had essentially ignored her the week before. "Still, I can't thank you enough for last night. You probably saved my life."

"No thanks needed," he said with a grin. "I'm just thankful everything turned out fine and that you're doing ok today. Also that you are listening to the doctor and taking it easy."

"When you sleep past noon and it's storming in the Keys, there's not much else to do but take it easy. So, now it's my turn. How did you end up living here in the Keys?" Maddy asked, determined to know more about his story.

Jason looked at her and heaved a big sigh. "Well, to begin with, I'm just here temporarily. I'm an architect and I restore old buildings and homes. I've been traveling all over the United States for the past ten years, moving from one job to the next. I love to see an old building or house go from looking like a run-down shack into a beautiful place to live or work. I got the bug for restoring homes and buildings from my dad. He was a general foreman on a construction crew for as long as I could remember. I used to go to work with him, and he taught me so much. He's retired now. Sometimes he and my mom will come and check out the project I'm working on, turning the trip into a vacation. I think he misses being in the middle of a good restoration. I came here a little over nine months ago to bring an old hotel back to life, but one day another man came to the job site and asked me about restoring an old beach house. As soon as I saw it, I knew I couldn't say no. But everything should be wrapping up on it in the next four to six weeks. Then it will be on to the next project."

"Where is the next great home to be restored?" Maddy asked, a little disappointment welling up inside her.

"Several jobs have been offered to me. I just haven't decided where I want to go. They're all good opportunities, so it's hard to decide."

"Do you have a permanent house somewhere?" she asked, wondering at the same time if that house had a permanent wife attached to it.

"I guess I could say yes and no. I own a house in Las Vegas, but I'm rarely home, so my parents live there. They take care of it for me, and I visit every so often. I guess my home is my suitcases," he smiled.

"Nothing wrong with that," she said. "I actually live with my parents right now, and I'm forty-eight years old! Something I thought I would never do. But since my only daughter married last year, and keeping up the large house I got through the divorce settlement seemed silly, I sold the house and moved in with my parents temporarily. They converted part of their home into a small apartment for me, which I insisted was not necessary, but they always have family visiting, so when I finally do find a place of my own, they'll be able to use it as a guest house. At least, that was how they explained it to me. I know they just didn't want me by myself, and I dearly love them for that." She laughed as she remembered those conversations and how insistent they had been. In hindsight, it had been a good decision, but at the time Maddy had been determined somehow to keep her independence.

Jason laughed. "Well, now I don't feel so bad. I'm forty-nine, no children, and still living with my parents too. Add to that a conniving ex-wife. So I guess we have a lot in common."

"I guess we do," Maddy said, smiling inside.

11

Before they knew it, Jason and Maddy had spent the entire afternoon talking about everything, from work and hobbies to likes and dislikes, and much more. Jason told her a little about his ex-wife's extramarital affairs that had led to their divorce and how this had helped him decide to live a nomad's life, traveling to different jobs instead of staying in one place.

"I wasn't running away from my problems, but being on the road helped me heal, I guess you could say—and forgive. Loving what I do has helped also, and I've been able to see and do so much around the country." As Jason explained all this to Maddy, a part of him couldn't believe he was opening up so much of his life to her. She was so easy to talk to and if he had been smart he would have just made sure she was okay and left. But she made it hard to leave. "My parents say that I'm just scared of being in a relationship again, and they're always trying to get me to come home to meet some woman they met that they think is just perfect for me. I guess since they retired they feel it's their job to play matchmaker." They both started laughing.

"Well, for me it's my daughter. She's always wanting me to go out or try an online dating service. I just keep telling her as nicely as I can that I'm just not interested in any kind of relationship right now. Besides, most people, especially men—no offense—when they find out you might have a problem or two, they run like the plague." Her voice lowered as she ended her sentence.

Jason saw the look on her face change from happy to sad. "You know, that's not always true. I guess some people just don't know how to handle a situation, so they don't want to get involved. But there are others that look at the person and realize how special they are. Those are the people you need to concentrate on."

"Wow, you sound like a therapist!" she said jokingly.

"I'll admit that I've seen one before. My divorce was pretty ugly, and talking to my dad and brother was no help. It was actually my therapist so long ago that suggested I take my passion for remodeling and turn it into a full-time business. Putting my energy into what made me happy helped me heal. I can't say I've forgotten what happened, but it's behind me now. So, now you know my weakness for old buildings. What do you like to do?"

"I like painting. Especially with watercolors. I've had people ask for prints or want to buy my originals, but I've always felt they weren't good enough. I actually brought my paints here to practice and my camera to get some good shots around the Keys. I also like photography, but I concentrate mostly on coastal scenes. Brought my computer with me to do some research about online galleries and to talk to some people about setting up my own online shop. I think it would help me heal physically and mentally from everything. Give me some independence that I feel I've lost over the years."

Jason asked, "Have you painted anything since you've been here? I'd love to see it."

Maddy was nervous about showing her work, but she nonetheless reached over to the table and picked up the folder that held two of her completed paintings. "I've only finished two, and they're small ones. I've been exploring the island instead, which is why I'm paying for it today, but with all the rain, I couldn't have planned it better." He stood up and came to sit beside her in the big chair. He was so close she could smell a very faint cologne, but it wasn't strong enough to bother her. In fact, he smelled really good. She kept peeking at him, stealing sideways glances, examining the little features she hadn't noticed before, like his chiseled chin and his very muscular shoulders. Her heart was beating a little faster, but this reaction was being triggered by being so close to him. And she liked it.

"Wow, these are good! This looks like your backyard and dock outside. And I'm not sure where this one is. Somewhere here in the Keys?" he asked. He knew he should move back to the sofa but he wanted the conversation to continue just so he could sit so close to her. She looked so cute in her pajamas, curled up in the blanket with her hair up in a ponytail. He really wished he could sit back and snuggle up beside her as she described her paintings.

"The second painting is Anne's Beach on Islamorada. That so far is my favorite spot in the Keys. But I'm a beach girl. In Charleston, I'm only about fifteen minutes from the ocean. Even though our beaches aren't like the ones here in the Keys, a beach is a beach as far as I'm concerned. I love the sun, sand, and water. Listening to the waves is the best." She could tell she was rambling again. Sitting close beside him like this made her nervous.

"I grew up in the desert, so being here is like a completely different world. But I have to admit I really like it here. It's probably one of my favorite places in all my travels over the years." And right now you are making it a much better place to stay, Jason thought as he handed the paintings back to her.

Just then Maddy's stomach growled loudly, embarrassing her. "Um, I guess I'm hungry," Maddy said as she rubbed her stomach and smiled up at him. She looked at her phone and couldn't believe the time. "It's already six thirty! I was supposed to eat hours ago. Would you like to stay?" she asked politely. "I don't have much because I need to go shopping, but I could probably throw something together for you." She indeed wanted him to stay, but she knew that she didn't have anything for a complete meal, just the small amount of food she ate. Now she was embarrassed by her boldness in asking him to stay for dinner.

"Thanks, but I really need to get back home. I was actually doing some work when I decided to come and check on you.

I probably should get back at it, since it's due in the morning. And sorry if I stayed too long. Time just passed by so quickly," he said to her as they both stood up, brushing so close that she could feel the heat radiating from him.

Jason definitely wanted to stay but knew he needed to leave. This was just a friendly visit he reminded himself. Nothing more but she was so easy to talk to, and she was beautiful even in her bright pajamas and no makeup.

"I'm glad you came over, and I enjoyed the afternoon. Thanks for letting me talk. Just hope I didn't bore you with all the details." But I do wish you could stay longer, Maddy thought.

"Something tells me that you could never be boring," Jason said with a smile. Suddenly, he decided that his self-imposed rule of no friends on this trip was out the window. He enjoyed her company and finally admitted to himself that he wanted to get to know her better. When it came time to leave the Keys, he would deal with whatever this relationship became at time.

"Thanks," Maddy said quietly.

"You mentioned that you need to go shopping for groceries. Since you're still on rest orders from the doc, I could take you tomorrow if you want. That way I can help you." Jason suggested this hoping she would say yes so that he could spend more time with her. Asking her out on a date right now didn't feel quite appropriate given her trip to the ER last night.

"Oh, I don't want to bother you with that."

"Would be no problem. I need a few things too, and we could go in the morning. Say around ten?" Jason asked, looking at her expectantly.

"Are you sure? I thought you were working on plans that were due at work tomorrow." Maddy said, but secretly she was thrilled that he wanted to take her shopping. Who knew she could get this excited about a trip to the grocery store!

"I'll drop those off early and then come back and pick you up. That way I can bring in your groceries for you. *All* the bags this time, and I won't accept no for an answer."

"Well, then it's a date. I mean, not a 'date'—but...you know. Yes, I'll go. That would be great." She stammered her way through her answer and saw Jason grinning at her, trying not to laugh.

"Why don't we call it a 'shopping date'?" Jason said to help her along, even though he liked the sweet blush that flooded her cheeks.

Maddy smiled and nodded her head yes. "Ok, then. A shopping 'date' it is."

She shut the door behind her and just leaned against it, reflecting back on the wonderful afternoon she'd just had. She was definitely enamored of Jason, no two ways about it. He was gorgeous, sexy, intelligent, and hardworking. He even had some past baggage of his own. All this made her just melt inside. He seemed too good to be true. Even her medical issues didn't seem to faze him. But right now, it was time for some food—and fast.

The phone rang just as she was finishing her dinner of rice and chicken. Before she could even say hello, Riley was already talking.

"So, how was your afternoon?"

"Actually, very relaxing, and Jason stopped by to check on me."

"I know. That's why I didn't call till I saw him going back across the street. You guys have been talking or whatever for over four hours! So please tell me what happened. Don't leave out anything!" Riley said desperately.

"Do you have a camera somewhere watching my house around the clock? How do you know these things? And I thought you had a picnic to go to this morning?" Maddy asked incredulously.

Riley laughed. "I just have my ways, and besides, it started raining. Now, what's going on, and is he as nice as he seems?"

Maddy sighed contently. "I had a great time, and I think he did too. He seemed more relaxed. And yes, so far it appears he's a really sweet guy. He's even taking me grocery shopping in the morning."

"I knew it." Then Riley burst out singing "Summer Nights" from *Grease*, putting emphasis on the words "summer lovin'" and making Maddy laugh so hard that tears came to her eyes.

"We are just going grocery shopping, Riley, so stop," Maddy said, but she still couldn't help but laugh. Just then she happened to see her reflection in the mirror and saw the huge smile that graced her face. She hadn't felt like this in such a long time, and it felt good.

12

Jason knew he had a large amount of work waiting for him at home, but it didn't matter. He'd just spent about the best afternoon he'd had in a long time with a most amazing woman. Maddy was beautiful both inside and out. Her sincerity was endearing, and she was so honest about her feelings, speaking her mind in a respectful way that made him more attracted to her than any woman he had met. Plus, he couldn't help but notice her beautiful eyes, her wavy blond hair, and the curves of her body. Her pajamas today had displayed her features quite well, and he just couldn't quit thinking about her.

But was she right about the medical issues and how people run away? He told himself he wasn't that kind of person, but in all honesty, he did give it a second thought. What if Maddy had another episode? Could he handle that again? He had to remind himself that they were only going grocery shopping, but he truly wanted to spend more time with her. And with that came the possibility of her having issues like last night. Did he want to get close with someone who had an illness like this? One that was so unpredictable?

As the questions swirled around in his head, the answer came surprisingly quickly. He liked Maddy—he couldn't deny it. Something about her, from the day he'd first helped her with her groceries, had him thinking about her night and day even though he had tried to keep his distance. He couldn't explain it, but he knew from experience that he had to listen to his gut, his intuition. Yes, she had some past and present issues, but so did he. If she was willing to accept him just as he was, then he would do the same with her. At that moment, he knew deep down that he was making the right choice. Not to shut everyone out of his life but finally let someone in. Suddenly, for the first time that he could remember, he couldn't wait to go grocery shopping in the morning.

13

Although it was just a trip to Publix this morning, Maddy was both nervous and excited. This was not an official date, but it felt like it to her. So much so that Maddy had hardly slept last night, and then she woke very early this morning. She was still tired from her ordeal at the hospital and now from last night's sleep deprivation, but somehow she was also energized. Even though they weren't leaving until ten o'clock, she had already eaten, taken all her medications, and dressed in one of her favorite casual outfits: an aqua-blue watercolor-print peasant top with white capri pants. Bohemian-style earrings and necklace completed her outfit along with her favorite flip-flops. Not that she needed to wear anything fancy, but yesterday he had seen her in her pajamas the entire afternoon, and the night before…well, she didn't even want to think about how she'd looked. So today she wanted to look her best. She was all ready to go, and it was only nine o'clock.

Just then her phone rang, and before Maddy flipped it over to the see the caller ID, she knew it was Riley. Her friend was relentless, worse than she had ever been in school.

"You ready for your grocery date? It just sounds so romantic," she said mockingly.

"If you don't give me a break, I'm not giving you any more info about him or me. You'll just have to suffer."

"I'm just kidding. You are so easy to pick on! But I'm really happy for you. And I can tell you're excited too. I don't think I've seen you like this since we were in college." And Riley was right. Maddy hadn't felt this way about a man since her marriage disintegrated, and the possibility of a romantic relationship with Jason had her jittery all over.

Just before ten, Maddy peeked through the curtains of the front window as discreetly as she could to see if there was any movement at Jason's house. Her timing couldn't have been more perfect. He was doing something right in front of the house. She wasn't quite sure what, but she couldn't quit staring. He looked ready for the beach in his blue T-shirt, khaki cargo shorts, and flip-flops. That was definitely one thing they had in common—their love of flip-flops—and had even debated yesterday which brand was the best. She smiled inwardly as the memory of her wonderful afternoon resurfaced.

As she continued to watch him, she determined he was certainly not wearing what she would have expected as work attire, so she could only assume he had been to his job site and already come back. Just to help her on their grocery date. That thought sent her happiness meter sky high.

"Wow" was the only word in Maddy's mind as she watched him approach her house. He looked great, and even though his smoldering good looks had not been lost on her before, today he seemed even more intoxicating. Cute, sexy, helpful, nice. Where was the flaw? Everyone had one, but right now she could not find a single one with Jason. Anyway, it was back to the real world in a few weeks, so why not enjoy this... whatever it was that was happening between the two of them? She hadn't allowed herself to just relax and go with the flow in such a long while that it felt strange and great at the same time. Her logical side was telling her to be careful, not to let down her guard, and so much more. But this was her vacation, so at that moment she decided to throw caution out the door and embrace what she was feeling, even if it would be for only a couple of weeks.

Jason wanted to make sure he was on time. He'd gotten up extra early to get everything done, even taking the redrawn plans to the job site way before the normal workday was to begin. He was glad the foreman had arrived early too, because he was really looking forward to this shopping excursion with Maddy. Yesterday had been the first time since he could remember that he had just felt like himself, completely relaxed with a woman, and it had felt good. He had been very wary of women since his divorce, so yesterday afternoon had taken him completely by surprise. It had been like a breath of fresh air. Maddy was smart, funny, sweet, beautiful, and damn sexy. They had talked all afternoon as if they had known each other forever. At least, that was how he was feeling this morning, and he hoped that she had felt a connection too. The problem for both of them, of course, was that this was temporary. She was on vacation, and for him, a job would soon be ending, sending him somewhere new. He had lived his life for the last ten years working on one project while always planning the next. His parents and close friends had told him to slow down a bit and just take some time to enjoy what he had accomplished, but for some reason he'd never been able to. But today he felt different, out of his comfort zone. He just wanted to enjoy this time with Maddy—even if it was just to buy groceries.

As he rang the doorbell to her house, Jason felt like he was a teenager going on a first date. Well, he wasn't in high school, but this was kind of a first date, wasn't it? No, they were just going shopping. At least, that was what they had agreed on last night, but for him it was more than that. He didn't really have anything he needed to buy. He was going just to be with her.

After giving herself a glance in the little mirror in the foyer, Maddy opened the door and felt her stomach flutter. He looked so good in his Jimmy Buffet–style outfit! She instantly wished they were heading off for an island adventure instead of shopping. And then she had an idea.

"Good morning," Maddy said as she stepped out the door. "Ready for this ultra exciting grocery shopping trip?"

"Definitely," he said as he gazed appreciatively at her. She was dressed as though she lived in the Keys year round, which fit her personality perfectly. She was so adorable, and what he really wanted to do was reach over and give her a good-morning kiss. But he restrained himself, deciding a smile would have to do.

As they got settled into his SUV, she decided to spring her last-minute idea. "I was wondering, would you be interested in going to the Seven Mile Bridge park for just a bit before we shop? I know you probably have to get back to work, so if we can't, I understand. I just wanted to go and take a few pictures, maybe sit by the water for a few minutes. It's been a while since I've been there, and if I remember correctly, it's pretty peaceful, and the scenery is beautiful. Plus, the weather seems to be cooperating today, much better than yesterday," she said as she looked at the beautiful blue skies above. She was probably asking too much, but she hoped he would say yes.

"I thought you were still supposed to be resting and just needed groceries?" he said in a slightly reprimanding voice, looking at her with a grin.

"Technically, you're right, but I would love to get some pictures from the bridge. For my paintings. But I know you have to work too. I'm really sorry. I probably shouldn't have asked, but I wanted to do something different than just sit at the house." Plus, it will give me more time with you, she thought.

"I would be more than happy to escort you to the bridge, as long as you promise not to overdo it. Remember that you're still under a doctor's orders. I love that old bridge too. While I've been here, when I just needed to think through a problem, I've often driven there to walk down to the park and sit by the water. It is peaceful." Jason sat for a second, lost in thought. "I say let's go!" he said, and he pressed his foot on the gas pedal and pulled out onto Highway 1.

The day was perfect for the forty-five-minute ride to visit the old Seven Mile Bridge, one of the Florida Keys' most fascinating landmarks. The bridge started out as a railroad until it was destroyed during a hurricane in 1935. Then the state of Florida turned it into a very narrow automotive bridge, until in 1982 a new, larger bridge was built close by. But a group of people had formed an organization to save the old bridge from being torn down. People could walk and bike ride across the little bridge until it reached Pigeon Key, a little island under the bridge. After that, a section of it was dismantled to keep people off the part of the bridge that was sagging and unstable. Even though it was old, it was still beautiful. Maddy remembered the first time she saw the bridge surrounded by the clear, aqua water of the ocean. It was breathtaking. Now she couldn't wait to get there, but this time it had extra meaning. She would be sharing it with Jason. This gave them an extra couple of hours together that they hadn't planned on yesterday, and this made her extremely happy.

When they arrived, there were not too many visitors yet, which was fine by Maddy. Fewer people around meant a more peaceful view. As she climbed out of Jason's vehicle and looked around, she was once again captivated by the near-perfect scenery. The water was a beautiful shade of turquoise, so clear that she had an overwhelming urge to jump in and swim. She had been in the Keys for over a week now and had only soaked in the warm ocean water once. She quickly promised herself she would make her beach trips a priority as soon as her energy was back to normal.

"It is so beautiful here," Jason said as he looked around at the bridge and the water below. "But it's hard to imagine traveling across it all those years ago. Just a bit tiny, if you ask me."

She laughed. "I have to agree with you on that one. I'm not sure I could have made it across and enjoyed the scenery at the same time. My eyes would have been closed till I was on the other side!"

As they walked down the steps to the small park by the water, Jason asked. "Are you sure about walking back up the steps? Remember, I don't want you to do too much."

"Goodness, now you sound like Riley!" she said with a smile.

"Well, I'm not your boss, just a concerned friend." Who would maybe like to be a closer friend, he thought, but this he did not say out loud.

"When we get to the park, let's find a shady spot. I've got my water, and I should be ok. Plus, after we shop, I promise not to do anything else for the rest of the day. I really want to be able to do some more island exploring, and I also need to plan my trip to Key West."

Jason was intrigued. "When are you planning on going?"

Maddy hadn't planned the date yet, but she wanted to go for a few days to tour the city, watch the sunset at Mallory Square, have some french fries at Margaritaville, and take the town trolley around to get some pictures of the old city.

"The date is still up in the air. I have to find a hotel that is close to Mallory Square so I don't have to do a lot of walking. But then, I suppose I could just use pedicabs. That was so much fun on my last trip there," she said, remembering the comedic man that had pedaled her and her dad around the city last time. That guy had turned out to be the best tour guide ever!

"I have some friends in Key West that own a bed and breakfast right off Duval Street. I can see if they have anything available. I just finished renovating one of their properties in Tennessee not too long ago. Let me know your trip date, and I'll see what I can do—if you're interested," Jason volunteered.

"That would be wonderful, but I don't want to put you out." Or maybe, Maddy thought in her imagination, we could go together. She could just picture spending time with Jason, exploring the old city. Thinking about it made her feel quite giddy.

At his next statement, Maddy could have sworn he had read her mind.

"You check your calendar, and I'll check mine, and let's see if we can go together. I could use a break, and I could be your chaperone. That way Riley won't go a little crazy on you when you say you want to go. I'll ask if they have two rooms available. If so, we'll be citizens of the Conch Republic for a few days. How does that sound?" Jason couldn't believe he had just asked her to go to Key West with him. What was he thinking? The words had come out before he'd really thought about it and he could just imagine what Maddy must be thinking about him. Asking someone to go on a trip after only knowing them for a few days? He cringed inside, hoping she wasn't thinking ill of him.

Maddy was so surprised at their seeming telepathy that all she could say was, "Sounds perfect to me, but I don't need a chaperone."

Pleasantly startled by her acceptance but dismayed at her interpretation of his suggested role, Jason quickly said, "I didn't really mean it like that. Let's just say a friend looking after another friend. Does that sound better?"

"Much better! And I think the idea sounds perfect," Maddy said as she turned to look back toward the turquoise water, a big grin on her face. She was going on a trip with Jason! This was clearly not the same Maddy who had traveled here on the train a little over a week ago. The Florida Keys were already having the magical effect on her that she'd been hoping for.

14

Their conversation as they rode back to grocery store was filled with more questions to each other about their respective lives, and they each shared more information about their divorces and their exes. Jason gave her a few more details on Andrea, the woman who had hardened his heart toward relationships, but he also shared more about his love for his career. He was passionate about what he did. When he talked about the homes and buildings he had remodeled around the country, his face and body language radiated happiness.

Maddy opened up about her marriage and her daughter's diabetic condition that had kept her so very busy over the years, elaborating that her ex-husband just wasn't the family type and that when things got rough, he bailed. She explained that in hindsight, she'd come to see this as a good thing—she and her ex were just too different. They had tried for twenty-five years to make it work, and it never really had. And even though their split came at a tough time, as she was going through back surgery, ultimately it was the best thing for both of them. She went on to brag about Hope and how she had finished high school and college before she was twenty. Now she was married, had a doctorate from Harvard after receiving a full scholarship, and was in the middle of her residency researching childhood mental disabilities.

"Did you have any children?" she asked him.

"No, Andrea wasn't into children, even though before we got married, she would tell everyone we were going to have at least four kids! I was quick to tell her that two was enough for me, but it was all just a show to her anyway. She had no desire for even one child, much less four of them. She was much more interested in how many men she could sleep with instead." The disgust in his voice was so apparent that Maddy decided a change of subject was needed.

At her sudden silence, Jason realized that his last sentence had sounded a bit harsh. "Sorry. Old memories, and I *am* truly over them. Just sometimes it's hard for me to believe that I let myself get duped by her. She was so heartless and cruel. Not just to me, but even to my parents. But let's talk about something more cheerful!"

"I'm sorry. I probably shouldn't have brought up the subject of our exes. But I know how you feel," she said softly.

"Maddy, it not a big deal. We've both been through a bunch of garbage. I'm just glad we can talk to each other. To be honest, I haven't talked to anyone this much about my divorce as I have with you today. Thanks for listening." As he finished his sentence, they pulled into the Publix parking lot.

"Ok, let's get your groceries inside first. I think you've been out too long, and you look like you could use a nap," Jason said jokingly as he stood beside her in front of the house.

"Are you implying that I look bad?" she quipped as she made her way up the stairs with just her tote bag, since Jason had insisted on bringing in all the shopping bags himself.

"No, you are definitely not looking bad," he said slyly, and she looked back at him with an impish grin.

"No, you actually look quite nice, but I just want you to follow the doctor's orders, and we strayed a bit by taking our little side trip to the bridge. Not that I didn't enjoy spending more time with you, but I certainly don't want to be the cause of your not being able to enjoy the rest of your vacation." He followed her up the steps to her house, concentrating hard on what he was doing, because this view of her was provoking other thoughts and making him want to stay with her instead of going back to work.

As he deposited the grocery bags on the kitchen counter, she found herself wanting him to stay. The morning had been so nice, and after yesterday afternoon, she'd discovered that she truly enjoyed being with him. Her eyes traveled to his lips, and she wondered what a kiss from him would feel like.

"What are you grinning about?" Jason asked as he caught her look.

"Just thinking about what a nice morning it's been. I really had a lot of fun, and it was great to escape the house for a bit." Nice cover-up, Maddy, she thought.

"I guess I need to get my food put up before the frozen stuff becomes mush," he said as he walked toward her front door.

"Yes, and I will have to educate you on healthier eating. Those TV dinners are full of all kinds of creepy stuff," she said playfully.

"It's the best this man can do for now. I'm not much of a cook, but if I can throw it in the microwave, it sounds good to me."

They had reached her front door, and as she gazed up at him, his smile melted her insides. Impulsively, she stood on her toes and gave him a quick kiss on the cheek. But as she started to back away, she felt Jason's hands gently touch each side of her face, and he kissed her lips…softly, warmly, tenderly. She felt the spark that flew between them, and she knew he felt it too.

15

"Well, hi there, everyone! Seems like you're in good hands," Riley said playfully to Maddy as she opened the gate. "Thought I would walk down here to check on you, since your little shopping trip took longer than you said, and I saw Jason's vehicle here. But it looks like you're doing just fine." Both Maddy and Jason had been so caught up in the moment that neither of them had heard Riley's approach.

They each stepped back, looking at one another and then at Riley as though they had been caught red-handed doing something wrong. Except this had felt very right to Maddy. If Riley hadn't shown up, would Jason have kissed her again?

"I wanted to take some pictures at the Seven Mile Bridge, and Jason was sweet enough to take me. It was my suggestion... and I know—I have to rest. And yes, as soon as the groceries are put away, I will. I promise I didn't overdo it, and—oh, I'm getting ready to eat and take medication. I think that's a full report." Maddy looked at Riley with her eyes opened wide as if to say "you came at the wrong time."

"Ok, you're off the hook. Hi, Jason," Riley said to him as he stood watching the two women exchange lighthearted barbs.

"Hi, Riley. I'll remind her next time to call you *mom*," he said with a smirk.

"Both of you can joke all you want, but I was truly worried. The only thing that helped was that at least I knew she was with you," she said, pointing at Jason. "But now that I know everything is A-ok, I'll leave the two of you alone so that you can have your privacy." With that, Riley turned and started walking back down the street toward her own house, a big smile on her face. Jason and Maddy stood in awkward silence.

"I gotta go, but if you need anything, please let me know. And one more thing. Have dinner with me tomorrow night. I'll even try to cook—or better yet, we can go out. You choose," he said.

"Are you asking me out on a 'real' date?" she queried.

"The real thing this time. But the more I think about it, there's a great restaurant on the water just a little way from here that I know you will love. That sounds much better than my microwave cooking," he said.

"Dinner with you tomorrow sounds great, as long as you don't mind if I bring some of my own food with me just in case," Maddy said, excitement pulsing through her.

"That doesn't bother me at all. I will pick you up at six thirty tomorrow evening. Ok?" Jason felt as anxious as the day he presented his very first blue print at the start of his architect career.

"Sounds perfect."

The rest of her day was spent sorting and storing groceries, taking a nice shower, and sitting outside by the water again, this time with her computer, looking at the pictures she had taken that day. She couldn't wipe the silly grin off her face. Just thinking about Jason had her feeling emotions she'd long ago put away on a shelf. She and Jason had taken some selfies on her camera phone, and she couldn't get past those to view her other pictures, the ones that were supposed to be her muses for her sketches and paintings. A passing tourist had taken a picture of the two of them next to the blue water, and she stared happily at it. Jason had put his hand at the small of her back, and Maddy remembered the sensation of electricity surging through her at the time. These feelings were actually making her feel vibrant and alive again. But lingering in the back of her mind was the thought that she would be going home at the end of the month and that Jason would be moving on to his next job soon after. So she decided to enjoy every minute of what they had right now.

The excitement of spending more time with Jason that evening had her once again awake much earlier than normal. She just couldn't sleep, but she also knew that if she was awake this early, she would need a nap this afternoon. She certainly didn't want to ruin her first "official" date with Jason. She went to the kitchen to get her medicine for the morning along with a light breakfast, sneaking a peek discreetly through the gap in the front window curtains at his house as she did so. Her timing was perfect yet again—he was just leaving for the day. Even though he had a casual, button-down shirt on with his blue jeans, he looked very much the professional businessman carrying his laptop case. And a very charming businessman at that, she thought. It seemed to her that he got better looking every time she saw him. Riley had told her when she'd arrived here that he was a "hottie," but at the time Maddy hadn't given it a second thought. Men were not on her radar. But now it seemed all she could do was think about the man across the street. She was glad she'd gotten to watch him leave for work today. Something to think about as she waited for evening to arrive.

The day seemed to drag by slowly as Maddy waited in anticipation. She had called Riley early that morning to give her the big scoop, and Riley couldn't contain her excitement.

"Please, please, please let me come and help you get ready! I can pick out the best outfit for you."

"I think I have decent fashion sense and can dress myself, but it would bring back memories of old times. Remember in high school when we would help each other get ready before going out? " Maddy asked excitedly. "There would be clothes everywhere, and my mom would come in and just shake her head," she said, laughing.

"Yeah, we were pretty messy, but we sure looked good when we left the house!"

"Ok, I relent. He's picking me up at six thirty, so come over a couple of hours before then. I know that's early, but I want to take my time and really look nice this evening. He's only seen me in beach clothes and a hospital gown so far. He's taking me to some nice restaurant on the beach, but he didn't give me the name."

"I wonder which one it is. I'm as excited as you are, I think," Riley blurted out. "I'll be there at four, and I promise to leave way before he comes to pick you up. But I'll be watching out the window when you guys leave."

Maddy rolled her eyes but was secretly happy that her best friend approved.

"I'm going to do my best to try to take a nap today, but… Riley, I'm so nervous and excited! I really like him. And I know it's only been a week, but—I don't know. There's just something about him I can't explain."

"Maddy, just enjoy it. All the feelings and emotions. Don't give a crap what others think, including me. This is your life— follow your heart."

"You are the best friend a girl could ever have. You know that, right?" Maddy said softly.

"Yes! You are so lucky. See ya in a few hours!"

Maddy spent the day doing things around the house to keep herself busy. She thought about going to the beach but didn't want to press her luck. She was on only her third day since being released from the hospital, and according to the discharge papers, she was still supposed to be resting. She was feeling better, though, having been taking it very easy and making herself drink extra water, but she thought the renewed energy really had more to do with Jason than anything else.

Thinking about him made her feel happy, and the smile on her face felt permanent. That was a stress reducer, right? She could now report that happiness did have some very positive side effects, whether you were ill or not. She decided to do a watercolor painting using one of the pictures she'd taken yesterday. Something she could show Jason when he came to pick her up. Maybe she'd even give it to him. The project kept her busy until she deliberately made herself lie down for a nap, and to her surprise, she actually fell asleep.

She woke abruptly to a knock at the door and panicked at first, thinking she had overslept, but it was just Riley—was it four o'clock already?—coming to help her get dressed the way they used to so many years ago. After excited consultations and outfit assessments with Riley, she ended up choosing her favorite maxi dress, a blue and lime-green print. She added a white cotton crocheted shrug and white sandals. And instead of wearing her hair straight, she decided to play up her waves by scrunching it into an attractive, natural curl as it dried. When she looked in the mirror, she felt right at home, as if she belonged on the islands. She and Riley both approved of the finished product. She was glad she'd let her best friend come help her. Moments likes this brought back so many happy memories of their old times together.

Riley left, bestowing many happy wishes for a terrific evening. As six thirty drew closer, Maddy had an urge to go check to see if he was coming yet, but she resisted it, not wanting him to catch her peeking out the window. She was trying to play it cool, but she was finding it difficult with this man. He truly had her excited, happy, and all turned around.

Sudden footsteps outside broke into her thoughts, and she knew her first date with Jason Burnett was about to begin.

16

When she opened the door to his knock, Jason was taken aback by what he saw. He had thought her beautiful from the first day he saw her from across the street, but the woman in front of him was simply stunning. Her normally straight hair fell around her face in soft waves, her eyes twinkled a beautiful hazel, and her soft lips beckoned kissably. Her dress gave her the appearance of an island beauty just stepping out of a magazine.

"Hi," Maddy said as Jason stood there motionless. Was he ok? He was just staring at her, saying nothing. But then again, she was a little overwhelmed by the sight of him as well. His dark hair, the sparkling brown eyes, and that dark stubble over his chin made him ever so sexy. His attire—dark jeans, a royal-blue pullover shirt, and deck shoes—made him look like he had lived here all his life.

"You look beautiful," he said as he took her hand and leaned in slightly to kiss her cheek. Maddy couldn't help but smile as a shiver ran up her arm.

He followed her to the passenger side of the SUV and opened the door. "If it's ok with you, we're going to have dinner by the water this evening, outside under the stars. And afterward, if you'd like, we can take a stroll down the nearby beach." Jason laid out his plans with a confident voice, but she could tell he was hoping they would meet her approval.

"It sounds wonderful. But may I ask, have I overdressed for dinner? If so, I can change quickly," she said.

"No way. You look perfect!" Jason said as he closed the passenger door.

A short drive later, they pulled into the parking lot of a restaurant called Lazy Days, which was located right on the water. Since the evening sky was clear and the weather near perfect, they chose a table on the outside patio that would allow them to watch the famous Florida Keys sunset as they dined.

"This is beautiful!" Maddy said as she took the chair he had pulled out for her. "I've passed by this restaurant before but never really looked at it. The location is great."

"The food is good too. I've been here a couple of times since I've been in the Keys with some of the guys from work. It's one of their favorite restaurants for a more upscale place. There are a lot of little diners along the Keys that are really good, much better than the chain restaurants," Jason said, wondering why he was talking about restaurants. Even though they had already spent time together, he felt quite nervous this evening.

"I also called ahead to see if they had some of the food you can eat, and since they did, I thought this would be the best place. Hope that was ok. Don't want you to think I'm being like Riley," he added quickly.

"Actually, that was really quite thoughtful of you. No one has ever done that before. Thanks!" She was now in awe of him. Manners. Good looks. Thoughtful of others. He was almost too good to be true. Where were the imperfections?

They ordered their meals, and she found she was indeed able to order off the menu, which was unusual. Again, all through dinner, they never ran out of subjects to talk about. They seemed to have so much in common, and Maddy loved it. She also enjoyed watching Jason—his body language, his smile, the way his eyes lit up when he was telling her something he was thoroughly excited about. The ease of their conversations amazed her. She couldn't remember ever feeling this way before. She wasn't sure she'd ever been this relaxed even with Hope's father. Everything was so different with Jason, and that simultaneously excited her and scared her.

"How was your dinner? I feel like you barely ate anything!" Jason said.

"It was delicious, and this place is amazing. Dining out on the patio, watching the sunset, listening to the waves. And spending time with an amazing man. Feels like the recipe for a perfect evening." And Maddy meant every word she said.

"I could say the same about you. You are an incredible woman, Maddy. I'm really glad you decided to rent the place across the street. For one thing, you're a huge improvement over the college frat boys that were there a few weeks ago! Much prettier—and quieter too!" He was joking but serious at the same time. "Would you like to walk on the beach?"

"I would love it!"

Jason took care of the check, and they headed toward the water. As soon as they reached the sand, they took off their shoes, leaving them sitting by a palm tree, and started walking along the dark shoreline. Just the slightest hint of the sunset remained in the distance, but enough light came from the homes, hotels, and restaurants lining the beach for them to be able to see where they were walking. Also, with the moon at half phase in a clear sky, they had all the light necessary for a romantic walk. Before they'd walked twenty feet, he reached for her hand, and she gave it. They strolled in silence for a little while, just absorbing the atmosphere and listening to the waves.

Before long, Jason slowed to a stop, looking briefly down at the sand and then to her. "Maddy, I hope I don't sound like an idiot, because I know it's only been a little over a week, but...there is just something about you. I feel energized, relaxed, and happy when I'm with you. I find myself thinking about you all day long. I want to thank you for helping me feel something again." Before she knew what was happening, Jason leaned down and kissed her lips so softly and gently that she felt molten inside. She didn't want him to pull away, but as they separated, she found her own voice.

"First of all, I certainly don't think you're an idiot, because that would mean I'm one too. I've thought about it for the last two days as well. How can I feel such a connection with someone I barely know? But there is something about you that I can't explain, and it has me thinking about you more than I should. You are definitely the most caring and thoughtful man I've ever met. As for renting the house across from you, I'm so glad I did." She reached up and placed her hand on his cheek. Then Jason's lips met hers again, and this time it was a deep, sweet kiss that sent all her senses reeling. She found herself intertwining her fingers behind his neck as she felt his arms wrap around her waist. A first, real kiss, on the beach under the stars in the Keys!

As they continued their walk along the beach, Jason decided the time was right to spring his idea on her.

"I was thinking about something today, and if you don't want to do this, there's no pressure, ok? Remember we talked yesterday about a trip to Key West? Well, I called my friend today, and they have two rooms available this Sunday for up to five days, however long you want to stay. I looked at my schedule, and I could go, but I might have to do a bit of work while we're there. That is, if you still want me to go with you."

"Yes."

Her meaning didn't immediately register in Jason's mind. "Yes what?"

"Yes, silly. I would love to go to Key West with you. Sunday sounds great, but I just need to know how much the room is. Then I can tell you how long I can stay."

"No charge. It's on the house because of all the clients I've referred to his hotels in the past," he said, much to Maddy's surprise and pleasure.

"Really? Are you serious? Can we stay Sunday through Wednesday? Will that fit in with your work schedule?" She fired the questions off so fast that Jason barely had time to register them all. Seeing her so excited and knowing she wanted to go with him made him one happy man.

"Sounds absolutely perfect to me," he murmured, pulling her in for another kiss under the stars.

17

The next morning, Maddy woke up smiling, remembering last night's magical evening. It had been idyllic, and every time she thought of Jason, the happiness that flooded her body made her tremble with delight. It wasn't long before the phone on her nightstand rang, and she knew who it was.

"Good morning, Riley," she answered quickly, without checking the display. She knew her friend was ready to fire questions at her at lightning speed.

"Tell me everything. I want to hear it all! " She sounded giddy with excitement, and Maddy was glad she had someone to share her story with.

"Do you have time to come over for some girl talk this morning before you start work? If so, bring your coffee and come to the house."

They sat on the back porch, taking in the splendid Florida morning while Maddy gave her friend the details about her date with Jason. Retelling what had happened last night allowed Maddy to relive every wonderful moment all over again. She described the restaurant, their beach walk, their first kiss, and then how they'd sat in the sand talking until they'd realized how late it was. Then he'd brought her home, leaving her at her front door with another kiss that left her weak all over. Riley barely said a word throughout, intently hanging on every detail that Maddy shared.

"And the best part is that we decided to take a trip to Key West together. We're leaving this Sunday and staying for a few days," Maddy said enthusiastically.

Riley's expression went from pure joy to a disapproving frown. "This Sunday? Don't you think that's a bit fast for someone you just met a week and a half ago?"

Riley's look was so serious that Maddy was truly surprised. She'd rarely seen her best friend like this.

"When you say it like that, it does sound fast, but there's just something about him. It's like I have known him for years instead of days. And you don't know what it's like to have someone accept you as you are when you carry around a lot of complicated issues, past and present. Not that I've gone on many dates since my divorce, but once someone finds out about my condition, they seem to drop like flies. It's not that I'm desperate for a relationship. Believe me that was not even a remote thought when I came down here. But this is different. Jason has provoked just the opposite. He basically rescued me that night I got sick, asking no questions. After taking me to the hospital, he could never have spoken to me again despite living across the street, but instead he went out of his way to check on me. We've talked, laughed, and shared so much now. We have much in common, and he even sends me silly texts during the day. He makes me smile inside and out. Last night, before we got to the restaurant, he even made sure there was food I could order. Little things like that mean so much.

"As far as the trip to Key West, he has a friend who owns a beautiful little bed and breakfast off Duval Street. He offered Jason two rooms for three nights—free! Two rooms, not one, so I don't think he assumes I'm just going to jump into bed with him...although I must say the thought has certainly crossed my mind. I'm not ready for that yet, but I think I might be ready for a relationship." She talked continuously, not giving Riley a chance to speak. She didn't want to hear objections to a trip that sounded so wonderful to her, one that she was truly looking forward to. "Riley, please be happy for me. You told me earlier to go for it and I deserved some happiness. And that is what I'm doing."

"Maddy, you know I'm not one to spoil a party. I love them! But I just hope you know what you're getting into. Especially when it's time for you to go back home, and he leaves for his next job. You're both here temporarily, and I would hate to see either of you get hurt, especially you. You are my best friend, and it's my job to make sure you are happy. I'll admit I haven't seen you this content in a long time, but I just want to make sure you know what you're jumping into," Riley said softly, being the friend Maddy had always loved.

What Riley didn't know was that Maddy had already thought about all those things. She just didn't want to give up this chance to live in the moment and be spontaneous, to experience some joy and happiness with someone who made her feel so special and cherished. Her life had always been full of planning, making lists, and following routines. Her outings most of the time were to hospitals and doctors' appointments. Even though this trip had been way out of her comfort zone, she'd still planned it as if she were building a house. For once she wanted to make a decision and just go with her gut. Just pack the essentials for four days away. Even leave her laptop behind. All she needed were some clothes, her food, medicine, a camera, and Jason.

"I know, Riley. I've been thinking about this whole thing with Jason from the moment he helped me that night. But for once in my life, I'm trying to just enjoy the moment instead of living in the future like I've always done. To be a little more like you," she said, grinning at her best friend. "I just want to do this. I want to go and have fun. Be spontaneous. I had planned on a few days in Key West anyway, so this is perfect, and the icing on top is that I get to go with Jason," Maddy told her friend.

"I was under the impression that the Key West trip was supposed to be me and you, remember?" Riley said with a slight smile.

At that, Maddy could tell she had convinced Riley this was a good thing for her. "You and I will go before I head back home."

"We'll see. I've been there so many times. I was mainly going so that I could show you the town. But I have to say, Jason will probably make a great tour guide!" Riley reached over and took Maddy's hand. "I don't blame you. Go and have fun, but please be safe. I just don't want to see you heartbroken, and I can tell you're falling for him—and falling fast," Riley said with mock grimness.

Maddy got up and gave her friend the biggest hug ever.

With the anticipation of the trip building, the next few days seemed to go by excruciatingly slow, but Maddy took advantage of the time to visit a local landmark or spend time painting using the pictures she had taken thus far of the Keys. Plus, she took naps and rested in order to be ready for her Key West trip.

Each evening was spent with Jason. One night they went walking along Anne's Beach, even going for an evening swim. For Maddy it was a bit unnerving, but his presence made her feel safe. They spent another evening at a beach bar listening to a local band play island music with a little bit of country mixed in. Maddy was instantly in love with the music, and by the end of the week she had already downloaded a bunch of new tunes to her playlists. But most of their time together in the evenings was passed either on her patio by the water just talking and watching the twinkling stars or curled up inside watching the latest home renovation show on TV, which Jason adored. She didn't really care what was on TV. She just liked that she was snuggled up next to him.

18

Sunday morning, Maddy was up before sunrise, needing no alarm. It had been a while since she had been to Key West, and her past trips there made her truly love the Conch Republic city. She had a long list of things she wanted to do there, but what she was looking forward to the most was just sharing this trip with Jason. She made sure the night before that she had packed everything necessary: the foods and snacks she could eat, her medication, comfy clothes and walking shoes, the camera for sure, and a couple of nice outfits for dinner. They hadn't talked about exactly what they would be doing, but she wanted to be prepared. As active as she wanted to be, Maddy knew she had to balance it with taking care of herself. She wanted this trip to be as perfect as possible; she didn't want to spoil it with a trip to the ER or a day in bed because she had overextended herself. Jason had been telling her all week that he wasn't going to let her do too much and that she just needed to accept that he was going to make sure she was taking care of herself. Plus, Riley had lectured him for what seemed like an hour yesterday on what she would do if Maddy got hurt or sick while they were gone. During the conversation, Maddy had felt much like a child being handed off between two divorced parents. Jason just smiled as he listened to Riley, knowing she was just concerned about her best friend's welfare. Maddy realized as she watched them talk how blessed she was to have two people so concerned for her.

They'd decided to leave around ten o'clock and to take their time driving down the long coastal highway, which consisted mainly of bridges connecting one Key to another. If Maddy remembered right, the drive was beautiful and scenic, so she had her camera ready and couldn't wait to capture more images that could be potential paintings or drawings. But most of her excitement stemmed from the fact that for the next four days, it would be just the two of them. Herself and Jason. They had grown much closer over the last week as they spent more time together, learning even more little tidbits about each other. Even small things, like Jason's intense love for dark chocolate. He seemed to always have a piece in his hand, insisting it was good for him. And she had begun to let her guard down too. Sharing things with someone new could be difficult, but Jason made it so easy—he just listened. She knew she was falling deep and falling fast for this man. Even though her head kept telling her "this is temporary," her heart insisted it was the right thing.

A little before their appointed time to leave, Jason went up to knock on Maddy's door, but it flew open before he could do so. An extremely attractive blonde was standing in front of him, exuding excitement, a huge smile on her face. A suitcase and a few handbags sat at her feet. Jason loved seeing her so happy and leaned in to kiss her good morning.

"Looks like you're going somewhere. I'm heading to Key West. Want to catch a ride with me?" he said, his eyebrows waving up and down.

"Most definitely!" As she reached for her bags, Jason caught her hand.

"No way! I've got that. You're going to get me in trouble with Riley doing stuff like that, and we haven't even left the street. I'm sure she's watching from her house, making sure I'm doing what I'm supposed to." Jason looked over at the house four doors down to see if he could spy Riley watching them.

"You're probably right. Let's not get on her bad side. I'll let you take the suitcase and the small cooler, and I'll grab my two tote bags and lock up." She looked around to make sure she hadn't left anything and that things were secure for the couple of days they would be gone. As soon as she'd double-checked everything, she went out to the car, totes in hand, and loaded them into the backseat. They were really going, she thought, and she could barely contain her excitement.

Before buckling her seat belt, Maddy leaned over and kissed Jason on the cheek. "Thank you for this trip, and most of all, thank you for being the adorable man that you are."

This time he leaned to her and kissed her fully and tenderly on the lips. "Yep, that's me. Just one big teddy bear. Seriously though, I'm the one who should be thanking you. You don't know how happy you have made me, something I really didn't think I would ever feel again."

They'd picked a wonderful day for a ride through the Keys. The weather was ideal, the partial clouds keeping the temperature nice. Just as Maddy remembered, the passing scenery was spectacular, and it seemed that everywhere she looked was a great opportunity for a photo—but of course they couldn't stop at each spot. Instead she made mental notes of the places she would come back to for exploration before she left the Keys. She had already been here two weeks, but it felt like she had only just arrived. The time was passing by so fast. She tried not to think about that, especially about the fact that she might not see Jason anymore. She had promised herself she would not dwell on that during this trip. Especially now, because he was sitting beside her, holding her hand as he drove, and she was getting lost in the beautiful views outside her window.

As they continued through each of the islands toward their destination, it seemed that each Key had its own special quality. On Marathon Key, Maddy made a note to come back to its Dolphin Research Center. She loved dolphins and wanted to see how these amazing creatures were cared for. Leaving Marathon, beautiful water surrounded them on both sides except for a few islands here and there. Then they passed quickly through several smaller Keys: Big Pine Key, Little Torch Key, Summerland Key, Cudjoe Key. In some places, they could still see the old railroad bridge that had once connected Key West to the mainland before the hurricane of 1935. Before Maddy knew it, they were on Stock Island, where the Key West Naval

Air Station was, and getting ready to cross over the tiny bridge into Key West.

As soon as she knew they were close to the city, Maddy pulled out her camera and started snapping pictures.

"I have to get a picture of the Key West sign for my scrapbook. So if it sounds like my camera is on autopilot, it is! I don't want to the miss the sign," she exclaimed.

"You do know we could just stop and take a picture. Might be a bit easier," Jason teased her.

"We can? Is there a place to stop? That would be fantastic!" As soon as she spotted the sign that said Welcome to Key West, Maddy began looking around frantically for a parking spot. Jason laughed.

"Also, remember that we're going to be here for more than a few hours. More like a couple of days?"

Maddy shot him a glance. "Yes, I know, but I can't help it. I'm excited! I love this old city."

But out of the blue, she suddenly felt a bit dizzy. Weakness was spreading through her arms and legs, slowly compared to last time, but she definitely felt a reaction coming on. While she knew something wasn't right, she didn't want to alarm Jason. And suddenly she remembered—in all the excitement of leaving for the trip, she had forgotten to take her meds this morning!

Without explanation, Maddy grabbed her purse, quickly got out her medication, and took it. She knew she had to get the medicine into her system right away in order to keep things from escalating out of control. She also took some liquid Benadryl to help keep the reaction at bay as much as possible.

"What's wrong, Maddy?" Alarm shot through Jason as he saw her quickly going through her tote trying to find something. She had also just missed the welcome sign she'd so desperately wanted a picture of.

"I'm having a reaction. Forgot my medicine this morning. I'm so sorry." She was speaking in simple sentences, and slowly, because weakness and a fuzzy head were beginning to overtake her. This was not how she wanted to start her trip, and damn it, she was going to nip this in the bud.

Jason quickly pulled into the first parking lot he could find. "Do we need to go to the hospital?" he asked calmly, even though he was on high alert after what had happened the last time. His instinct was telling him to take her straight to the ER without asking.

"No, I'll be ok. Just have to let the meds get into my system. I am so sorry," she said slowly. "So sorry. Just so sorry."

"Don't apologize, love. It's ok," Jason crooned sweetly in her ear as he cradled her on his shoulder. He could tell she had gotten a bit sleepy, probably from taking all the medication at once. She had been so excited to see the city when they drove in, and now she was too tired to enjoy it. The best thing, he thought, would be to get to the bed and breakfast and settle her in her room for some rest and food.

"I'm ruining the trip already. I can't believe I forgot to take my medicine." She was still talking a bit slowly, but she was more coherent now.

"You're not ruining anything. You just forgot. Maddy, we all make mistakes. We forget things, and we are not perfect. I wish you wouldn't be so hard on yourself. Right now, we're going to head to the inn and get checked in. Then we'll order some takeout or fix something in the room. Ok?"

She nodded her head in agreement. They were going to be here for four days, so she would take the remainder of the day to rest and relax. As long as Jason was here with her, it really didn't matter where she was.

19

When they arrived at the bed and breakfast, it was love at first sight for Maddy—everything was just like she had imagined. Although the drugs had made her tired, she was still able to appreciate the little inn painted in tropical colors and the beautiful palm trees that lined the walkway. Thank goodness she was feeling better and had averted a full-blown reaction. When they entered the reception area, Jason was immediately greeted by the owners, Lonnie and his wife Sara.

"Thanks so much for letting us stay here. This is Maddy," Jason said, introducing her. "I haven't seen the place in a while. It looks great!" Jason continued as he filled out some paperwork for Lonnie.

"We learned from the best, using some tips and tricks you used on our other properties," Lonnie said, praising him. "Come on, let me show you where you'll be staying."

Their rooms were side by side on the first floor, so Maddy didn't have to climb any stairs. When she opened her door, she felt immediately transported to a little tropical paradise. To her left was a large bathroom with its own stand-alone shower next to a large tub with jets, like a mini-Jacuzzi. The pale blue painted walls and the colorful coral tile floor made her feel she'd just stepped into a house right on the beach, and the little mermaids, sea turtles, seahorses, and other ocean creatures that adorned the tiles in the shower area and the edges of the wall reminded her that she was indeed on a little tropical island. Moving into the larger room, she spied a queen-sized bed with a lovely bamboo frame and headboard. The coverlet and sheets nicely complemented the coral-colored walls and the various works of art depicting popular scenes from around the city. In front of the bed stood a matching bamboo dresser that supported a flat-screen TV, and beside the dresser was a bamboo chair and footstool. Two French doors beyond the bed opened up to a beautiful inner courtyard and pool area that was surrounded by banyan and palm trees, with the beautiful blue sky above still clearly visible. The room was indeed like a lush tropical escape, a little piece of the island just for Maddy.

As Jason came into her room with her first two bags, she suddenly remembered she should be helping with the luggage.

"I forgot about our things in the car! I was just so mesmerized with the room. This place is gorgeous! I had no idea! Let me help with the bags," she said, turning quickly toward him, only to find that her balance was still slightly off. She swayed toward the bed.

"I don't think so," he said adamantly. "You're a bit wobbly. If I let you go outside, our neighbors next door will think you've already paid a visit to the little bar across the street."

She sent him a "smart ass" smile and then laughed. "You're probably right. I am a bit foggy, but I really want to do something. Duval Street is right there, and I want to explore. Just let me take a nap. I promise I will be better, and maybe we can go somewhere for dinner? I really don't want to start this vacation by staying in the room." Her eyes pleaded with him, and she had the cutest pout on her face. Jason couldn't resist her when she looked at him this way. She didn't know it yet, but he was putty in her hands.

"If I remember correctly, Riley made me swear almost in blood to take care of you and that if I didn't, there would be hell to pay when we got back. So I think the best thing for you is that we get some take-out dinner, maybe eat outside in the courtyard, let you get a shower, and then I'll personally tuck you into bed." That last statement had his mind exploring several different options.

Tuck me into bed, she thought? That might prove interesting.

"I have a counterproposal. I take a nap, get a shower, and then we walk to the nearest restaurant for dinner. Then you can tuck me into bed. How about that?" She was disappointed, because this was in no way how she'd imagined their first night in Key West. She had hoped they could celebrate the sunset each evening in Mallory Square, walk Duval Street at night, and explore the city by day.

"Listen, I know you had plans, but we're going to be here for a few days. Indulge me...please? Let's order take-out dinner and rest. Then tomorrow we'll be ready to go."

"Ok, but only if you'll stay for a while after we eat. Maybe watch some TV or a movie, unless you are too tired. I know all my problems can be overwhelming—at least, that's what some people have told me. My dad calls me high maintenance." Maddy smiled, but Jason sensed the tinge of sadness in her voice.

He looked at her sweetly. She still didn't realize that he wanted to be with her and take care of her, but then they had only known each other a short time.

"Maddy, I'm not tired, and staying with you here tonight sounds wonderful. As a matter of fact, I think one of my remodeling shows will be on," he said playfully. "But seriously, I don't know about what other people say or think, but you don't overwhelm me. I love being with you, taking care of you, watching you smile, making you happy. Because you make me happy," he said softly as he went to sit beside her. He reached out and took her into his arms, tucking her close and hoping she could feel how he felt about her.

He had no idea how those words impacted her. No one had ever told her that they wanted to take care of her, to be with her no matter what the circumstances. He said it with such a sincere voice that by instinct she knew it came from his heart. She was smiling inside as she looked up at him.

"Thank you. You'll never know how much that means to me," she said and then kissed him sweetly.

After they decided on dinner—a burger and fries for him and a baked potato, unseasoned green beans, and baked chicken for Maddy—Jason went to settle into the room next door while they waited for their meal to arrive. His room was identical to Maddy's, its floor plan just opposite to hers. Being the architect he was, he couldn't help but examine all the workmanship that Lonnie had put into the details of each room. The tropical island atmosphere was truly well captured. He would have to take some pictures for future reference should he be asked to come up with a coastal or island theme for any upcoming projects. He unpacked and decided to take a shower to freshen up before heading over to spend the rest of the day and evening with Maddy. He didn't care if they went anywhere or not, just as long as they were together. That was all that mattered to him.

Next door, Maddy also unpacked her bags and took a shower. Her medicine had kicked in fully now, and she was feeling much better despite being somewhat fatigued. The side effects of the antihistamines were at times as unpredictable as her illness. Sometimes the medication just took away the reaction, and at other times she felt like she had a bad case of the flu. Right now, she was at a point somewhere between the two possible scenarios, and the shower's warm water was helping her relax. She felt fortunate to have realized what was happening before it was too late and that the episode hadn't progressed to anything worse. Even so, she felt somewhat embarrassed that it happened just as they were entering the city. She just wanted this to be the "perfect" getaway, but she supposed she should to take that word out of her vocabulary. But then again, Jason felt perfect to her.

Since they were staying in for the evening, she put on one of the bright, repurposed T-shirts she had made by adding tiny seashells around the neckline. Another one of her craft projects that had actually brought her some customers when people started asking for shirts of their own. Next, her white capri pants and her pink flip-flops brought her evening outfit together. Her reflection in the mirror showed her an island girl minus the dark tan. She didn't mind having pale legs. And the bright colors always lightened her mood and made her feel good.

A knock at the door signaled both the start of her date for the evening and the arrival of the food. As she swung open the door, the aroma of burger and french fries assailed her nostrils, and she suddenly realized she was very hungry. But the cause of the flutter in her stomach wasn't the food; it was the man standing in front of her.

If she was the island girl, then he definitely was the island guy. He had showered and changed into a peach-colored Margaritaville T-shirt, jean shorts, and brown leather flip-flops. With his hair still wet and a little tousled from his shower and with that constant dark stubble along his jaw and chin, he was so sexy that Maddy momentarily forgot about the food.

"Oh, it smells so good! I didn't realize how hungry I was until you were standing there with the food." She helped him carry their dinner to the small table outside her bedroom doors. It was positioned perfectly under two palm trees and had a bright umbrella covering. The chairs were big and comfortable with padded cushions that felt like pillows when they sat down. As she helped set the table, she continued thinking about Jason more than the meal. Here they were, by themselves, having dinner in one of the most romantic spots she had ever seen, in a city that she loved. And the man sitting across from her was so striking that the food itself was secondary. But she reminded herself that sex was not on the menu, at least not right now. If she and Jason ever reached that place in their relationship, it would be because they had made a commitment to each other, and they were nowhere close to that at this point. She was sure he must have been thinking along the same lines, because he had suggested getting two separate rooms.

She had promised herself after her divorce that if she ever contemplated a committed relationship again, she would take it slow—no rushing into the most physical, intimate side of things. Hormones play havoc on the dating populace, and she had learned the hard way the first time. She didn't want to make that mistake again. But looking the way he did tonight, he sure made it difficult! Plus just the way he made her feel—it was more than special. Ok, Maddy, pull it together, she thought to herself. Let's try to concentrate on the food.

Little did she know that Jason's thoughts were very close to her own. From the moment she'd opened the door to her room, she'd overpowered his senses. She was a beautiful vision, fresh and sweet from her quick shower, her outfit making it seem she'd just been walking along the local beach. She wore just enough makeup to give her a fresh glow, even though in his opinion she didn't need any at all. She had dried her hair in the wavy natural style he liked so much. Most importantly, she appeared to be doing well after her little mishap with her medication earlier, which was good to see. But the combination of her pleasing appearance, being here in this tropical atmosphere, eating outside in the lush green setting, and knowing that their rooms were separated only by a thin wall made him want her in ways he had been thinking about since the day he first saw her. Maddy was so different from the other women that had passed through his life since his divorce from Andrea. But he promised himself he was going to do this the right way, and for the first time in a long time, he knew he wanted a relationship, even if it had to be long distance, even though they would both be going separate ways in a few short weeks. He would figure something out soon, before she went back to Charleston, and their time together would also help him gauge whether or not she wanted the same thing he did. Even though a conversation about the direction of their relationship hadn't come up yet, he had been thinking about it over the last few days. But now was not the time to broach the subject. While he didn't think it would scare her off, he still wanted to take things slowly. His first impressions were that she was reacting to him the same way he was to her even though when they first met he had tried his best to avoid a connection to her. They were like two magnets drawn to each other, the pull getting stronger and stronger each day they were together.

"Again, this isn't exactly how I envisioned our first evening in Key West, but in truth it's really perfect. The food is great, we have this beautiful courtyard all to ourselves, and I have the most attractive man sharing this romantic dinner with me. How lucky can a girl get?" Maddy asked as she smiled and blew him a kiss across the table.

"Honestly," he said, looking at her appreciatively, "I believe *I'm* the lucky one here." Jason drew her hand to his lips and gave it a soft kiss, sending goosebumps up her arm once again.

Dinner was wonderful as they sat outside eating their take-out meal under the darkening sky. For some reason they started telling stories about the crazy things they'd done as children, both laughing so hard at times that Maddy thought she might choke on her food. Jason's laugh was infectious, and she would get the giggles just because of his laughter. He made her feel so good, like they were the only two people in the world at that moment. How had she become so blessed? she thought as she gazed at the man sitting across from her.

"I think it's time for me to walk you home, my dear. We have such a long way to travel," he said, kidding her as they gathered up the leftovers and dinner plates. As they entered her room and shut the doors behind them, he wrapped his arms around her and grinned. Then, lowering his head until they were ever-so-softly touching foreheads, he murmured, "Thank you for coming with me. I've not been to Key West to just relax and enjoy the city in a long time. And never with a stunning woman by my side. I am so looking forward to these next few days with you, Maddy. More than you can imagine."

The kiss that followed those words was slow, full, and deep, making Maddy's legs tremble and sending a fluttering feeling throughout her body. Just being in such close proximity to him was starting to have that effect on her. She was not denying it. She was falling for this man who was sweeping her off her feet.

"What are we going to do tomorrow?" she said, still wrapped up in his arms. "There is so much to see and do that I don't know where we should start."

"I suggest we tour the city. There is a great trolley that will take us all over town, showing us the highlights of Key West. We can get on and off wherever we want. After lunch we'll come back here for a while for you to rest, and then we can go watch the sunset at Mallory Square. And if you get tired at any time, we can just come back to the inn and relax, maybe even watch a movie. Let's promise each other something—that we are going to relax, have fun, and just enjoy our time together."

"Sounds like a wonderful plan to me," she said softly before giving him another kiss good night.

20

The next morning they ate breakfast in the quaint little dining room near the check-in area of the bed and breakfast. From there it was just a few steps to Duval Street, the main roadway of the city. To keep Maddy's walking to a minimum, they flagged a pedicab to take them to the nearest trolley station. Maddy loved the pedicab and the wonderful man that pedaled them to their destination. By the time they reached the trolley, both felt they knew the city quite well as their cab driver had filled them in on the sights they'd passed along the way. But this was nothing compared to the trolley ride and their very colorful tour guide, who gave them complete information about each sight they passed and how it had made Key West what it was today. He also offered interesting tidbits of offbeat Key West lore that only a local would know. Maddy and Jason took the trolley once around the city, not getting off but making mental notes of the places they wanted to go back and visit, like the Hemingway House, the marker for the southernmost point in the United States, the Key West Shipwreck Museum, Fort Zachary State Park, and a bunch more. After their trolley ride, they decided to walk down Duval Street, taking their time and enjoying the sights. Maddy couldn't wait to see it at night and was looking forward to watching the sunset at Mallory Square that evening. By now it was past time for lunch, and they were nearing Margaritaville, a restaurant Maddy wanted to go to even if they didn't have anything for her on the menu.

"Are you sure you want to eat here?" Jason asked dubiously as they looked at the menu posted outside the establishment.

"Definitely! I have some snacks with me, and I'm going to try the french fries. I've always wanted to go here, and this is the original restaurant. Please?"

"You have twisted my arm yet again. I'm not always this easy, you know," Jason said with a grin. And they both walked in, singing along with the song playing over the speakers: "Cheeseburger in Paradise." After placing their orders, Maddy took pictures of just about everything, from the swirling hurricane mural on the ceiling to the street signs and birds that decorated the restaurant.

"Are you having fun so far?" Jason asked as he scooped a nacho off his plate.

"I'm loving it! There are so many places I want to go back and see, but I know we can't do everything in just a few days. I had no clue this city is so full of history. I'd love to get more still pictures so I can turn them into paintings. There are so many potential shots here that I don't know where to start. I love the colorful architecture. I feel so relaxed, and the vibe this city exudes is just so peaceful and friendly. I love it!"

And she truly did. Her own hometown of Charleston was very historical and had plenty of beaches nearby, but being here was different. She dearly loved her hometown but these small islands were so laid-back, and she liked that. This was the first time she had really thought about home since coming to the Keys. She wondered what Jason would think of Charleston and her little apartment attached to her parents' house. That in turn made her think of some of the things she still wanted to sort out before she boarded the train back north. With Jason now part of the picture, things were just a bit more complicated. But she was determined not to spoil the here and now by thinking about such things.

Jason couldn't help but grin at Maddy's exuberant enthusiasm. She was like a little kid in a great big candy store wanting to try everything at once. Being with her was infectious. Her laughter, her smile, her willingness to try things, even though most people with a condition like hers would probably stay home, afraid to walk out their door. She had a fighting spirit, but it was also gentle and loving at the same time. This girl, this woman, was becoming integral to his life, and the thought of her leaving soon made him feel a bit lost. But for now, he was going to just be with her and enjoy every single second.

As the plates were being taken away, Maddy asked, "Ok, what's next?"

"Nap time," Jason said as the waitress put the ticket on the table for their meal.

"Goodness, you sound like a kindergarten teacher," she said with a snicker. At the same time, she saw him start to pay for their meal and immediately grabbed her wallet. "This is for mine," she said, handing him a ten-dollar bill.

"No, this little vacation of ours is on me. I want to do this for you. Please?" he asked, looking at her with those eyes that were so hard to resist.

"I thought we were splitting everything, especially since you were able to secure the rooms for free. At least let me pay my half. I insist."

"No way. This is my getaway gift to you, so don't ruin it for me." Jason looked at her with such sincerity, and she knew she could not deny him. She relented and smiled.

"Thank you Jason. Not just for lunch or the trip. Thank you for accepting me just as I am and making me feel so special. You truly are an amazing man!"

"Well, you make it very easy." And he flashed her that smile that melted her heart.

They found a pedicab as soon as they walked out the door and were able to take a leisurely ride back to their little bed and breakfast. Taking a nap was hard with so much still to see and do, but as soon as Maddy walked into her little room, she obediently lay down on the bed and closed her eyes. She began to think about the wonderful day they had had so far. Before separating to go into their respective rooms, they made plans to meet in a few hours to go to Mallory Square to watch the famous Key West Sunset Celebration, a nightly occurrence that was very popular in this little paradise. But he didn't let her go without kissing her again, leaving both of them breathless and wanting more. They parted, grinning at each other like two teenagers dealing with their first crush. Except they both knew this was more than a simple attraction.

21

Sunset was to occur at 7:35 p.m. that evening, and they both wanted to make sure they were there early. If Maddy's memory served her correctly, lots of artisans and street performers filled the square as everyone gathered, waiting for the sun to sink below the horizon. She wanted to see it all, even though Jason kept reminding her they could come back each evening if she liked.

She had slept for a little over an hour and was feeling good after her nap. She freshened up her makeup, scrunched her hair a bit, and grabbed a lightweight sweater just in case it got a bit chilly after sunset. She also ate a little snack before leaving and made sure this time that she took all her medication. She didn't want anything to ruin the evening like the previous night, even though she had to admit that as it turned out, last night had been wonderful, just the two of them.

This time *she* was knocking on Jason's door, expecting him to be surprised that she was ready to go, but he opened it before she could finish.

"Am I running late, or are you early? I was just coming to check on you. You look gorgeous, as always," he said, enveloping her in a hug and giving her a big kiss. If he kept this up, they might not get to the square. She loved his gentle hugs, sweet caresses, and kisses that left her wanting more—he made her feel so special that she was finally ready to admit that she may be falling in love with him. It felt so right, but it was scary at the same time. Maddy hoped and prayed that he felt that special connection too.

Since the pedicabs had all retired for the evening, they decided to walk down the street to the square. After Maddy's nap, she was sure she would be able to walk there, since it wasn't as far as it seemed. But Jason cautioned her that when they were ready to come home, they would be taking a cab. Finding one would not be a problem on Duval Street, since there were so many bars within a one-mile stretch. Jason's priority was making sure Maddy was taken care of, and finding a cab on a street lined with drinking establishments would be simple since he was sure many could not make it back to their hotel or home without a safe ride.

The little trip down to the square was wonderful. They walked hand and hand, every now and then stopping for a passionate kiss with no thought to those around them. Every time Jason caught Maddy off guard with his sensuous lips, the delicate flutter inside her grew more intense.

And even though Jason hadn't said anything to Maddy about the feelings he was developing for her with every minute they spent together, he knew it wouldn't be much longer before he would have to let her know. He found himself thinking about her constantly, almost to the point of forgetting what he was doing. She was so utterly different from other women he had dated. He knew his best friends would probably say she was the complete opposite of his "type." But since he'd met Maddy, he couldn't help feeling that he was falling in love with this woman. At first he tried to deny it. Maybe it was simple lust that he felt—he had many thoughts about what it would be like to spend time wrapped up with her, skin to skin. But deep down, he knew there was more to it. They had known each other for only a few weeks, but to him it felt like months, maybe years. He had shared more with her in this short span of time than he had with any other person, ever. To hell with the opinions of others, he thought. The only people that mattered were himself and Maddy.

As Maddy had expected, Mallory Square was packed with people of all types, dressed for the celebration of the sunset in outlandish outfits of every kind: bikinis, tuxedos, pirate costumes, and a myriad of others. She couldn't help but laugh at some of the more extreme clothing, sneaking a picture or two so she could show everyone back home. Jason seemed to be enjoying the people watching too, laughing and pointing out the odd outfits she missed. They also stood, arms around each other, watching the street performers do their acts, from juggling on a unicycle and dancing with fiery hula-hoops to playing musical instruments of all kinds. But Maddy's favorite thing was going from one artisan booth to another, all of them showing off their own form of artistic talent—paintings, jewelry, you name it—and Maddy loved it all. Jason bought her a silver sea-turtle necklace with a beautiful opalescent shell inlayed as part of the turtle's shell. She immediately put it on, and he thought it looked absolutely breathtaking against her soft skin. At another booth, Maddy found some decorative ceramic tiles, each depicting popular areas around Key West, and she hoped to put them in her future home. She was also able to talk with the artist, asking questions about how she'd started selling her work, something that Maddy wanted to do with her own watercolor paintings. Jason stood back and just watched, mesmerized by Maddy's enthusiasm and kindness as she talked to each person about their particular craft. She was definitely in her element.

"I love this! I think it would be so neat if I could sell my artwork like this."

"Maybe you could. Your paintings are beautiful, at least the ones you showed me the other day. Have you ever sold a painting?"

"Just a few here and there, but nothing consistently. Up to now, it's always been just an off-and-on hobby for me. I've always felt like I needed to improve, learn more techniques. But watching these people here sell what they've made, sharing it with everyone, it gives me the desire to do something with my own paintings. Something I'll have to look into when I get back to Charleston. I had planned to do more painting while I was here, but I'm finding that other things occupy my time," she said, sliding her arms around his firm, muscular waist and reaching up to kiss him. "I've been a bit distracted." She smiled deviously at him.

"If I'm the cause of your not being able to release your inner artist, please let me know. I'll be sure to leave you alone so you can get creative." He winked at her.

"I rather like the distraction, so I'll tap into my artistic side later!"

The crowds at the square grew larger as the sunset time drew near. Hand in hand, the pair slowly made their way down the pier to the cement wall and found a spot just big enough for one person, so Jason pulled Maddy up onto his lap. They sat together watching the sunset, which was so gorgeous that her camera seemed to work nonstop as she captured as many images as she could. One was sure to be a future painting, she thought as the camera clicked away. But just before the sun sank fully into the sea, she put the camera away and laid her head on Jason's shoulder, relaxing as he wrapped his arms around her. They watched quietly as the sun completed its evening journey, both lost in their own thoughts and thoroughly content.

"That was so much fun!" Maddy said as they started walking away from the square. "Everything from the artisans to the street performers was simply amazing. And some of the outfits those people were wearing! I guess anything goes down here." Suddenly she stopped and turned to face him. "But the best part was sitting on the pier with you, watching the sunset. I know there were hundreds of people around, but it felt like just the two of us there on that little cement wall. Thank you for such a wonderful time."

Jason grinned. "You're welcome. I've been to Mallory Square many times with friends, but I can honestly say I've never had as much fun as I did with you tonight. Come to think of it, you make everything better when you're with me. You're my little lucky charm."

"Thank you," she said softly, looking up at him. She wanted to pinch herself, because it was so hard to believe that he wanted to be with her even though he now knew everything that she was dealing with in her life—and it didn't matter to him. Maddy never thought she would find anyone like Jason, ever.

"Are you hungry," Jason asked, breaking through her thoughts as they started walking toward the inn.

"I guess a little, but I think I'd better eat a snack in my room. I've had a few foods today like that bite of Key Lime Pie that I don't normally eat, so a safe snack is probably a good idea for me tonight. I'm sorry. But let's stop and get you something," she said, not wanting to spoil the mood.

"That's ok. I have some food back in my room too, so I think I'll do the same. I know it's early, especially to all these people, but it might be best for us to head back and for me to make sure you get some rest."

Maddy groaned. "Now you sound like Riley *again*."

"No. This is just me taking care of you. I have selfish reasons for making sure you're always ok." With that he gave her a quick kiss and hailed a cab.

Their day had been very busy, and he just wanted to make sure that Maddy hadn't done too much. She did look a bit tired, though she was alluring as ever. He was drawn to this woman, never wanting to let her out of his sight. Feeling this way toward her felt good, but it was also unnerving. His past romantic relationships had always had a negative ending. Even though he didn't feel this was a possibility with Maddy, the old memories still haunted him. But damn if he didn't want to tell her how he truly felt. He decided to step up and take a chance.

The cab dropped them off right in front of the inn where they were staying, and they walked down the palm-tree-canopied path to their adjoining rooms, holding hands. This path led them past the courtyard and pool area where the trees gave way, opening to the sky above and giving guests a beautiful view of the stars overhead.

"Want to sit by the pool in the lounge chairs and stargaze for a little while?"

"Aren't there too many trees?" Maddy asked.

"Come here and see," he said, knowing she would be surprised when she saw the area he was talking about. She followed him along the little pathway to a set of two large, comfy loungers sitting at the pool's edge and looked up.

"Oh, wow, you were right!" she said, stunned by the beautiful night sky.

"Want to share a chair with me?"

"I would love to," she said with no hesitation at all.

By the time she had put down her little tote and shopping bag that held her goodies from this evening, Jason was already lying in the lounger. He scooted to the side, leaving just enough room for Maddy to join him. As they both lay back, looking at the stars above, Maddy was sure this was the most romantic thing she had ever done. As she settled in beside him, her body practically molding itself to his, she had never felt so content. Everything for once felt so right.

For a minute or two, both were silent, peering up at the twinkling night sky. A gentle, soft breeze was blowing and with barely any lights shining around the recreation area, trees along the edges shielding the lights coming from the other rooms, it was a perfect night for gazing up at the stars. But the best thing for Maddy was lying nestled up to Jason, feeling his muscular, toned body pressed up against hers.

"Do you know any of the constellations?" Jason asked her as they both gazed upward.

"I used to when I was younger. When Hope was a little girl, we had a telescope we tried to use to view the planets and stars. We weren't very good at it, so we finally gave up and would just go out and lie on blankets, and I would tell her what I knew about the star patterns. But when meteor showers occurred, we would get up early with our beach chairs, set them up in the front yard, and count how many shooting stars we could see. When she went to college, I didn't really have anyone to watch the night sky with anymore. I've only watched one meteor shower since. I love to do that, but it's better when you have someone to share it with. But the stars amaze me. I think part of it is that I love science-fiction movies and books so much."

"You do? I do too! Most people snicker at me when I tell them that, but I love those movies, especially all the special effects!" At this, Maddy laughed and lifted a hand, signaling him to give her a high five, which he promptly did.

"So...something else we have in common. We are sci-fi nerds," she said laughingly.

Spontaneously, he hugged her and kissed the top of her head. But she wasn't satisfied with that, and she turned her head to give him a real kiss, one so full of tenderness that both of them were left relaxed and content.

As they both snuggled in the lounge chair, Jason decided it was time to let her know just how he was feeling. He loved her. He knew that with every fiber in his being. But just as he began to utter the speech he had prepared in his mind, a feeling of anxiety washed over him. It was almost as though he couldn't breathe and a conversation began inside his head. "What are you thinking?" He told himself. "There is no way you could fall in love with someone this fast. It's ludicrous! And why would you make a commitment to anyone? You know how it always ends. Maddy will not be any different. She is leaving soon and so are you. You are just caught up in the moment. Don't say anything you are going to regret or worse hurt this woman." The thoughts were coming at him so fast that he almost didn't hear her speak.

"Jason, are you okay? You almost feel like you are trembling," Maddy said as she looked at him cautiously.

"I'm fine. Just thinking."

"About what or is it private?" she said smiling at him.

That smile. It was her smile that let him know that he was right. Things were different this time. Not like anything he had experienced before. Suddenly he felt his body calm down and he found the courage to tell her what he wanted to say.

"Maddy," Jason started, "I know this is going to sound a bit crazy, maybe even a lot crazy, because I've only known you for a few weeks, but..." He paused, took a deep breath, and finally said the words he had been thinking about all day. "I love you. You are a remarkable woman, and every second I'm with you, see you, watch you smile, even the times you've cried, this feeling for you grows deeper and stronger. I've never felt like this. Ever." As he finished his declaration, he still wondered if he'd said all of this too soon.

Maddy was stunned by his revelation, but even so, a feeling of joy washed over her. She felt exactly the same way but had been afraid to say anything for fear of driving him away. Now it seemed she had nothing to worry about.

After a few seconds of silence, she sat up and faced him. She wanted to look him in the eyes before she said anything.

"Jason, I've fallen in love with you too. But I thought it was just me being too emotional. Even chalked it up to hormones or something. I've kept telling myself it's not possible to feel this way about someone so soon. Plus, it's hard for me to believe that someone could love me knowing the things I have to deal with, namely a weird illness that keeps me and everyone else in my life constantly on guard. But I honestly feel that God put me in that house in Islamorada for many reasons, one of those being to meet you. I truly love you, Jason." And that was all that was said between them. He reached up and folded her into his arms, kissing her fervently as if to seal the declarations they had just made to one another.

Even though they still had eyes only for each other, when they drew apart a few moments later, they looked around to see if anyone else had joined them out in the pool area, but it was still just them. Then they looked back at each other and laughed just a bit, happy to finally know how the other felt. They snuggled back into the chair to continue looking at the stars, but now each was thinking only about the other.

After about an hour, Maddy knew that while she would probably be content to stay here in Jason's arms all night, she needed to go to bed. The hard part would be to go to her room by herself, but if her feelings for Jason were true, they wouldn't need to solidify them by making love. She couldn't kid herself that she didn't want him. She'd dreamed of feeling him lying beside her in the most intimate way. She hadn't been with anyone in a very long time, but she wanted this relationship to be solid, not built on just a physical attraction. She wanted the romance, time to get to know this most caring man even more before their relationship moved to another level. She only hoped Jason would understand.

"As much as I don't want to get up and leave you and this comfy chair, I think it's time for me to go to bed. I'm looking forward to our boat trip tomorrow and don't want to spoil the fun. I'm sorry," she said as she reluctantly started untangling herself from him.

"No, you're probably right. But it feels so good to lie here with you."

They had both gotten so comfortable that getting out of the lounger was proving to be quite difficult, and they both laughed as they struggled out, almost falling into the bush beside them. Again, his laughter was so contagious giving her one more reason why she had fallen for this man.

When they got to Maddy's door, Jason pulled her as close as he could to him, kissing her with one hand on her cheek and his other arm wrapped tightly around her waist.

"I meant what I said tonight. I truly love you, Maddy. But I'm going to follow your lead here. I want this to work, and I know we have some hurdles to overcome, but let's agree to just take things one at a time. No rushing, just enjoying what we've found, because right now I feel like I won the lottery tonight. Let this be the beginning of a beautiful love story."

His words made her melt inside. "I agree, and..." After giving him another kiss, she whispered, "I love you." With a reluctant sigh, she turned the key in the lock and went into her room.

22

Maddy woke up the next morning once again with a smile on her face, something that had become practically an everyday occurrence since meeting Jason. It's probably been there all night, she thought as she stretched to get out of bed, remembering everything from the night before. He loved her! But as soon as she started moving around, she could tell that yesterday's activities might have been a bit too much—her body ached from head to toe. She didn't want to change any plans for the day, since they were only going on the glass-bottom boat tour—something she was very excited about. They hadn't made any concrete plans for after their boat ride. But one thing that gave her the incentive to get up and moving was that she couldn't wait to see him. Just knowing that he was right there on the other side of the wall sent a sudden rush of heat flowing through her body. Actually, when she had looked into his room, she'd noticed that his bed lined up with hers, the headboards in the same place. So all that separated them as they slept at night was that tiny wall. She went over, touched it, and imagined her love just on the other side.

Her cell phone suddenly rang, bringing her back to reality. He was calling already! Without looking at the display, she quickly picked up the phone and said, "Good morning, sexy!"

"Wow, good morning to you too!" Riley chirped. "I guess I don't have to ask how *you're* doing."

"Oh crap, I thought you were Jason," Maddy said, embarrassed. "What are you doing? How are you?"

"Was calling to see how the two, I guess I could say, 'lovebirds' were doing, but you especially. Hadn't heard from you and wanted to check on ya. So, spill the beans. What's going on…and don't give me that shit and say 'nothing.' No one answers their phone like that unless there's a story behind it."

Maddy smiled. "I love the way you act like my mom. That's one of the reasons you're so special, Riley."

"Ok, someone has taken a happy pill and still hasn't let me know what is going on," Riley said impatiently.

"I don't really have a lot of time, because I need to get ready. We're going on a glass-bottom boat tour this morning, and I just woke up."

"Alone?"

Rolling her eyes, Maddy answered. "Yes—*alone*!

"Well, that's no fun. He is one fine man. What's the problem?" asked Riley.

"There is no problem. That's just not me, Riley. But I will let you chew on this till I get back in a few days. He told me he loved me!" Maddy said giddily.

The answer she got back was not what she expected.

"Um…isn't that a bit soon? You've only known him for a few weeks." Riley's voice was suddenly flat.

"You sure know how to deflate my happy balloon. Is it soon? Maybe, but we both feel the same way. There's more to it, and I will talk to you when I get back home. But to satisfy the real reason you called…yes, I'm fine. Had a little hiccup the first day I was here, but it was my fault. I forgot to take my medicine, because I was so excited about the trip and being with Jason. I'm a bit tired today, but I'm taking it easy, as promised, and Jason is taking good care of me."

"Listen, Maddy. I just don't want to see you get hurt, ok?" Riley said with true concern.

"I won't, Riley. I promise we will talk when I get home. Right now, just be a little happy for me, please? I haven't felt this in a long time, and you know what I've been through. I just want to take things one day at a time and enjoy the moment. Please can you do that for me?"

"I won't be Debbie Downer, but we will indeed have a long chat when you get back." Now she sounded more like the Riley she knew.

"I promise," Maddy said before hanging up the phone.

As she headed to the bathroom, the room phone rang, and this time she knew it had to be Jason.

"Good morning," she said sweetly into the phone.

"Good morning to you. Hope you were able to get some restful sleep," Jason said as he reflected on how his night had been just the opposite. He'd dreamed about her all night long. Not that that was such a bad thing, but his thoughts didn't lend themselves to sleeping. Just the opposite! Since telling her his true feelings, his emotions were all over the place. And he couldn't help but replay the conversation he had with himself before he told Maddy how he felt. He loved her, he knew that but deep down in the core of his being, he feared this emotion.

Those faraway memories of when he'd previously let his guard down, trusting someone completely, had ended in disaster. His ex-wife had completely trampled any kind of faith he might once have had in another woman. That's why his relationships after the divorce had always tumbled into an abyss. But he wanted what he had with Maddy to be different. He wasn't sure exactly what to do to break the cycle, but he felt in his heart that Maddy was totally different. Could he let himself go and just jump into this relationship, finally having true happiness? He was going to take a chance—on himself to trust his instincts and on Maddy with his heart. To let himself be vulnerable. He knew this would be a battle in his own mind, but the thought of her made this mental hurdle easier, so he was going to rely on her and how she made him feel. Hopefully this awareness would guide him to just be himself instead of the guarded man he had turned into. And now, hearing her voice on the phone told him instinctively that he was making the right choice.

"Yes, I got some sleep, but I have to admit I was a bit restless. Especially knowing you were so close by," she replied playfully. "I'm just now getting dressed and should be ready to go in about forty-five minutes. I had a phone call from Riley this morning, so I'm running a little late. Hope that's ok."

"We've got plenty of time before the boat leaves. I just couldn't go another minute without saying good morning. Thought about surprising you in person, but I figured you might still be in bed. Not that it would be a bad thing, but..." he trailed off in midsentence, laughing.

"Phone call or in person? I think I would have preferred an in-person greeting, but I'm glad you called instead. I look a mess!"

"I'm sure we would disagree on that statement. How are you feeling?" Jason wanted to know so he could help her not to do too much. Even though they still had today and tomorrow here, she'd told him yesterday about all the things she still wanted to do while visiting the city, knowing full well they couldn't do even a fourth of what she desired. He was having to help her pace herself, but he couldn't help but get caught up in her enthusiasm and childlike excitement over the smallest of things. It was irresistible, and he loved it.

"To be honest, I'm feeling fine. Just a little tired. Comes with the territory, but I'm ok. I can't wait for the boat ride today." She was excited about the glass-bottom boat and going out to the reef, hopefully to see the ocean creatures where they lived.

"This will work out perfectly. I found out this morning that I have to attend a few online meetings this afternoon. So we'll go out in the boat this morning, and then you can have an afternoon of leisure while I work. We can decide later what we want to do tonight. How does that sound?" Jason asked.

"Perfect! I'll get ready as quick as I can. Do you want to eat here at the inn?"

"That sounds great. The food was really good yesterday. Oh, and by the way..." Jason paused. "I haven't changed my mind, and hope you haven't either."

"Changed my mind? What are you talking about?" Maddy was puzzled by his statement.

"I love you, Maddy." She heard a click on the other end of the line before she could say anything, leaving her smiling back at the phone in her hand.

A little while later, she met him at the small eating nook in the lobby. She was ready for the boat trip, her backpack filled with all of her essentials for the day. He was reading the local paper as she walked toward him and didn't notice her. Despite the serious look on his face, all she could really see was an attractive, caring man who had told her he loved her. This man loved her! As she continued walking, she began to wonder what he saw in her. Not that she was putting herself down, but the men she had met since her divorce had just never stayed around very long, especially once they found out about her illness. But Jason had. It was as if all that didn't matter—they had just clicked from the moment they'd met even though at first Jason had been a bit distant. It was only last night that they'd finally admitted the deep affection and love they had for each other. Maddy hoped he wasn't regretting it, but then she remembered his earlier phone call, and the doubt vanished from her mind.

"Hi there," she said as she hooked her tote bag onto the chair across from him at the small table. She loved this little space where all the guests came for a homemade breakfast prepared by Lonnie and Sara. Fresh muffins, croissants, toast, eggs, ham, bacon, and fresh fruit were always available. She was so tempted to try just a bite, but she also wanted a fun trip and didn't want to take a chance, so for now she just ate her own breakfast. Anyway, it was Jason's company she enjoyed much more than the food.

"Good morning, beautiful," Jason said, standing up and giving Maddy a kiss before they both sat down. She looked lovely this morning, he thought as he watched her across the table. He honestly couldn't get enough of her, and last night, after he'd escorted her to her room and made his way to his, he'd had a rough time lying in bed knowing they were mere inches from each other.

"Good morning to you, handsome," she said as they began their breakfast.

"Yes, it's a gift. I just wake up every day looking completely awesome," he said arrogantly and then snickered.

She laughed too and then stuck her tongue out at him like a three-year-old.

"What time do we have to be at the pier?" Maddy asked as she pulled her food out of her pack.

"We have to be there by ten fifteen, so we need to go soon. The boat leaves at ten thirty. As soon as we're through, though, I have to come right back. My meetings, which were supposed to start later this afternoon, have been moved up a bit. I'm really sorry—I know we were going to try to go to the Hemingway House and the buoy marker. Maybe we can do that tomorrow before we leave. But I would still like to go back to Mallory Square again tonight. Maybe even take a walk this time down Duval Street and check out the shops along the way if you want." Jason didn't want to disappoint her, even though they'd both known even before leaving on the trip that this might happen. He would probably be on the phone all afternoon, because some new work requests had come in that needed to be evaluated, and this afternoon was the only time he could meet with Maria, the best virtual assistant ever. They had been working together for quite some time now, and she was part of the reason he was doing so well in his business. Plus, the head foreman on the current home renovation had hit a few snags and needed his opinion on some alternative solutions.

"That's no problem. Don't worry about me—I'll be fine. I'll probably rest up, watch a movie, or better yet, go sit in the shade outside and sketch. I've got plenty of inspiration around the pool area or sitting on the front veranda, where I can do some people watching. That's always fun, especially in this town. But I do have one request. If possible, I do want to go parasailing tomorrow before we go home. It seemed like each Key we passed through on our way here had parasailing tours."

"You want to parasail?" Jason said, more than a little shocked.

Maddy could tell she had surprised him.

"I've always wanted to try it but just never did. Either there wasn't enough time, we were short on money, or someone would talk me out of it because it's a little scary. But it looks exhilarating! Want to do it with me?"

Jason looked at her with a surprised grin. She seemed as excited as a child on Christmas Day, so much anticipation showing on her face. "Well, maybe. I'm more a feet-in-the-sand kinda guy. But we were going to take our time going back, anyway, and maybe stop by a beach or two. I think we can add parasailing to the agenda," he said, wondering how he could ever say no to her.

23

The glass-bottom boat was located at the dock at the end of Duval Street. To Maddy, it seemed like everything in Key West revolved around this street. At least, this was where most of the tourist activity occurred. The rest of Key West was quieter and more laid-back. All she knew was that she loved it all, and having someone special to share it with made this city and the trip even more magical.

People were already boarding the boat when they got there. Jason purchased their tickets, and they went up the ramp to the large boat that would take them out to the reef to view the sea life. Maddy could hardly contain her enthusiasm. She had always been drawn to the ocean and its creatures. Most of her drawings and paintings reflected this love of ocean life, beaches, and palm trees. For today's trip, she'd brought along her regular digital camera as well as her iPhone so she could get more photos.

Jason, on the other hand, was a bit nervous. His past experience with boats and the ocean had not been that pleasant, but he didn't dare tell Maddy. He was just praying he wouldn't get seasick. When Maddy had seen the advertisement for the glass-bottom boat tour, she was beyond thrilled and asked about going. Of course he couldn't say, "No, we can't go, because I get seasick." It was too embarrassing, and he didn't want to disappoint her. So instead, he readily agreed while cringing inside. Whatever her hold over him, it was very hypnotic, because getting on this boat was the last thing he wanted to do. But watching her excitement made it worth the risk of seasickness.

As it turned out, the morning boat was only about half full, which suited Maddy just fine. More space to move around and take pictures. Jason was carrying her pack for her, so she had a camera hanging from her shoulder and her phone wrapped tightly in her hand. The boat was big and had two decks: The top was open, with rows of benches for watching the passing scenery, and the wind was blowing strongly. The second deck was enclosed and air conditioned, and this was also where the glass bottom was. The captain had warned his passengers not to watch the passing water through the glass as they traveled because it could cause seasickness, something Jason immediately heeded. This deck also had two doors on the bow of the boat that opened up to a place to stand up front and enjoy a windy ride to the reef.

They went to the top deck outside as the boat pulled away from the dock and together watched it shrink into the distance. But when Maddy looked over at Jason, she could tell something wasn't right. The expression on his face was different, like he was troubled.

"Is everything ok? You look like something's wrong. Are you worried about the meetings this afternoon? We didn't have to go on this trip. I would have been fine back at the inn. Just as long as I'm with you, I don't care," she said, finishing her sentence with a small kiss on his cheek and threading her arm through and around his.

"Everything is fine but…this is embarrassing. I get seasick easily."

"Why didn't you say something? We didn't have to take this boat trip," Maddy said, feeling terrible, as if she had somehow forced him to come.

"I wanted to try it. But I started getting that queasy feeling as soon as we stepped on the boat. I keep telling myself it's all in my head."

"You've got to start telling me these things. I can't read your mind, silly. There were a lot of other things we could have done, but since we're already on our way, the best thing for seasickness is fresh air. Usually if you stay outside with the wind blowing in your face, it helps. Plus, put pressure here," she said, pointing to a spot on the inside of his lower arm about two inches above his wrist. "This is an acupressure point that relieves nausea. Oh, wait!" she said, quickly digging around in her backpack. "I forgot I'd brought these!" She pulled out two gray terry cloth wristbands and handed them to Jason. "I use these when I feel a little sick. They're called Sea Bands, and they work like a charm. Now, put these on like so," she said, taking his wrist into her hand and putting the gray band right over the pressure point. "See that little inside button? That actually puts pressure on the point I just showed you, so this should help." She looked up at him, and he just seemed to be staring at her. "What's wrong? Did I grow a third eye or something?"

"You are just so damn cute the way you take care of things. I think that backpack has something for just about everything inside it! Thanks for taking care of me and not laughing. I really hated to admit that the sea gets the best of me at times, or at least it has in the past," Jason said hesitantly.

"You'll be fine. Just hold my hand like this," she said as she gently wrapped her hand in his, "and give me a kiss. That kind of magic takes care of everything."

"So, now you cast spells? I'm learning more and more about you every day. Should I be scared?"

"I'm harmless," she said, laughing. It seemed their conversation was taking his mind off the potential of getting sick. Then Maddy lead them to the deck below then out the door to the bow of the boat where Jason could feel the air on his face. They wrapped their arms around each other as they gazed out at the horizon. The view was amazing, and although the boat bobbed up and down with the swell of the waves, Jason seemed to be doing quite well.

"Hey, I think your wristbands are working. So far, so good!" Jason said, pleased that he was feeling ok.

"I'm surprised they're doing the trick. You didn't follow all my instructions."

"What do you mean?" he said with concern.

"You forgot the kiss." And she didn't have to tell him again. Before she knew it, his lips were on hers, giving her a gentle but intense kiss as his hand caressed her back. As he pulled away, she whispered, "Jason, you have truly stolen my heart. I love you—I really do. I ask just one favor: please don't break it."

"That won't happen," he promised. But could he really make that promise? They were going their separate ways shortly, and how would they make this work? And what about him? Could *she* be the one to change her mind and break *his* heart like the women of his past were so prone to do? He knew this relationship was different from anything he had experienced in his life, but his mind was getting in the way. He had already declared his love for this woman, so if he wanted this to be real and permanent, he had to dispose of these limiting thoughts. He had to put a stop to these internal negative conversations in his mind.

The boat trip to the reef was intoxicating for Maddy. They did stay outside on the bow of the boat, where they watched the crystal aqua water, so clear that even though it was at least twenty feet deep or more, she could see right to the bottom. To her great delight, a small school of dolphins began swimming ahead of the boat as if leading the way to the reef!

"So, where are you right now?" She heard Jason's voice and realized she had gotten lost in old memories while watching the dolphins play in front of her.

"Just watching the dolphins. It's like our own private show."

Jason had been watching the playing mammals swim and jump too, but it was Maddy that captivated his attention.

The boat started slowing down to take its position over the reef. Maddy and Jason made their way through the door and over to the glass floor that separated them from the sea. The boat's captain came across the loudspeaker and introduced a young woman named Ella who would point out and name the various sea creatures and fish they would see. Maddy was not disappointed. They saw beautiful fish of almost every color, a moray eel, a lobster, a sea anemone, and even a very large grouper. But the best thing of all was the pair of huge sea turtles that swam by the glass a couple of times, acting as if they were checking out the boat and its passengers. Maddy was mesmerized, almost forgetting that Jason was standing beside her.

Jason had to admit the ocean show had been pretty good. Prior to this, he had only seen sea life like this in an aquarium, so seeing them in their own habitat was amazing. But once again it was Maddy that stole the show. He loved the way she enjoyed the small things. Maybe it was her illness that had made her appreciate the things most people would take for granted. He felt she was teaching him a lesson on how to just be present.

"Oh, I hope, hope, hope these pictures turn out! Those sea turtles were amazing, as were the dolphins on the way to the reef. The scenery, the water—I loved it all!" she said excitedly as she and Jason made their way off the boat to the pier. Jason was glad to be back on land, even though the boat trip had been great. And no seasickness!

"You really love the ocean, don't you?" Jason said as they walked down the shaded side of the street, keeping Maddy out of the sun as much as possible. She admitted to him that she'd probably gotten a little more sun than she should have, so she took some extra anti-histamine medication as a precaution.

"I do. I love the ocean, the beach, the palm trees, even the sand most of the time. There's just something so soothing about the beach and the waves. I've been all around the United States, visited some beautiful places. When I got to travel out west, I loved the deserts, the Rocky Mountains, the Grand Canyon. The Grand Tetons are magnificent, but I just like to visit. When it comes to the beach, I know I could live there, no questions asked. I used to always kid with my ex-husband that when we won the lottery, we would move to the beach. He would just laugh at me and say we were moving to the mountains. Basically it was always what he wanted, and my dreams were just that—dreams. When Hope was young, I would take her to the beach as much as I could. That always seemed to help me get through the rough patches." As Maddy talked, Jason could tell she was reminiscing, because her voice got softer, and part of it sounded melancholy.

"Sorry. I've rambled so much that we're almost back at the inn."

"I'm glad you shared that with me, because I wanted to know, Maddy. I want to know everything about you. Gives me ammunition," he said playfully.

"Ammunition? What do you need that for? Are you blackmailing me because I haven't told you the good, juicy stories yet? Now I might just have to censor myself," she said with a sly smile.

"Well, you don't seem like the type that would have a sordid background. As for me, that's another story," Jason said as they turned onto the little path leading to their rooms.

"What have I gotten myself into? Is your past full of meanness? I'm really good at snooping, so you might want to think about sharing your bad side with me before I find out on my own."

Jason laughed. "I have to admit I was a bit of a rebel when I was younger. Did get in a bit of trouble but learned my lessons quickly."

"Like what?"

"You know, a bit of drinking, tried a drug or two, crazy car stuff guys like to do. Maybe even riding on the hood of a car going around fifty miles per hour one time."

"Are you serious? You could have killed yourself!" Maddy said in disbelief.

"Yeah, that's what the cop said when we got caught. My friends and I were always walking that fine line. It's a wonder none of us got seriously injured or went to jail."

"Sounds like I've fallen in love with a scoundrel. My reputation will be ruined, oh my," she said with her best southern accent, fanning herself with her hand.

"Yes ma'am, you have, so you might want to rethink your decision," Jason said in a very authoritative voice.

"Never." By this time they were at the door to her room. She reached up and kissed him, but that wasn't enough. His arms enveloped her tightly as he kissed her again.

"Thank you for this morning. I had a wonderful time, and thanks to you and your Sea Bands, the boat ride was great. Now it's time for a little bit of work. If you need anything, let me know." He kissed her once more and headed to his own room.

24

When she finally sat down, she suddenly realized how tired she was from the morning's activities, but thoughts of Jason still occupied her mind. She would have loved for him to come and share the afternoon with her, but she knew in her heart that probably would have led to allowing him into her life in a very private and intimate way. She wanted him, it was true, but the time wasn't right. Although what setting could be more romantic than this beautiful bed and breakfast inn surrounded by a lush garden? The sexual tension was definitely in the air—it increased each time they were together—and she knew that eventually their relationship would reach that level. But her intuition told her to take it slowly, and the feeling she received from Jason was that he was holding back too. She just hoped he wasn't having second thoughts about telling her he was in love with her. She didn't want to end her vacation in the Keys on a sour note.

One thing she did know was that when she got back to her little getaway house on Islamorada, it would be time for some of that soul searching she had originally came to the Keys for. She could look back right now and see that since she'd been here, she had more or less run away from facing the questions and decisions she'd intended to address while on her trip. When she'd found Jason, all those things she'd been so concerned about had mostly disappeared because she found herself preoccupied with this wonderful man. But as she sat in her chair looking through the double doors leading to the pool, she knew that she wanted—no, needed—to go back to Charleston with a plan for her health, her family, and her life.

Maddy freshened up and fixed herself a small lunch using the microwave in the room. Then, as she lay down to take a nap, she realized how happy and content she felt. Not the "fake it till you make it" type of happiness, but a feeling of complete bliss, both mentally and physically. It seemed her body was taking some positive cues from this cheerful state. The itchiness that plagued her on a daily basis back home was much better, as were the other symptoms that accompanied her illness. She'd always known that stress was a big component in triggering her reactions, but maybe the beginnings of a new relationship was creating some sort of buffer in her body, releasing chemicals that calmed down her system. If that were the case, then Jason was the best medicine for her. She loved the feeling of being in love and cherished by someone who was truly a caring and, most assuredly, a very sexy man.

As she lay in bed relaxing, she thought this might be the perfect time to check in with her parents. Her mom and dad had promised they wouldn't call her so she could have the alone time she needed, but they'd also reminded her more than once before she left that should she need them, they were only a phone call or plane ride away. She loved her parents immensely, and they'd been her rock through all the mess she had gone through, especially recently. Two and a half weeks had passed since she'd talked to them, so before she took her much-needed nap, she decided it was time for a check-in.

"Hi, Mom!" Maddy said as soon she heard her mother's voice.

"It's about time you called, young lady. I know I said I wouldn't bug you, but do you know how hard that is? How are you? How are the Keys? What is your house like?"

"And I love you too," Maddy said, chuckling a little. "I'm sorry I haven't called. Things have been fine, but I did have a bit of a rocky start. Ended up at the hospital the first Saturday I was here, but everything's fine now. Please don't worry," Maddy said quickly, knowing her mom would stress out immediately.

"We knew about that already."

"What? How? Oh, my gosh. Riley. You are in cahoots with Riley! No wonder you said you wouldn't call. How did I not figure this out before? Now I know why you and Dad were so ok with me and this trip!" Maddy was putting it all together now as she lay there with the speakerphone on.

"Can you blame us, especially me? I was one worried mom when you were just *thinking* about going on this trip, so I had to do something. Thank God for Riley. She's given us updates almost daily, sweet thing that she is. Sorry to spy on you like that. Well, it's not really spying. Just Riley and me talking, that's all," her mom said as smoothly as she could.

Maddy wanted to be upset, but how could she, really? Her parents were being parents, and to be honest, she would probably do the same thing if Hope had approached her as a single woman wanting to run off somewhere by herself. But just how much information had Riley given her parents?

"So, how often do you and Riley have these little chats?" Maddy asked coolly.

"Oh, about every two or three days."

"You've got to be kidding. Mom, you know I'm a grown woman, don't you? If there were anything wrong, I promised both you and Dad that I would call. So, what has Riley been saying?"

"Well," her mom started, "she described the house you're in—and by the way, it sounds really lovely. Said you seemed to be doing ok, maybe a bit tired. She told us about your trip to the ER and how this lovely gentleman across the street helped you to the hospital. And her latest update was to let us know that you were still doing ok but had decided to take a trip to Key West with said gentleman across the street. Don't know much from there."

Riley! Ugh! Just wait till she got back to the cottage. They were going to have one serious talk. Why had she told her mom about Jason? Now her parents were going to think she'd just come down to the Keys to run away and find a man.

"So, tell me a little about this Jason. I think Riley said that was his name," her mom said, still cool as a cucumber.

Maddy took in a deep breath and sighed heavily.

"Listen, Mom. He is a sweet man. It's like we're best friends, and yes, we are in Key West together, but in separate rooms. Nothing trashy is going on. Friends taking a trip together." She just wasn't ready to tell her parents how she truly felt about Jason. She wanted to give it more time, to see what kind of decisions they would make about their relationship when it came time to go back home.

"Sounds like a nice gentleman. Glad he was there to help you that night you had to go to the hospital. That's one of the main things I've worried about since you've been on this trip of yours. I still don't see why you couldn't have picked a place closer to Charleston."

"Mom, you know how much I love the Keys, and it was the perfect place to come because Riley lives here. Didn't know she was your personal spy and my babysitter, though!"

"Maddy, don't get so upset. Your dad and I put Riley up to it, but I have to say she was all for it. Could tell even on the phone she was smiling ear to ear when we asked her about keeping an eye out for you."

Sounds like Riley, Maddy thought.

"Mom, I have to go. Jason is doing some work in his room and I was getting ready to take a nap. We went on a glass-bottom boat trip this morning, and the sun got to me a bit. I'm ok, just needed some extra medicine, water, and rest. I will call you again when I get back from the trip. And even though Riley and I are going to sit down and have a serious conversation about privacy rights, thank you for looking out for me. I love you, Mom, and tell Dad I love him too!" Then she clicked the disconnect button.

As she settled into the pillows, she noticed it had gotten quite a bit darker in her room, and thunder rumbled in the distance. A thunderstorm made the best weather for taking an afternoon nap. She quickly changed into something a bit more comfortable, grabbed her blanket, and got back into bed. But before she could get very snug, she heard a slight knock at the door. She got up, hurried to the door, and looked through the tiny peephole to see Jason standing there, the rain beginning to fall in the background. Another lightning flash and clap of thunder startled her; it was so immediate and loud that she knew the storm was just about over them.

"Come in before you get soaked!" she said, opening the door and pulling him inside. "I thought you were working. Are you done already?"

"Seems the Internet service is out, probably because of the storm, and I can't reach any of my people on the cell phone. Was hoping I could come and keep you company for a while till the storm blows over. You know I'm scared of the thunder," he said, his eyebrows raised.

"Aw, you poor thing. Come here and I'll protect you," Maddy smiled.

"Were you getting ready to take a nap?" Jason said as he looked at her bed, the blanket and pillows in a heap as if she had just gotten up.

"Yes, but I'd rather spend the time with you, unless you want to lie down with me. I mean take a nap, not anything else. I mean...no, I don't have to take a nap. But just lie down on the bed. No, that didn't come out right either." Maddy rolled her eyes and looked down at the floor. Nothing she said was making sense, and she didn't want it to seem like she was throwing herself at him.

He went over to her bed, fluffed one of the extra pillows, and scooted the blanket over to the other side. He then motioned for her to join him. She went and lay next him, and he gently put the blanket over her. She nestled beside him and he wrapped his arms around her. The room was quiet except for the rumble of thunder, the heavy rain outside, and their breathing. This feels so right, Maddy thought. And she felt so loved.

Lying with Maddy was what he had imagined it would be. The desire to carry things further grew stronger each moment he stayed there, touching her—but he didn't. Lying in the bed and holding her made him feel like he was protecting something immensely precious to him, and he was. Every second they were together she became so much more a part of his life. Those thoughts he was having of getting hurt again were fading with every moment. But lying beside her like this was wonderful for him. As for intimacy between the two of them, it would come in time, but he couldn't deny that he thought about it, especially with her so close to him.

As the storm raged on outside, the two of them fell fast asleep, wrapped in each other's arms.

25

When Jason awoke, he looked down to see Maddy sleeping peacefully beside him. He had no idea how long he had slept, but the storm was over and a very light rain was falling. As he gently slid his arm from underneath her, she stirred and turned over, still sleeping soundly. He kissed her forehead softly so as not to wake her, got his phone off the nightstand, and slipped out of the room quietly, heading back to his own.

When he saw the time, he realized he'd been with Maddy for a little over an hour. Hopefully he would be able to reconnect to his meeting now, because many things still required discussion and he wanted to finish as soon as possible. But before calling Mr. Ruthner, his next potential client, he decided to call Maria to make sure everything was still on track with the permits she was securing for him for the present job site.

"About time you called today," she said, not even saying hello. "I know you're on your minivacation with your latest female conquest, but there's still work to be done, young man!"

Even though Maria was at least ten years his junior, at times she acted like a combination boss/mother. They had worked together for some time now, and she was the best assistant he'd ever had. And being able to work remotely—she from her home in New York and he from wherever his next job took him—had worked perfectly for them. She was a genius at getting just about anything done and was proficient on the Internet and all the necessary software programs needed in his line of work. He felt lucky to have found this gem of an assistant.

"The permits you asked for are done and should be delivered to the job site by five o'clock today. Mr. Ruthner called about thirty minutes ago and said that your online meeting had been disconnected and wanted to know what was going on. I assured him that as soon as I could get in touch with you I would let him know. Since I couldn't reach you either, I checked the radar and saw that you were probably in a bad storm, so I figured the Internet access was down."

"You didn't tell him I was in Key West, did you?" Jason asked cautiously.

"For goodness' sake, no!" Maria cried. "All he knows is that you're on a job in the Keys. But he's very anxious to hear your plans for the renovation of his home and your bid on the work, even though he pretty much told me you had the job. You also have two other clients that want to talk to you, but they want their projects done at the same time as Mr. Ruthner.

You're just getting a little too big for your britches, Mr. J.," she remarked, calling him the nickname she had given him several years ago.

"Send me an e-mail containing all the information on the other two potential clients so I can go over it. I might be able to work something out. I'm getting ready to call Ruthner again, because the storm has finally let up here. I should have a decision about the next job site within a few days. We're leaving tomorrow to go back to Islamorada…and Maria, she's not a conquest. She's different," Jason said thoughtfully.

"Oh, crap. I can hear it in your voice! You're actually falling for someone," Maria cried delightedly into the phone. "I knew this day would eventually come, but you sure did take your time."

"How do you do that? It's like you women can read between the lines. Really freaks me out sometimes," he said. "But I'm not sure where this is heading. She's on vacation and I'm working, but Maddy's just not the same as the other women I've met along the way. But that's enough for now. I've got to get back to work."

"Not yet. I have some other news for you, and it ain't about work. I've taken a few phone calls in the last week from Andrea."

Jason froze in dismayed silence. What in the world was Andrea calling him for? They hadn't talked in at least five years!

"You've got to be kidding! Are you sure it was Andrea?"

"Well, that's who she said she was."

"What did she want?" he asked, irritation in his voice.

"Just keeps asking where you are and how she can reach you. I keep telling her you're on a job site and can't be disturbed. Then she asks *again* where the job site is, and I tell her that due to client privacy, I can't give out that info. Then she gets all annoyed and hangs up on me. She's called three times in five days, each time apologizing for the time before, but then that bad attitude rears up again when I won't give up your whereabouts."

"Thanks, Maria. For the information and for being my bodyguard. I want nothing to do with that bitch. Sorry!" Jason was having a hard time dealing with this irritating piece of news.

"No problem Mr. J. I completely understand. As far as I'm concerned, she's a witch *and* a bitch by the way she treated you. I better never see her. She won't look the same after this New York girl gets through with her," Maria said confidently.

"At least she doesn't know where I am, so I don't have to deal with her. If she keeps calling, just hang up. You don't have to put up with that, and neither do I. But if you do find out what she's calling about or why she's trying to talk to me, let me know." Jason's voice was now venomous as old, bitter memories crept into his consciousness.

"Don't let this spoil your time with, um…what was her name, again?" Maria asked innocently.

"It's Maddy, and like I said before, this is different. Get back to work, and I'll talk to you later," Jason said with a smile in his voice that Maria recognized immediately.

"Tell her that Maria says hi, ok?"

"She doesn't even know who you are!"

"She will eventually," Maria said and hung up the phone.

Maddy woke up to find that Jason had left her snuggled up in the blanket he had tucked around her. This had been one the best naps ever, what with the thunderstorm and being held in Jason's arms as she fell asleep. She could tell that the storm was over by the sunshine that now peeked through the curtains of the French doors. She looked at her phone and saw that it was already four thirty. A three-hour nap! Her medications had done their job for sure, but she wondered how long Jason had stayed.

She decided to get dressed for the evening and then give Jason a call. That way, if he was ready for their night out on the town, she would be too. She picked out her aqua maxi dress with its halter-top bodice and resolved to tuck her thin white cotton sweater into her tote just in case it cooled down during the evening. Then she chose her favorite white slip-on sandals decorated with clear stones. Once she was dressed and had restocked her tote bag, she decided to go knock on his door instead of using the phone.

It took only a few knocks on the wooden panel before the door opened wide to reveal Jason standing with a phone to his ear. She'd forgotten about his meetings! She motioned she would come back later, but he mouthed the words "come in," so she slipped quietly into the room.

As Maddy viewed the floor plan again, she saw that she'd been right about the bed. If they removed one thin wall, their headboards would be touching. Her body tingled knowing that he slept so close to her at night. Memories of the afternoon nap they had shared and how deliciously romantic it had been wafted back to her. She could have stayed with him like that the rest of the day and into the evening, but she was quite positive such a nap would have turned into something more.

"I've looked at the pictures my foreman sent me and the list of items yet to be done. Things are moving along, just a bit slower than I anticipated. We've had a few problems with the bathroom floor, which put us behind the tentative schedule I initially gave you, but I'm still confident we can be done on time," Jason said. He was deep in work mode. Maddy had never seen this side of him and now watched in fascination. He was completely in his element, phone in one hand and work papers spread out on the table before him.

Though she couldn't hear the other side of the conversation, by the look on Jason's face, the answer he'd given must have satisfied his client. That was a good sign, she thought, because she would have hated to spend their last evening in Key West with him being annoyed about a work issue.

"I'll call you Friday morning to give you an update. If there are any snags you need to be aware of, I'll let you know. The house is going to be stunning, Roger. You and Margaret picked out beautiful decor to restore this home." There was silence on Jason's end while the other party talked again, and then the conversation came to an end.

"I'll see you then," Jason said, and he hung up the phone.

Jason now turned to her and quickly gave her a kiss. "I'm so sorry about that. The storm really put me behind on my meetings, but I just finished up. You look beautiful! And rested. Give me just a few minutes, and I'll be ready to go. I just need to freshen up a bit and change clothes," he said, giving her another quick kiss.

"That's fine. I'll go sit out by the pool and wait for you. It's nice out now—the thunderstorm cooled everything down a bit."

"You don't have to leave."

So Maddy nervously put her bag on the bed and sat in the little chair at the table by the window.

"So, how was your nap? You must have been really tired, because when I left, you didn't wake up. You were sleeping pretty soundly...and looked so cute wrapped up in your blanket." She looked up at him and caught him winking at her—and taking his shirt off at the same time. She knew that Jason was built, but she had never seen him shirtless this close up. The muscular arms she was very well acquainted with were only the beginning. His chest and abs were toned and muscular as well. She realized that even though they'd been swimming before, it had been dark, so she hadn't really seen him without clothes. Then she realized he hadn't seen her, either. This made her nervous about tomorrow, because they'd planned to visit a few beaches on their trip back. She definitely didn't have the figure of a woman who worked out, because she couldn't. Intense exercise actually triggered bad reactions, so she had to be careful about her exercise regimen. She had started walking a few months ago, but in her case it was a slow process because she had to build up her walking time very slowly. As for muscle toning, she used stretchy bands, but she was not consistent with their use, even though her doctors were pretty adamant about her exercising. Now she wished she had listened to their advice. She hadn't expected to fall in love with someone down here, especially a very muscular, sexy, man who just happened to live across the street. She'd actually thought it didn't matter what she looked like, because she would probably never see anyone she met here again—this was just a vacation. She knew worrying about this wasn't going to give her a model's body overnight, nor did she want one, so she pushed the thought out of her mind and concentrated on watching Jason as discreetly as she could.

"My nap was wonderful. I slept for three hours! But the best part was cuddling with you while it stormed outside. I know it wasn't good for business, but I was secretly glad the Internet access went down." She gave him a shy smile from across the room as he continued getting ready.

"My nap was great too. I did end up falling asleep for a while, but I like your assessment of our little situation. Lying in bed with me probably was pretty fantastic," he said sarcastically. She looked at him and shook her head as she smiled.

"So, now the true Jason Burnett shows up. In love with himself. I knew that you had to have a flaw somewhere, and finally here's proof," she said as she rose and walked toward him.

"The best part was watching you sleep." By this time she was standing in front of him, and his arms wrapped themselves around her waist once again.

"You are a stunning woman, Maddy. Beautiful in every sense of the word." He kissed her again, something she just couldn't get enough of when she was with him.

"Now, please go sit back down," he said as he turned her around, "or I won't be ready in time to see the sunset at Mallory Square."

"Yes sir," she said with her back to him and the biggest grin on her face.

By their calculations, they still had one hour till sunset as they left Jason's room. They found a cab quickly, and before they knew it, they were at the Square along with an unusually large crowd of people.

"Seems there's some type of event or festival going on tonight," Jason said as he looked around.

"The Tall Ships Celebration started today, so it will be pretty busy around here for the next five days or so," their cabbie informed them as they disembarked.

"I guess, since we're leaving tomorrow, we picked a good time to head back home. Everyone is packed in pretty close," Maddy said with a smile, a little sad, though, that their trip was coming to a close. But right now she wanted to get a good view of one more sunset over Key West.

Carrying Maddy's backpack on his shoulder and holding her hand behind his back, Jason led the way slowly through the crowd. There were so many people that by the time they reached the edge of the pier, all the good seats were gone and the sun was already starting its descent into the ocean. They had made it just in time, and it was beautiful! After the storm they'd had this afternoon, the clouds left behind were lighting up in brilliant hues of orange, pink, yellow, and purple as the sun sank lower and lower in the western sky. They stood together, Maddy in front of Jason and his arms wrapped around her, watching nature's picture show. But she wanted something more. She turned around and looked into his eyes.

"Jason, thank you for this wonderful trip. It means more to me than I can ever say. I've had the best time, and it's all because of you. You've given me back a piece of my life that I thought I'd lost for good. Even though we both know things have moved a bit fast, I do love you," she said. She put her hands on his face, stood on the tips of her toes, and gave him a kiss so soft and sweet that Jason craved more. When they finally pulled away from each other, the throng of people around them had already started to disperse. So they stood just holding each other, looking toward the ocean and the spot on the horizon where the sun had set, leaving small streaks of light seeming to burst from the depths of the sea.

"I think we missed the sunset," Jason said very lovingly.

"I don't think we missed a thing," Maddy said as she kissed him again.

26

Maddy had wanted to check out all the art vendors one more time, but tonight the crowd was just too thick. Jason reached for her hand and they made their way through the throng of people. But instead of heading down the street, they ducked into the Ocean Key Resort right by the square.

"What are we doing?" Maddy asked as Jason guided her through the lobby.

"If I remember correctly, you asked to go to a really nice restaurant this evening, since we were leaving tomorrow. So, here we are."

Delighted, she followed him through the hotel to the resort's restaurant, Hot Tin Roof, and it was beautiful. The hostess led them to a table for two that overlooked the pier and Key West Harbor. Even though it was getting darker outside, they could still make out some of the details around them. The little flickering candle on their table made it so romantic, and it felt to Maddy like she was living some kind of fairy tale. Jason had thought of everything, spoiling her, and she was loving every minute of it.

"This is breathtaking," Maddy said as she took her seat and looked out over the water.

"Thought you might like this restaurant. I've been here before, and it's really good. Plus—I checked, and they'll prepare food especially for you." He smiled at her, and she felt like putty in his hands. She knew they had to head back tomorrow, but she didn't want to go. These last few days had been so wonderful. But for now, she was going to enjoy this romantic dinner by the water, under the moonlight, with the man she loved.

Their dinner was wonderful, both the meal itself and the atmosphere. As usual, they never ran out of things to talk about. Afterward they strolled down Duval Street, watching the people—things were getting rowdier by the minute. Even though it was quite a bit noisier and more people were milling about, it was still fun. Maddy wanted to go into every little shop and art gallery, but she decided that would have to wait for another Key West trip. Just then they strolled by a jewelry store, and Maddy saw it—the souvenir she wanted from their trip.

"Can we go in here?" she asked excitedly.

"Of course," Jason answered, wondering what had her so eager.

She went straight to the little case in the front window and found what she was looking for—a beautiful silver bracelet in the shape of dolphins. As the store clerk came over, she asked to try it on. It was perfect.

"I love this! It looks like the dolphins are jumping one after the other. It reminds me of the ones we saw on our boat trip this morning." She twisted the little bracelet around her wrist, admiring the shiny silver.

"We'll take it," Jason told the girl.

"But I don't even know how much it is, Jason," she said quickly.

"Doesn't matter. Let it be my gift to you. A remembrance of our Key West trip."

"I can't let you do that. You've done so much already."

"Maddy, I want to get this for you. And hopefully every time you look at it, you'll think of me."

Before she knew it, the dancing dolphins encircled her wrist, and they were walking out of the little store. She would indeed think about this trip every time she saw the bracelet, and most definitely, her thoughts would be of him.

The next morning was bittersweet as they packed their bags into the car and started on their drive back to reality. Maddy's parasailing trip had been cancelled due to strong winds off the coast. But even though she never got to parasail in Key West, she was sure other places closer to her rental house would provide an opportunity. Riley was bound to know somewhere.

They stopped at the local grocery store to pick up a few picnic items for the trip home. They were planning to stop at two beaches today: Bahia Honda State Park, which she had only passed by on her two previous trips to the Keys, and then on to Anne's Beach, her favorite, where she and Jason had taken their evening swim. Maddy also wanted to take some pictures at some other favorite spots so she could get more ideas for paintings, which she was looking forward to starting on when she got back to her home away from home.

But before they left the tiny island, they went to the buoy that marked the southernmost point of the United States, where Cuba was only ninety miles away. A fellow tourist kindly took their picture there, but they also did some crazy selfies with their phones. The next stop was Smathers Beach, again for more pictures and to walk in the powder-white sand of the beach dotted with palm trees and to dip their toes in the clear blue water of the Atlantic. Then, reluctantly, they said good-bye to Key West.

The day had turned out to be beautiful, with partly cloudy skies and a temperature in the low eighties. Maddy picked out some Jimmy Buffet music on her iPad and plugged it into the car's speaker system, and it wasn't long before they were both singing to "Margaritaville." Every now and then, she would ask Jason to slow down or pull over if possible so she could snap a picture or two. And, thankfully for Maddy, the cars heading away from the island were few and far between, posing no obstacles.

Before long, they turned into Bahia Honda State Park, a picturesque place with plenty of parking, a changing area, a souvenir store, and an ice-cream shop. They'd put on their swimsuits before leaving the bed and breakfast that morning, so they were already dressed for swimming. As soon as they were parked, they grabbed Maddy's backpack and their towels and set off for the beach.

Maddy instantly fell in love with the beautiful scene before her. The white coral sand and clear blue water were amazing and completely relaxing. They laid out their towels and were quickly out of their T-shirts and shorts and heading into the water. Jason kept coaxing Maddy deeper and deeper, something she wasn't quite confident about, but he held her as they bobbed up and down with the small waves. They could see all sorts of tropical fish swimming around them that at least didn't look menacing, but she was still nervous, having once encountered a barracuda that had come too close, grazing her arm and scaring her so badly she'd had difficulty going for a swim again for a while. But the fish swimming around them now were harmless and looked like brightly colored specks of light dancing in the water.

"Very slowly...turn around," Jason suddenly whispered in her ear. This terrified her, and she froze like a statue in the chest-deep water.

"What is it?" she whispered back fearfully. "Is it a shark? What is it?"

"Shhh! No, no, no. Just look."

She turned around slowly to see a graceful dolphin come up out of the water and dive back down again only five feet from her. She was too shocked to say anything, but tears came to her eyes. This was incredible! Just then a second dolphin swam by so close she could almost touch it.

"They're so beautiful! I can't believe they're so close. I wish I could touch one. Should we move away or stay put?" she asked, not knowing if they really were safe.

"I don't know. I've never encountered a dolphin this close before."

But before she knew it, the first dolphin swam by her, and she tentatively reached out her hand and gently rubbed the creature as it swam by. It was as if this dolphin knew she was a friend, that she wasn't a threat. And she was ecstatic!

By this time, other people on the beach saw what was happening and started heading into the water, hoping to get a closer look at the pair of dolphins swimming around Jason and Maddy. Within a few minutes, though, the mammals turned to swim away, but not before one came close to them once more, allowing both Jason and Maddy to give it a little rub good-bye. Then the pair swam off toward the wide expanse of the ocean.

Maddy watched them till she could see them no more, mesmerized by the experience. They headed out of the water then, and as they reached their towels on the beach, Maddy still couldn't believe it! It was as if the dolphins had come especially to see them. She'd heard that dolphins used more of their brain capacity than humans and that they could sense when someone was sick or in trouble. She wondered to herself if they could actually tell she had a chronic illness. She would never know, but the experience was something that was forever etched in her memory. And she had been able to share it with Jason.

"Can you believe that? I can't wait to tell everyone! If my camera had been waterproof, that would have been beyond amazing." She grabbed him and hugged tightly. "Thank you, Jason."

"Hey, all I did was take you swimming and tell you to turn around. They came to you, Maddy. There must be something about you they liked. I know there's a lot about you *I* like!" He smiled at her, giving her that "let's get into trouble" grin.

"You'll have to give me a list one day of all my most wonderful attributes. It would be good for my ego," she said with a laugh. "And I'll go ahead and give you a list of yours. I like everything about you," she said as she ran her hand down his chest and around his waist.

"If you keep touching me like that, we might have a very delicate problem here on this beach!"

"Ok, I'll be a good girl. I promise," she said, raising her right hand.

They both took a quick shower at the changing rooms to rinse off as much sand as they could, and then they decided to have their lunch at one of the many shaded picnic tables. Jason had picked up a sandwich at the deli, and Maddy had applesauce, water crackers, and almond butter. She really wanted some veggies, but she knew that once they got home she could go back to eating more like she was used to. She was very thankful she hadn't reacted to anything in Key West, except for being tired. Her medicines were doing their job, and she also had her protector to keep her on track.

Since they'd spent much more time at the park than they'd planned to, they decided that except for Maddy's occasional photo stops, they would head straight home from there. She couldn't wait to see these pictures on her computer, and Jason had been so accommodating, stopping just about everywhere Maddy thought could be a potential piece of artwork. Plus, these pictures would be her respite once she was back home in Charleston. When she needed a break and a getaway, she would have her photos to transport her back to the memories of her month long retreat on these enchanting islands.

As they drove the last few miles toward their homes, Maddy began to think again about what had really brought her here. She was trying to determine her next steps in life. What were her passions? What did she want to accomplish? How could she regain her health? But now she had additional questions on her list. What about Jason? What about their relationship? What would they do? She loved him, she truly did. She felt it all the way through her body and into her soul. They would have to talk about this soon, but not now. In a few days, she hoped they could take some time together and find a solution.

"You're awfully quiet. Are you getting tired, or are you just lost in thought?" Jason asked as he watched her gaze out the window at the turquoise sea.

"Actually," she said, "a little of both. The swimming at the park, petting the dolphins in the wild, eating lunch by the ocean—all that has made this such a wonderful day, especially with you. On the other hand, the sun has tired me out and I'm starting to itch a little all over. But you know, when we were in the water, it seemed like all the muscle and nerve pain relaxed and disappeared. It was truly wonderful. I was also thinking about the reason I came to the Keys in the first place—to try to get my life together and make some crucial decisions. I've avoided thinking about them...but then, I've had a major distraction." She reached over and ran her fingers through his hair.

"Are you blaming me? I'm the problem?"

"Yes, and you are one hell of a distraction. The best one I ever had." And she leaned over to kiss him on the cheek.

They made the turn onto the road heading toward home. It seemed they'd been gone so much longer than just four days, but at the same time, the trip had passed too quickly. As they pulled up to Maddy's house to unload her suitcase and bags, Jason noticed a red sports car parked in front of his house, and someone was sitting in the driver's seat. He couldn't tell who it was, but he knew he wasn't expecting anyone today. As they took the bags out of the trunk, Jason looked over just as his unexpected visitor got out of the car. He stopped so suddenly that Maddy ran right into him.

"What's wrong?" she said as she looked at the expression of stone on Jason's face.

"Andrea is here."

27

"It's about time you got here! Been waiting here all day except to run up to the deli for a sandwich or a potty break." The woman walked over to where Jason and Maddy were standing and gave Jason a sticky lipstick kiss on the lips. Maddy stood there shocked.

"Well, aren't you going to introduce us, sugar?" she asked, leaning closer to Jason and wrapping her arm around him.

After shrugging out of her grasp, and with a very irritated look, Jason spoke.

"Andrea, this is Maddy. Maddy, this is Andrea, my *ex*-wife," he said, exaggerating the word *ex*. "What the hell are you doing here, and how did you find out where I was?" Maddy could hear in his voice that the longer Andrea stood there, the quicker Jason's irritation was turning into anger.

"Oh, Jason, you know I have my ways. Of course, I called Maria, but she just gave that standard answer of hers. You really need to do something about her. No personal skills at all. I'm surprised you still have a business if your clients have to go through her in order to speak to you. She's so rude!" Her voice was sickeningly sweet, and Maddy felt a rising sense of dread with every word she uttered.

Andrea then turned to Maddy.

"Maddy, it is *so* nice to meet one of Jason's, um…shall I say, 'friends'? And I just love your name. Is it short for something?"

Maddy stood speechless, not sure what to do. Jason seemed made of granite as he stood between the two women, his hands balled into fists at his sides, his eyes staring at the dark brunette who wore far too much makeup for a Florida vacation.

"Ah…yes, it's a nickname my father gave me as a little girl. It was nice meeting you. I'll just get my bags and go."

"I'll help you," Jason said quickly.

"Don't mind me. I'll just go wait at your house, sweetie," Andrea crooned, looking directly at Jason. She turned and strolled away in her too-tight miniskirt and four-inch heels.

As they set the bags down in the foyer of Maddy's house, Jason immediately erupted. "I had no idea she was coming here. I don't even know how she found out where I was! My job sites are kept confidential because most of the people who hire me don't want their personal addresses known. Let me find out what is going on, and then she is out of here."

Maddy was still shaking, her confidence in their relationship taking a beating. Here was this beautiful woman—who Jason used to be in love with—waiting for him at his house! By the looks of her, Maddy felt she could in no way compete.

"Are you ok? I'm so sorry you had to meet her." Jason took her into his arms, giving her a loving hug and a kiss. "Just remember that I love you. Nothing will ever change that, I promise."

She looked into his eyes and said nothing. She was still completely stunned by the fact that his ex-wife was here in the Keys, and who knew what she had up her sleeve. If everything Jason had told her about Andrea was true, no way was this good.

Maddy looked up at Jason. "I know you love me, but something feels off. Everything has been wonderful, almost like a dream, and now it's like we've been slammed by fate. I do believe in you, and I do love you. Hopefully this is just a bump in the road." She stroked his cheek, and he kissed the palm of her hand as he turned to walk out the door.

Maddy couldn't help but watch out her kitchen window as Jason strode back to the car to gather his bags and then walked across the street to his house, where *she* was. Andrea was eagerly awaiting him at the front door, but Maddy could tell by Jason's body language that this woman certainly was not welcome, and that made her feel a tiny bit better about the situation. But when they both disappeared into the house, her imagination went wild as to what was happening inside.

Jason threw his bags onto the living room floor and then turned on Andrea.

"So I'm going to ask you again. Why in the hell are you here, and how did you find me? What's going on, Andrea?

And you better start with the truth from the beginning, because I know how you like to skirt around it."

"Is that the way you greet your wife? Thought you might be a little happier to see me," she crooned sweetly.

"Happy? You've got to be kidding. When we went our separate ways ten years ago, it was the best day of my life. Should have been yours too, since you had someone else already lined up to take my place with his large stash of money. I do feel sorry for all the other men you've probably fooled over the years." His anger was starting to get the best of him, so Jason tried to breathe deeply and calm down.

"I haven't fooled anyone. I can't help it if a gentleman likes me and wants to spend some money on me. *You* certainly didn't," she said, her voice suddenly flat.

"We were just starting out. I made enough money to keep us afloat, and I was working fourteen-hour days!" he yelled.

"I was working too!" she said, now trying to sound hurt.

"You call answering the phone for your lover at his real estate office a job? He must have paid you with sex, because you certainly didn't bring home much money." She went to slap his face, but he was quicker and caught her hand.

"Do not touch me or try that again," he said as he let go of her wrist. "You have five minutes to tell me why you are here, and then I want you gone. I will call the cops if I have to."

"No, you won't. Would be kinda awkward if you told them you wanted to kick your wife out, especially when you just got back from a little tryst with your lover across the street. And poor little me has nowhere to go." Her pout suddenly turned into the sly look of a fox.

"You mean *ex*-wife," Jason corrected her.

"Oh no, sugar, I mean *wife*. We are still married, and I believe we are coming up on our eleventh anniversary. Isn't that so sweet? Maybe we can celebrate here in the Keys," she said as she walked around the little island house.

"What the hell are you talking about?"

"About three weeks ago I was contacted by a man that worked for my attorney back when we filed for divorce. Seems we signed the papers and have our own copies, but the clerk somehow forgot to file the papers with the court. When the attorney found out the mistake, he contacted me to let me know that legally we are still married."

Jason felt like he'd been punched in the stomach. No way was he still married to this vile woman!

"You aren't playing this game with me, Andrea. What do you want? Money? That's usually your deal. Are you really desperate enough to make up such an absurd story? Are you stupid enough to think that I can't contact my attorney to find out you're lying?"

"Oh, it's true, all right. I have all the papers and information with me just so I could show you. But I'm sure by now your lawyer has a copy too. You still use Dave Peterson, right? I made sure my lawyer sent the papers to him yesterday after I found out where you were staying." She continued walking aimlessly around the house, ending up right in front of him.

"How did you find out where I was?"

"Sweetie, it's easy to find a paper trail, and with your handiwork being so well known now, all I had to do was ask a few people the right questions. Then I just put two and two together. Seems your hotel project here in the Keys was a pretty big deal and made the news in the architecture circles on the Internet. Easy peasy!"

Jason was livid. Still married? There was no way! This had to be a joke, but if it wasn't, there had to be a way to get this fixed and fast. This woman was not going to wreck his life a second time, especially now that Maddy was part of it.

"So, where is our room?" Andrea continued in that sickening voice that made Jason cringe every time she talked.

"There is a hotel on the main street. I suggest you get a room, because you aren't staying here. We will talk in the morning."

"You going to kick your poor wife out into the street? Wonder what the authorities would say. Wonder if I could claim domestic abuse? There are all kinds of ways we can make this ugly—or keep it clean." Now *this* was the Andrea that Jason knew. She was showing her true colors.

"What do you want?"

"It seems that since we filed for divorce, you've made quite a name for yourself. Actually have a thriving company, something I thought you would never do. I'm definitely surprised you've made the kind of money you have. All I remember is your taking on pitiful little remodeling jobs. You were pathetic back then, but it seems times have changed. You know, in most divorce cases, couples split all assets fifty-fifty. Yes, that sounds about right to me from all the research I've done, and I've verified that with my lawyer. Give me 50 percent of your assets, and then we can sign the papers again, making sure this time they're properly filed and we're legally divorced."

"There is no way in hell you're touching anything of mine. I've worked hard to get where I am, and I'm sure you've just slept your way through men to have whatever you call a life. By the way, who is your latest fling? Is he lurking around here somewhere?" Jason asked angrily.

"Why, no, sweetheart, I've changed my ways. You're my darling husband, and I wouldn't dare have an affair, unlike you with that woman across the street." She smiled, but she stiffened at his comment, her body language giving her away. There was definitely someone with her here in the Keys. But right now Jason was furious at her for bringing Maddy into this, and he wanted her out of the house so that he could think.

"Leave Maddy out of this. We will talk tomorrow. Write down your number, and I'll call between jobs. *After* I call Dave."

"I guess a little overnight reunion is out of the question. Oh well. There's a nice Marriott right up the road, as you say, so I guess that will do while we settle our differences. Later, sugar." And she turned and strode out the door.

28

Maddy couldn't help but watch, as discreetly as she could, the house across the street from the front window of her little kitchen. She wondered what was happening inside. The car was still parked where it had been when they'd arrived back from their trip. What was being said? What did Andrea want? Was she trying to reunite with her former husband? Maddy knew that Jason wouldn't have anything to do with that woman after the stories he'd told her, but stranger things had happened, and Maddy was worried. What if he *did* decide to try a relationship with Andrea? The possible scenarios swirling around in her head had her stress level soaring off the chart. She had to calm down, not only for her mental well-being but also for the sake of her physical body. She knew all too well that if she let things get out of hand, she would end up in the hospital again, and she vowed that wasn't going to happen.

To keep herself busy, she unpacked and started a load of laundry. She then fixed herself a snack and took some extra anti-histamine to keep her system from going crazy. Next she decided to upload her photos to the computer to start assessing the images she'd captured on the trip. But she was continually drawn back to the front window to check if Andrea was still at Jason's house. Ugh! She had to stop torturing herself! She finally decided to just immerse herself in her photos, putting some relaxing music on in the background. She was doing her best not to worry, but she wondered if things would be the same now that Jason's whirlwind ex-wife was in town.

Looking at the photos, especially the selfies, brought back so many happy memories of the trip. They looked so happy—silly and goofy at times—but she could tell the two people staring back at her were totally in love. She found one she especially liked and made it her laptop's screensaver. As she stared at it, though, tears began to well in her eyes. Insecurity was creeping in, and she had a sinking feeling that this new development in her relationship with Jason was a bad sign.

A little over an hour had now elapsed since they'd arrived back home, and Maddy had received no call from Jason. Finally she couldn't stand it any longer and checked the window once more to see if *she* was still there. As she looked out the window, Maddy watched as Andrea walked out the door toward her car, dialing a number on her cell phone. She conceded that the woman was beautiful, but there was also a phoniness about her, as if she were a plastic Barbie doll. She was almost too perfect physically, which usually meant plastic surgery for sure.

Before long Andrea was speeding away down the street in her red car. Maddy wanted so badly to call Jason to find out what had happened, but she decided to wait—when he was ready to talk, he would contact her.

As soon as Andrea was in her car, Jason was on the phone to Maria.

"Well, hello, Mr. J.! How was the trip? Glad you're back, because I have some work for you," she said so quickly that Jason barely understood her.

"Maria—Andrea found me here in the Keys."

"What? How? I promise you, Mr. J., I didn't say anything. I gave her no information at all. That sneaky little bitch! Oh… sorry," she said reluctantly.

"No need to apologize. I feel the same way right now. She just dropped a bomb on me, and I'm going to need your expert skills to help me do some investigating. You and Dave. He's probably already gone for the day, so I'll call him in the morning."

"What's happening down there?" Maria asked, concerned.

Jason told her everything, from start to finish. How Andrea had threatened to take him for half of his possessions and money. Even that she'd hinted at throwing in some stupid, trumped-up domestic-abuse charge for not letting her stay at his house.

"Oh my! That woman has gone mental! I'll start by digging up the papers from your divorce. I have them filed away and scanned on the computer. Once you talk to Dave, let me know what to do next."

"Maria, I need you to do some research. See if you can find what Andrea has been up to these last years. Anything, good or bad. Knowing her like I do, she's probably been using people, because she is so damn lazy. You can work that Internet like no one else I know."

"I'm already on it. And…Mr. J.? Please don't worry. I know that's easier said than done, but this is going to work out. Don't let this spoil your new relationship with Maddy. She seems like a real sweet woman, someone perfect for you."

"Wait, how do you know what she's like?"

"You just told me how good I was on the Internet. I've looked her up and everything. Nice girl from what I can see, and you deserve someone like that," she said sweetly.

"Thanks, Maria. I'll call you in the morning after I talk to Dave. Right now I've got some explaining to do to Maddy. Andrea was waiting for us when we pulled up to the house, so Maddy got to meet her. I have no idea what she's going through right now, and I don't want her to worry."

"Just a little advice? It will be hard for her not to let her imagination run on about you and how this will affect your relationship. It's a woman thing. Just hang in there, boss!"

"Thanks, Maria," Jason said as he hung up the phone. He leaned back in the chair, momentarily spent.

Maddy heard the knock on her door just as she was sitting down to do some sketching. She'd found a few pictures from the trip that she thought she could develop into effective drawings. She'd been doing everything she could think of to keep herself busy and her mind occupied with thoughts other than what was possibly being said over at Jason's house. But when she looked through the little peephole in her door and saw him standing there, she didn't know whether to be happy or hesitant. She wondered what he had to say.

"Hey," she said as she swung open the door.

"Hi. Can I come in and talk?" She didn't like the tone of his voice, and the mental high of the past few days with him started to fade away ever so slightly.

"Of course." He walked into her house nervously, looking around as if he didn't know what to say or do. The air was thick with tension.

"To begin with, I'm sorry you had to meet Andrea," Jason began. "Had it been left up to me, I would never have seen her again, and I would *never* have exposed you to her. I sometimes wonder what I saw in her all those years ago."

"You must have loved her at some point. You don't strike me as the type of man to marry someone for anything but love. At least…that's the Jason I've come to know," she said as gently as she could.

"I guess you're right, but she still pisses me off. I think about how stupid I was, believing all her lies. And I'd truly let all that go, but when I saw her today, all those old feelings came back." He hesitated and began again. "Maddy, I promise that what I'm about to tell you, I had absolutely *no* knowledge of. I'm still trying to comprehend everything she told me."

"Ok. Just tell me, Jason."

Then the words began to just tumble out of him. The fact that he was still married and that Andrea wanted to get a new divorce. That she wanted half of everything he'd worked hard for these years since she left. How she intended on fighting for what she felt she deserved even though it was *his* hard work that had gotten him to where he was today.

"You're still married?" Maddy said, shock in her voice.

"Andrea says we are, but I know we aren't. I called my assistant, Maria, as soon as she walked out the door, and when it comes to doing research, Maria is the best. I mean, she can find *anything* on the Internet, so she's looking up a few things for me now. She's also e-mailing my divorce documents to me so I can go over them, and I have a call in to my lawyer, Dave, but I'm sure I won't be able to talk to him till tomorrow. Everything just feels surreal, like I'm in a bad dream. I just wanted you to know what's going on. I don't blame you if you want to jump ship on me."

"Jump ship? You mean…leave you?" Maddy asked.

"I mean, this could get ugly, and Andrea is a snake. She will do whatever it takes to get what she wants, including hurting those around me. I don't want this to cause you too much stress. I care for you too much to let you get dragged through the mud. And I have a feeling I'm going to walk through a real mud pit." There was a hint of defeat in his voice.

Maddy walked over to the chair where he was sitting and knelt in front of him. His eyes looked like he had been sleepless for days. Just a few hours ago, they'd been bright and cheery.

"I have to admit this is a lot to digest. And maybe I don't know where this will lead, but Jason…" She lifted his chin and made him look at her. "I'm not going anywhere. I'm right here, and I hope I'm still right here too," she said softly as she settled her hand on his chest next to his heart.

"The last few weeks have been wonderful, and most of it has been because of you. When I had a serious problem, you stayed right with me—and you didn't even really know me! For me, this isn't affecting the closeness we have. If anything, it makes me more protective of you, so just know that I don't plan on abandoning you. But the thing you have to keep in mind is that you can't let her take away from you all that you've achieved, materially and mentally. We haven't talked much about your business, but she doesn't deserve any portion of what you've worked so hard for. And you've also accomplished a lot by letting go of her and the hurt she caused you. Again, don't let her bring that back into your life. I know it will be tough, but I'll be here. I'm not going anywhere, so lean on me if you need to."

He pulled her up into his lap and cradled her in his arms. That was exactly what he wanted and needed to hear. This woman would stand beside him. He suddenly had no further reservations at all about her role in his life. She was and would be his. He had learned more about her in the short time they'd been together than he had in any other relationship or friendship in his life.

"I don't know what will happen in the next few days, weeks, maybe months, but if I know Andrea, it will be dirty. I don't usually play that way, but she started this game, and I might have to resort to my own devices to finish this," Jason told her in a warning tone.

"Hopefully it won't come to that, but let's just take it one day at a time. I love you, Jason." Then Maddy kissed him to reinforce that she meant what she'd said. They sat in silence for a bit longer, just holding each other for comfort and adjusting to this blow to their fledgling relationship.

"I have to be on the job site early in the morning, and then I'll probably be on the phone most of the day. I'll call you when I have more details about what's going on. Don't send any e-mails or texts. No telling what she would do with them. If she's right, then she can accuse me of having an affair, even though I know she has someone with her here in the Keys. She went for staying at a hotel way too easily, and she mentioned the Marriott. She might have a room there, but for sure someone else is in on this game of hers. And if that's the case, I need to find who she's working with." Maddy could tell that his wheels were turning, trying to put plans into place.

"Remember, one day at a time. But if I were you, I would keep a little written journal so you can keep your notes straight, starting with her sudden appearance this afternoon. Better yet, if you don't want to admit you have a written document that could be used against you, and if you trust her, we could give Riley the information as this plays out and let her keep track. Would love to see Riley in a courtroom. That judge wouldn't know what hit him. Plus, she knows everyone on this Key. She's Islamorada's social butterfly. And she loves snooping, so maybe we can get her to help." Now Maddy was planning just like Jason.

"You think she would?"

"Are you kidding? I didn't tell you that I talked to my mom yesterday while you were working, and she already knew practically everything I'd done since I've been here. She's in cahoots with Riley! So, you let me know, and we can talk to Riley... only after you have decided how you want to handle this."

As Jason stood up to leave, he kept his arms wrapped around Maddy, and they walked that way to the front door.

"I knew there was something special about you the day I saw you from across the street. I love you, Maddy Sumner!" he said as his mouth met hers for a goodnight kiss.

29

After everything that had happened, neither Maddy nor Jason slept well that night. As she lay awake in her bed, Maddy tried to think the situation through. Less than twenty-four hours ago, she and Jason had been in a perfect little bubble. Their trip had been wonderful, they were learning more about each other every day, and love was blossoming. Now, however, they were faced with an ugly situation, one that Maddy wanted to eliminate once and for all, and sooner rather than later. Even though she knew she was in love, she admitted to herself that Andrea's being in the picture had brought her back down to earth, made her think "real world" thoughts. Was she crazy to think that a true relationship could have developed this fast? Hadn't Riley warned her before she'd left on her trip? And her mom, too? As she ruminated over and over about everything happening in her world, she soon became so exhausted that sleep finally found her.

In the house across the street, Jason too was tossing and turning in his bed. No position was comfortable, and sleep was elusive. Though he didn't know what was going through Maddy's mind, he thought maybe all this was a sign that he was never meant to have someone as good as Maddy in his life. He knew he loved her, but it seemed something always stood in the way of his finding true happiness with someone. Maybe he was doomed to remain single the rest of his life. He'd accepted that fact long ago, but meeting Maddy had changed that, and he'd felt deep down that he had found his true soul mate, the one meant only for him. Now he was beginning to doubt again, wondering if it was just a cruel joke his mind had played on him. All because of Andrea.

Even though they had gone their separate ways ten years ago, off and on he would still hear about her ongoing she-nanigans, usually from a man she had just dumped who was looking for her. His answer to all of them was the same: he didn't know where she was, and he certainly didn't care. She had been through a string of boyfriends, but he heard a ru-mor that she had remarried. Apparently that wasn't true. Only twice had she contacted him since their divorce: Once, two years after they split, she had run into a bit of money trouble and Jason had loaned her $3,000, which she had promised to pay back within a month. But he'd known as soon as he hand-ed the money to her that it was gone for good, and he'd hoped she would be too. She made her second appearance about four years ago when they had accidentally run into each other in Las Vegas while he was home helping his dad take care of his mom when she was sick. It was at the grocery store where they had always shopped, and Jason was stocking up his parents' kitchen. When he saw her, she was practically glued to the man she was with, who looked to be at least twice her age— they were practically making out in the produce section of the store. Then she spotted Jason across the aisle. She introduced him to the man, and Jason realized both were on their way to a very drunken night. It was the next day when she showed up at his parents' house that really pissed him off. She was trying to be all sweet and concerned, but Jason saw right through her act. As he ushered her to the door to leave, she started going on and on about how she still loved him, that she was sorry for all the affairs, that she wasn't like that anymore—and that she wanted him back. Jason reminded her swiftly about her "date" last night and how they seemed to be having lots of fun in the grocery store. That got him a slap in the face, but at least she left, and he hadn't heard from or seen her since. Until now.

Why now? He had finally, after all these years, found someone he wanted to be with every minute of every day. In the short amount of time they'd been together, Maddy had changed his life. Their relationship was still at a new, fragile stage. She'd said she would stand right there with him, but he had been hurt too many times before, and it was hard to believe that any woman would follow through. This was driving him crazy, because he knew Maddy better than that. But why did his thinking always go back to feelings of being alone and betrayed? Maybe because that was all he'd really ever known.

30

Just as he'd said, Jason was gone when Maddy looked out her little front window when she awoke. Originally she had planned on a trip to Anne's Beach today since they didn't go yesterday, and then on to the store to restock her refrigerator. But after the stress of yesterday, coupled with the fact that she'd hardly gotten any sleep last night, she was exhausted. She could feel it all over—every muscle and joint ached. It felt like she was breathing through a filter, and the nerve pain that had seemed to disappear the moment she'd arrived in the Keys had decided to reinvade. She was dehydrated. At least those were the only symptoms she had, knowing that things could be worse. She had to get food, so a trip to the grocery store would be all for today, even though the beach was calling to her. Maybe Riley would go with her. After all, she knew her best friend would want to know every last detail of her trip. And Maddy really needed someone to talk to about Andrea.

"It's about time you called me," Riley said, answering her phone.

"Good morning to you too," Maddy said tiredly.

"For someone who just got back from a lovely trip to Key West with Mr. Right, you sound a bit off. Are you ok? I hope so, because I'm craving details over here."

"Do you have time this morning for a trip to the grocery store with me? I also need to get a prescription refilled at Walgreens. And I definitely need to indulge in some girl talk."

"That doesn't sound good. I have a small project I'm finishing right now, so give me about an hour and we'll go. Why don't we go have some lunch first? We'll be there early, so we can avoid the crowd," she said. Maddy didn't have the heart to tell Riley she just wanted to go shopping and come straight home. Maybe even crawl back into bed.

"I'll pick you up in a bit," Riley offered before Maddy could ask her to drive, and she was so thankful. She was really feeling off today, but at least she knew why.

Riley was true to her word, and soon they were off to the little bar and grill down the street. Maddy loved this little place because of the view of the water and its tiny, private beach with lounge chairs nestled under palm trees. It was so relaxing. She had been here before on both of her previous trips to the Keys and had pictures of herself lying in the chair relaxing, the wind gently blowing from the ocean. At home, when things were tough, she always imagined herself there, giving her the mental vacation she needed. And even though she could only eat the french fries they served, she was able to bring the rest of her food with her. Riley had a grilled cheese sandwich with fries, one of the things Maddy missed terribly. But today, the food didn't even tempt her. She was too tired and deep in thought over the events of yesterday.

As soon as they got their orders, Maddy checked out the little beach outside. Seeing that it was clear, she and Riley grabbed their plates and headed to the lounge chairs by the ocean where Maddy hoped they could talk privately. Once they'd settled into the comfy loungers, Maddy began giving Riley all the details of the trip, and Riley hung on every word. But suddenly Riley stopped her.

"Ok, let me get this right. You mean to tell me that you went to a lovely and romantic bed and breakfast inn with this man who may just be the love of your life, and you didn't have sex? You have got to be kidding me!"

"No sex, but that's not to say we didn't come close a time or two, and believe me, it was on my mind *a lot*! But Riley, I've been through too much, and so has he. I just feel this is the right thing for me. As bad as we both wanted to take that next step, I felt—and he must have, too—that we needed to wait. And boy, were we right."

"What do you mean? I could tell through your whole story, even though it sounded like you both had a fantastic time, that your voice seems...I don't know, blah?" Riley looked at her, confused.

"The trip was wonderful, but when we arrived home late yesterday afternoon, Jason had a visitor waiting on him," Maddy said in hushed tones, looking around again to make sure they were truly the only ones on the private little beach.

"You mean that red car parked in front of his house? There was someone in it? I saw it parked there for the last two days but thought it belonged to one of the neighbors," Riley said.

"She has been waiting for two days?" Maddy exclaimed.

"She? Who is *she*?" Riley asked, a bit loudly.

"I swear, Riley, you should be the head of your Neighborhood Watch committee."

"I already am, remember? What's going on, Maddy?"

She spent the next fifteen minutes telling Riley only the pertinent information about Andrea, the supposed ex-wife that Jason might still be married to, and her demands from him in order to grant the divorce.

"She wants half of everything he owns?" Riley exclaimed.

"And she could use our relationship as more fuel for this powder keg," Maddy said sadly.

"I don't think so. Someone like that is bound to have her own little trysts here and there. But you're right. When it comes to money and lawyers, it's like sharks and blood."

"Please don't say anything. And Jason may need your help, but right now everything's on hold until he gets more information from his assistant and his lawyer. It's a mess," Maddy said, leaning back in the lounger and looking up at the sky. Retelling the story was making her exhaustion even more pronounced.

"If I can help, this is right up my alley. I'm not a vengeful person, but when I see someone getting the raw end of a deal, it lights my fire. Carter says sometimes I need to keep my mouth shut, and he's probably right, but it's so hard! Most of the time, karma does the job. What goes around, comes around," Riley said with a smile. "You just let me know if you or Jason need anything. But in the meantime, and don't take this the wrong way—you look pretty bad."

"Well, *that* really cheered me up!"

"No, you know what I mean. You look very tired, and I've seen your hands shaking just a bit today. Is that part of your symptoms? I mean, I've never seen you do that," Riley said with concern.

"I'm just tired, and my muscles are letting me know. They'll sometimes seize up and shake, but I've only noticed it when I'm stressed, when I've done too much, or when my blood sugar is low. In this case it's probably a combination of everything. That's why I want to get my prescription refilled. I had cut back on the dosage because I was feeling better, but with everything going on, I think I should have it on hand just in case."

"I have an idea. Give me your shopping list, and I'll go for you. You go home and rest. Hopefully Jason will have some good news when you see him this evening. And I hope to hell I don't see some brown-haired woman down there. There's no telling what I might do," Riley said with a sly smile.

"Ok, now, you promised you wouldn't do anything unless Jason asked. Please, Riley, promise me again," Maddy said very emphatically.

"Ok, but I will admit it will be hard. It's just not my nature to sit and wait."

"Thanks. As for shopping, I can't let you do that. It won't take that long to get what I need."

"No, you are going home. And unless you want me to guess at the food you need, you'd better make a grocery list."

Maddy knew there was no stopping Riley. "Thank you," she said.

As Maddy wrote out a grocery list on her napkin, Riley asked, "Maddy, how has all of this affected your feelings toward Jason?"

"As crazy as it sounds, I love him. It's only been three weeks, and I know I'll be leaving for home shortly, but I really love him. And please don't laugh or tell me it's too soon. But I do wonder if love is enough. Maybe we were just meant to be together these few weeks and nothing more. I really don't know, except that he's a good man, he cares about me, and the love is there. I feel it with every fiber of my being. But where to go from here? I'm lost right now."

Riley hugged her friend when they got up to leave the tiny beach. "You know I don't believe in the whole love-at-first-sight thing, but with you and Jason it's different. When I see you two together, it's like you just *fit*. Like two pieces of a puzzle that have found each other. Maddy, don't let that go because of this woman. It will work out. How, I don't know. But like you said, he's a good man, and he's good to you. Plus, I've already talked to your mom, and we're working on the wedding details!" Riley started laughing which made Maddy smile.

"You and my mom!" Maddy cried, shaking her head, but she laughed and hugged her friend back. "Thank you. That means more to me right now than you can imagine."

As soon as Riley dropped her off at the house, Maddy lay on the couch to try to relax. She hadn't heard from Jason all morning, but she figured he had to be busy. She hoped to see him tonight, but with everything he was dealing with, she didn't know what would happen. Right now she was exhausted, so she lay on the sofa with a big fluffy pillow, waiting for Riley to return. But she was soon fast asleep.

The next thing Maddy knew, she had awoken to a loud banging noise. In her head it sounded like a jackhammer, and she couldn't figure out where it was coming from. Startled out of a sound sleep by the loud sound, she felt disoriented, and then after a moment she realized someone was at the front door. It must be Riley with the groceries, she thought.

Getting up to get to the door was proving to be a feat in itself. She got up slowly and wobbled through the family room to the door. Looking through the peephole, she was suddenly fully awake. Andrea stood on the other side. You have got to be kidding, Maddy thought.

She looked at herself in the foyer mirror, straightened her hair into somewhat presentable shape, and opened the door.

"Hello there. Sorry to come by unannounced, but I thought maybe we could have a girl-to-girl chat, seeing as how you are having an affair with my husband," Andrea said as she strode past Maddy and into her home without even being asked. Maddy couldn't believe the audacity of this woman. She wanted to kick her out immediately but decided she would first find out Andrea's motive for barging into her house. But the fact that Maddy wasn't feeling too well was probably a sign she should not take this any further and ask her to leave. But she couldn't help it. She wanted to know what had made the little witch stop by.

"Hmm. Cute little house. How long have you owned it?" Andrea asked.

"First of all, hello, and of course, come on in." Maddy's tone was sarcastic as she walked over and sat in a chair across from where Andrea had decided to make herself at home.

"Oh, I'm sorry. Were you busy? Look a little on the tired side though, for which I don't blame you since you just got back from an intimate trip to Key West with my husband."

This woman was unbelievable! Andrea had dared to insinuate things about Maddy's trip with Jason by insulting her and acting like she herself was Miss Innocent? And now to accuse her of being with *her* husband? No way, Maddy decided. She wasn't putting up with this.

"To answer your first question, this isn't my house. I've rented it for a month, not that it's any of your business. As far as my looking tired, I was taking a nap when you decided to bang on my front door. And people with manners don't just barge into someone's home without being asked. I didn't ask you to come here, so I would appreciate it if you would leave right now. What's going on between you and Jason is your problem and has nothing to do with me."

Andrea laughed a little and looked at Maddy with a smirk. "Oh, but honey, it does involve you. You see, Jason and I are still married, and you seem to be the one he has eyes for right now. My timing couldn't have been more perfect—seeing the two of you drive up yesterday, unloading your suitcases from your little lover's trip? Like I said, perfect for me. Just more ammunition for my court case."

"Court case? From what I've been told, you have been divorced or apart for ten years! I don't see—" and before Maddy could finish her sentence, the door to her house swung open forcefully and Jason walked in. He was fuming.

"What is going on here?"

"Hi there, sweetie. Me and…what was your name, again? Oh, that's right—Maddy. We were just having a little girl talk. Now you've ruined the mood." She put on a ridiculous pouting face. Maddy had never before beheld a woman with such evil intent. She could read between the lines of everything Andrea was doing, and she knew Jason could see it too.

"Andrea, this little issue is between you and me. Maddy has nothing to do with it, and you will not bother her anymore. Do I make myself perfectly clear?" Jason's voice was as hard as stone. To Maddy, he sounded like a different man.

"But darling, that is where you're wrong. Just like I was telling your girlfriend here before you walked in the door, she's dating *my* husband, and she just went on a trip with *my* husband. Don't you think that will sound just lovely in a court of law?" Andrea stood there, facing him with a sickening smile.

"Andrea, you will leave now before I call the police for trespassing. I will not put Maddy through this, and you will not bother her again. Do you understand?" Jason sounded menacing now.

Maddy was still standing there as if watching a scene out of a movie. It was so surreal. Even worse, though—everything suddenly went black.

31

When she opened her eyes just a few minutes later, she found herself lying on the couch. Jason was sitting on its edge beside her, and Riley's voice was discernible in the background. A blood pressure cuff was tight around her arm, and Jason had a needle in his hand. As soon as he saw Maddy's eyes open, he told her to drink. She just stared at him. Everyone seemed far off but close by at the same time. When did Riley get here? Where was Andrea? What was going on?

"What happened?" Maddy asked, slurring her words a bit.

"Sweetheart, you passed out. I got you to the couch, and Riley came in with your groceries at the same time. We called the paramedics, and they should be here any second. I have your Epi-Pen here, but since you woke quickly...here, drink this water and take this dose of Benadryl. We need to get your blood pressure up." Jason talked to her sweetly as he stroked her hair.

She could hear Riley's heated voice in the background and caught vestiges of conversation.

"Get your skinny ass out of this house, and if you come back here, you'll wish you hadn't." That was Riley.

"So, that's a threat? Wow, this just keeps getting better and better." That was Andrea. Maddy was beginning to piece things together.

That did it. Jason had had enough. "Riley, come and help Maddy." He walked toward Andrea like a bull looking at a red flag.

"What I ever saw in you I can't imagine. You barge into someone's home, cause trouble, and the very person you were attacking has a medical condition that you might have made worse, maybe causing a trip to the ER. It blows my mind that you are so damn heartless. I don't want to see you here or at my house ever again. We will contact each other via phone or through our lawyers, and that is it. If I do see you, I will put a restraining order on you so fast you won't see it coming, because as of right now, if Maddy has any repercussions from this little visit of yours, the fault will lie with you. No judge in this land would refrain from writing an order to keep you away from her. As for our little divorce issue, you might have bitten off a little more than you can chew."

The ambulance pulled up just then, and the medical team streamed out of the van. Seeing that things hadn't quite gone the way she'd intended, Andrea picked up her handbag and stormed out of Maddy's house.

By the time the paramedics finished checking her out, Maddy was much better and didn't even require her shot. The water for hydration along with the medication was working its magic. Her pressure was getting back to normal, and even though she was still exhausted, she was feeling better, which meant no trip to the hospital. So this was basically incident number two, and Maddy had been determined at the start of her vacation that there would be zero. But this one was the culmination of exhaustion and a pushy ex-wife—probably a little too much for anyone to handle.

As Riley was showing the paramedics out the door, Jason sat on the couch cradling Maddy in his arms. "I am so sorry. I had no idea she would come here and talk to you. Do you remember what she wanted?"

"We actually hadn't gotten too far before you came in. I'm still a little fuzzy-brained, but she was making it sound like we were having some sort of illicit love affair, saying how she was the victim because you two are still married. She kept emphasizing the married part." Her brain fog lifted bit by bit the more she talked.

"We'll talk more later. Right now, just rest," Jason said soothingly. But something told Maddy he had more to tell her, and she wanted to know now.

"The EMT guys are gone and said that actually you were doing good. I filled in Steve, the paramedic, about the pushy bitch that was here, so he said he could understand why you... well, your body reacted the way it did," Riley said.

"You already told Riley?"

"We started talking at lunch today, and she was the one who saw Andrea's car parked in front of your house for the last two days. So I gave her a basic synopsis of what was going on," Maddy said, wondering why Jason sounded agitated.

"Sorry, Riley. Just a bit edgy with everything going on," he said apologetically.

"Don't worry about it. I'd be more than irritable with someone like that hanging around me," Riley said.

Jason looked at her and sighed. "As a matter of fact, I want to know if you might be able to help me with something. Maddy told me last night you would be perfect for the job."

"I'd love to! What can I do to help?"

"I haven't really digested all the information I learned today, but some local snooping is going to be in order. Even though I've been here for quite a few months, I still don't know the area and the people here like you do. But right now I really just want Maddy to rest, and we can talk tomorrow," Jason said, looking back to her and seeing she was thoroughly exhausted.

"I agree. That's why I insisted on getting her groceries. As for your ex-wife, I would love to help you get rid of her once and for all. You don't mess with my friends, and that includes you, Jason." She gave him a quick peck on the cheek and whispered in his ear, "Thanks for taking care of Maddy. You're a good man." She looked back at her friend, who was struggling to sit up, intent on saying good-bye to her.

"You," she said, pointing at Maddy, "lay your butt back down like Steve told you to. You might think you're fine, but you still need some rest. I've put your groceries away, and we shall talk tomorrow." With that, she went out the door, leaving Jason and Maddy alone.

"Jason, tell me what you found out," Maddy pleaded.

"Haven't you been listening? You need to rest. I promise we will talk tomorrow."

"I'm fine. Actually, I'm embarrassed that I let someone like that get to me, especially since she's your ex-wife. I can only imagine what she must think of me now," she said, depressed.

"Who gives a damn what she thinks? That she actually came here is what has *me* boiling mad. If she wants to attack me, let her. I can take it. But she'd better not mess with those I love, especially you.

"I have to go back to work. So rest—take a nap. I'll be back in a few hours to fix us some dinner, and we can just relax tonight. Try to forget about what just happened."

To Maddy, it seemed like only a few minutes had passed before Jason was back at her house to spend the evening with her. Clearly she'd fallen asleep again.

"I thought Riley went grocery shopping for you today," he said as he stared at the mostly empty refrigerator and kitchen cabinets.

"She did, but I don't eat a great variety of foods. Plus, I didn't get a lot since I'll be going back home next week." This was the first time she'd brought the subject up. Secretly she wished she hadn't said anything. The last twenty-four hours had already been rough, and thinking about being apart was the last thing she needed right now.

Jason said nothing. With all the worry over Andrea's arrival in the Keys, he had forgotten that Maddy would be going back home soon. In his mind, Maddy just lived across the street, like a permanent resident of these islands. This immediately dampened his spirit even more. Andrea in town, Maddy leaving soon. No way. It should be the other way around, and with the things he'd learned today, he was sure that at least one of these women was leaving sooner than she thought—and it wasn't going to be Maddy.

"Then we're ordering in. I will heat up your potato and green beans and fix you a piece of grilled chicken. Personally, if it's ok with you, I think I could devour an entire pizza," Jason said as he grabbed items out of the refrigerator and cabinets and then dialed for a pizza delivery.

"As long as you're here, anything sounds perfect to me."

32

As soon as they finished eating, Maddy quickly fell asleep. Jason picked her up gently and put her to bed, making sure her phone was beside her along with her water and medicine. It was funny, he thought. He knew just what to do for this beautiful woman he had fallen in love with so quickly. Taking care of her was like second nature, and he loved every minute of it. She made him feel loved and wanted, and he hoped he made her feel the same way. As he watched her sleep, he wanted to make sure she was ok, happy, and loved. She brought out the best in him, and he was so glad that she was here with him, wanting to be with him. When he'd first seen Andrea yesterday, he'd immediately had a sinking feeling that Maddy would leave him, but so far her reaction had been just the opposite. He had much to tell her tomorrow, and he hoped that it wouldn't change their relationship, because if she decided to leave him, he wasn't sure if he could handle it.

Maddy woke up around midnight to the realization that someone had put her to bed. Jason. The last thing she remembered was eating dinner with him and watching an episode of *The Big Bang Theory* so they could have a bit of a laugh after all the drama that had taken place only a few hours before. He was right about being hungry—he had practically inhaled almost an entire pizza, claiming that he hadn't eaten all day. But he had made sure to fix her meal first before he ate. And he knew just the right foods. He had been more observant over the past week than she'd thought, and that made her feel happy inside. He really cared for her. If not, he wouldn't have known. Then she saw the telephone, water, and medicines all lined up on the table beside her. Tears came to her eyes, not of sadness but of happiness—it flooded through her when she thought of how he protected her and took care of her, making sure she was safe. Suddenly she remembered that he had news for her about his ex-wife and that they were going to discuss things tomorrow. Now wide awake, she contemplated what this news could be. She took a quick shower and decided to read a little, hoping that would help her fall back asleep, but no luck—she found herself at the window in the kitchen, looking at the house across the street. Maybe he was still up and she could call and thank him. Yes, his light was still on, but she also realized he had to be tired himself from his busy day, so even though he couldn't see her, she blew him a kiss good night and headed back to bed.

Maddy woke early the next day to beautiful Florida sunshine streaming through the blinds once again. She had finally fallen back asleep last night, although it wasn't as restful as it could have been. She was still a tiny bit tired but so much better than yesterday, thank goodness. She decided she needed some alone time today, and that meant visiting her favorite spot—Anne's Beach. If she got there early enough, she could take everything she needed for a beach trip and find a choice shady spot under a tree. Her sketchbook and camera were going along, as was her journal. It was time to start making a plan for life after her retreat to the Keys, and what better place to do this than sitting under a mangrove tree on the beach. She did promise herself to tell Riley and keep in touch with her today, but after all the events of the past few days, she needed some time to herself, just to think. Coming to the Keys was supposed to have been a time and place of refuge, but just the opposite had occurred. She'd had two episodes that required medical attention, and now a spiteful woman was hounding her. But the best part was that she had fallen in love. Something she didn't think would ever happen again. If anything, her life had become more complicated since coming to South Florida, but was that good or bad? She needed to do some soul-searching, and she could only do that by herself.

After donning her bathing suit and cover-up, she began to pack her tote with what she needed for the day and assembled her snacks in the rolling cooler. Everything rolled, so that would help her get things to the beach, even though it really wasn't that far from her car if she got there early enough to get one of the premium parking spots. Getting everything down the stairs was the biggest chore, but she could do it. Once she was in the car, she decided to call Riley. Maddy knew that after what had happened the day before, she would try to talk her out of going, so she purposely waited until she was on the road.

"Look who's up early today. Figured you would sleep till at least ten o'clock. How are you feeling?"

"Riley, do you ever just answer your phone by simply saying hello?" Maddy asked, laughing.

"What's the fun in that? Ever since caller ID, I just go ahead and start the conversation as soon as I pick up. You know, gets the ball rolling. So, you didn't answer my question. How are you feeling? And how is Jason?"

"To answer your first question, I'm feeling fine. Maybe a bit tired, but really good considering everything yesterday. So good, in fact, that I'm going off by myself today." Maddy held her breath for Riley's reaction.

"Do you really think that's a good idea after what happened? Don't you need to just take it easy all day?"

"Riley, I'm tired of taking it easy. I promise I'm not going to go overboard, but I've got to get away by myself for a while. The whole reason I came to the Keys, except to spend time with you, was to try to put my life back together, to take time for me instead of everyone else. I needed time and space. It's been a whirlwind since I got here. A good one, I'll admit. Meeting Jason has been an absolute dream for me, but now with this stupid divorce mess, a hateful ex-wife who doesn't care who she stomps on, and having these episodes of mine causing me to seek medical help while on vacation—this wasn't in my plan!"

"Maddy," Riley said softly, "when does anything ever go as planned? Yes, you came to the Keys with one thing in mind, but sometimes you just have to go with the flow. You have to learn that you can't control everything. Then maybe things wouldn't seem so hard to you. Granted, I don't know what it's like to have an illness like yours, and I can't say I know how you're feeling, because I don't. We all have things we have to deal with, and this just happens to be yours. As for the other distractions when you got here, I would call Jason the best distraction you've had in a very long time, and I've known you since you were four years old. If you feel the need to get away today, I understand, but do me a favor, please? Just let me know where you are, and I promise I'll check on you by phone and not come bug you."

"Actually, that's why I'm calling. I'm going to be at Anne's Beach parked in the second parking lot as close to the beach as I can. I'll have my cell phone with me, but if I don't answer, I could be swimming. I'll check in with you periodically, and I'm not sure how long I'll be there, because I have to stay in the shade when possible. I just really need some time alone away from this house. I know that I probably sound pathetic, but I hope you understand."

"I'm just a call away. I'll be here working most of the day, finishing a project, so just let me know if you need anything. And promise to be careful."

"I promise," Maddy said as she hung up the phone and turned into the parking lot.

The beach was only ten miles from her house, so she was still close to civilization, but with nature surrounding her like this, she felt far away. Only one other car was there as yet, which was perfect—she'd gotten here before the crowds. When Maddy got out of the car, she realized she really didn't have as much stuff as she'd thought she would: her roller cooler, her beach tote, and a folding chair. Everything hooked to the cooler, so that made it easier for her to trek to the beach. She found the perfect spot under a low branch of a mangrove tree about ten feet from the water's edge. She turned around, surveying the scene, and found she had settled in a spot not too far away from an older gentleman—probably the owner of the other car in the lot.

"Good morning," he said as Maddy settled down into her chair.

"Good morning. I didn't see you there at first. Am I a little too close? I can move down the beach some if you'd like."

"No, you are fine. I'm not staying much longer anyway. Just came out to watch the sunrise on the beach," the man said, even though he was lying on a towel in the sand with another towel under his head and a hat over his eyes, as if maybe he had been sleeping. At first she thought he might be homeless, but then she remembered the other car in the parking lot, a nice one at that.

"So, how was the sunrise?" Maddy said to keep the conversation rolling.

"Same ol' sunrise. Kinda silly for me to come here to this beach looking out at the water when the sun rises in the east behind us, but I just love it here. Been coming here for years."

"I have to admit, this is only my third time to the Keys, and this is by far my favorite beach too. The sand is beautiful, the water so clear and warm, these little mangrove trees give you some shade so you don't need a beach umbrella, and for the most part it's nice and quiet."

"For someone who hasn't visited here that much, you really know the details of this place pretty well. How long are you staying this trip?" he continued.

"I've been here for almost a month. I leave next weekend." As she said the words, a feeling of sadness washed over her.

"How has your trip been so far? Hope us locals have treated you nice. We usually do our best, maybe get a bit rowdy sometimes, but it's all in fun. We try to adopt an easygoing lifestyle down here."

"I know. I wish I could bottle it up and take it home with me," Maddy said, secretly wishing she could stay here in this little paradise a little longer.

"You *can* take it home with you. You just have to make a mental note of what it is about this place, or the Keys in general, that makes you feel the way you do when you are here. When you get back to your real world, to the best of your ability, live your life like you are a permanent resident here. Pretend if you have to. Tell yourself to relax each day, to appreciate the beauty all around you. Enjoy nature like you are doing now, watching sunrises and sunsets. The things you do on vacation do them when you're home. Of course, if you work, you just figure out a way to incorporate them into your life."

Maddy smiled and said, "You would make a great therapist. But thanks for the ideas, and you're right. Maybe one of these days I'll be able to live here. I would move right now if I could, but it's always something to look forward to."

"I moved here twenty years ago after just one visit," the mystery man continued. "My wife and I came for vacation, went back home, and sold everything we didn't want to bring with us. All the children were married, and we had lived in the mountains of Tennessee all our lives. Of course, the kids thought we had lost our minds, but we put everything in a U-Haul truck and came down here without even a place to stay. But we were in an apartment within a week and then a house just six months later."

"So, you retired down here?"

"We aren't really retired. Don't like that word. We just moved. I work, if you want to call it that, by doing a little day trading on the market, and I have some clients. I also do a few odd jobs here and there. My wife writes a blog about the Keys that keeps her pretty busy and brings in some money too. We did leave our 'careers,' if you want to call them that, but we love what we do now. Just like today. I can come here, enjoy a sunrise, relax, and then work when I want. The whole atmosphere here is perfect for us, and it didn't take long for the kids to find out how much they loved it here too. Two of our three children have already moved down here with their families."

Maddy loved talking to the older gentleman. He seemed so full of wisdom, so relaxed, and certainly enjoying his life. He was at ease with the direction his life had taken, and she envied him. He had a sense of purpose and clarity that she was still seeking. A huge part of her would like to sell everything she owned and move here, just like this man and his wife had done so many years ago. But it felt so risky and scary to do something as audacious as that.

Just then she noticed more cars pulling into the little parking lot and more people finding special places along the beach to set up for the day, just like she had.

"Well, time for me to go. It was nice meeting you, young lady. I hope you enjoy the rest of your stay here with us. And maybe one day you will be able to call yourself an islander. Take care," he said as he picked up his towels and walked toward his car.

She sat back and just stared out at the water. It was beautiful and relaxing, just what Maddy needed after the stress of the last couple of days. Even though Jason had said they would talk today about what he'd found out about his situation with Andrea, she was leaving that behind for the moment. For now, she was just sitting, marveling at the relaxing scenery before her, and thinking about what she wanted out of life once she returned home.

What did she truly want to do with her life? What was her passion? Her values? She was finally at a time and place where she could think about these questions, the first time in three weeks that she was actually giving her future a thought. She desperately wanted to regain as much of her health as she could while remaining as independent as possible. She had read a bit and done some research about people who had faced illnesses even more severe than hers and were making headway toward living a normal life with only minor adjustments. Most of all, she wanted to take her art to the next level. She wasn't sure what to do exactly, but she knew it would involve her watercolor paintings and the drawings she'd posted to Facebook and Instagram. People had asked for prints, had suggested calendars, coloring books, art journal workshops, and more. She just didn't know how to put this all together, but now she felt a little bit of clarity, at least in a direction for herself.

But the more pressing issue was her relationship with Jason. She had met and fallen in love with a possibly married man. With that thought, depression came over her again. Not about falling in love, because she knew Jason was meant for her, but for all the baggage they both carried into this brand-new relationship. She should have guessed that at their ages they each had things in their past to deal with, but she'd never thought it would be this complicated—she with her illness and he with a vengeful ex-wife bent on destroying any happiness he might find. Would they be able to work around these issues? She just didn't know.

Even though she knew in her heart that her love for Jason was very real, she also knew that sometimes circumstances could keep people apart. She didn't want that for them, but she had to face the fact that it was a possibility. Suddenly the tears started to flow, and she was so glad that she was a bit removed from the other people that had joined her on the beach so that no one could see her crying. But something about crying released some of the pent-up stress, and after a few minutes she felt better. She knew that she was down here for a reason.

Maybe she didn't have a solid plan for when she arrived back home, but she thought back to the conversation she'd had with the older man this morning. He was relaxed and lived each day in the moment, not fretting about the future. Anyone who could just take a vacation, go home, pack up everything, and move here was, in her book, living life fully. He didn't let fears and not having a thought out strategy, like the one she was seeking, stop him from making a decision and going with his gut instinct. Suddenly everything felt clearer in her head. She needed a plan, yes, with everything that was on her plate, but she had to allow herself flexibility. This would be so different, certainly out of her comfort zone, but the longer she sat there with her thoughts, the lighter and more positive she felt, more so than she had in years. So she closed her eyes and relaxed in the thought that she was making progress. The best part was that in her mind, Jason was part of the flexibility she had never allowed herself. She just prayed that it was meant for them to be in each other's lives.

33

"Hey there." She heard it as if from a distance. She wasn't quite asleep, just in a very relaxed state, so she knew who it was. She opened her eyes to see him standing beside her chair, his own chair in hand.

"Is this little area taken?" Jason said, gesturing at the spot beside her.

"I did have it designated just for me," she said, gesturing with a wide circle of her arms. "But I think I can make an exception for you."

"Thank you, because this is exactly where I want to be."

"So, it seems Riley told you about my getting-away spot?" Maddy asked with a smile as she looked up at him.

"Yeah, I wore her down. But it didn't take long, I have to say," Jason said, laughing as he looked down at her lying in her chair, as stunning as ever.

"I'll bet," Maddy said, picturing in her mind Jason trying to find out where she was and Riley holding out. No, it would have been just the opposite, actually. Riley probably called Jason and told him to "get your ass out there and make sure she is ok, because you have some explaining to do." Yes, that was the more likely scenario.

"She said you came here to be alone, and I don't want to spoil that if you truly want some time to yourself, but I was also hoping we could talk. My foreman has everything under control at the construction site, so I decided to take the day off...well, sort of. I went to the house and saw you were gone. I knew you wouldn't go off without telling Riley, and luckily for me, she was home. She warned me that you might be a bit angry with her for ratting you out, but don't be. I was pretty insistent and promised her that if you told me to leave, I would." Jason still stood with his beach chair in one hand and a bottled drink in the other.

"Of course it's ok. I've been here a few hours, just relaxing and thinking. There is just something about this beach, so I packed up my stuff for the day and came out here to try to make sense of everything that has happened these last few weeks. Also got to talk to a nice gentleman, a local, who was really sweet. We were the only two people on the beach for quite a while, and it was nice," Maddy said, her eyes closed.

"Another man? So now I have some competition?" he said, half joking and half serious.

Maddy laughed. "You know how silly that question was, right?" She opened her eyes to see him shrug his shoulders.

"Come on. Put the chair down and get comfortable. We have the best spot on the beach."

Jason had to agree with that. It was beautiful here under the tree, and the water was particularly clear and bright. The temperature was about eighty-five degrees, but it was definitely cooler in the shade of the tree. Best of all, her presence made the spot perfect.

"So, did you come so we could talk about you know who?" Maddy asked, knowing the answer to the question already.

"Yes," he answered. His voice held no emotion.

"If it's good news, let's talk. But if it's going to ruin the moment, let's wait till later, back at the house."

"What if it's a little of both? I'll let you decide—talk now or later?"

Maddy was intrigued. He didn't come right out and say it was hopeless, so that made her feel better.

"Ok. Let's talk now."

Jason unfolded his chair and set it up next to her, put his towel down, and secured his drink in the sand. Before he said one word, though, he leaned over and gave Maddy a kiss, a very passionate, lingering one that helped sweep away some of the nervousness she felt about the upcoming conversation. It seemed to her he hadn't held her or kissed her in a long time, even though it had been only one day back. But right now that one day felt like one month.

"Now, I don't want to talk, but we are in public," she said teasingly.

"I know how you feel," he replied as his hand traced some sand down her arm and he held her hand for a moment. "But

I just had to do that. Every time I see you, I want to touch you and be with you. Hold you and kiss you. I can't stand the thought of your going back home next week." Jason looked at her, and she could have sworn his eyes held a sadness. "We'll talk about that later. Now let me get you up to speed on what I know about why my bitchy ex has made a reappearance." And so Jason began.

"First of all, if it weren't for my amazing assistant, Maria, I wouldn't know any of this. As I said, she is the best snoop on the Internet. If you want to find anything, ask her. Remember I told you how I'd called her the other night after Andrea left? I knew I couldn't call Dave, my attorney, until the next morning, but Maria I can call just about any time. As soon as I told her that Andrea had found me and about her accusations, she started researching. She called me back yesterday morning before I could even call Dave, which was a good thing because she had a wealth of information for me. To start with, the bad news is that Andrea is right. Officially we are still married. We both signed all the necessary papers, but they were never filed at the courthouse. The office clerk for my lawyer at the time had a car accident on the way there. Even though the accident wasn't bad, she ended up in the hospital for an overnight stay. All the documents she'd had with her were scattered everywhere in the car, and all were thought to have been recovered and recorded. But apparently our divorce papers did not make it. Since I've retained my original papers, thanks to Maria, and we have evidence of the accident, it should be an open-and-shut case according to Dave, who I talked to after getting this information from Maria. But she also uncovered that Andrea has been on a bit of a…shall we say, boyfriend shopping spree, and it looks like she's been conning older men out of their money. Not huge amounts that would bring unwanted attention, but enough that she's probably racked up a good little fortune. Most of these men, very wealthy ones at that, lost only what they consider small amounts to her, so nothing was ever reported to the police."

"So, she takes money from a man, and when she's finished she moves on to someone new to prey upon? How much money has she taken?" Maddy was interested.

"Seems she's skimming anywhere from $40,000 to $90,000 each time, enough to keep her living the lifestyle she's always wanted and not have to work. Apparently the money is being kept in a little offshore account so she wouldn't have to pay taxes. At the same time, she's collecting disability from the government, claiming she has some illness that prevents her from working, but Maria couldn't find out what that was. At least not yet. Her disability money isn't enough to live on, but it leaves her free to be able to con these men, because they feel sorry for her."

This infuriated Maddy. Andrea was the type of person that made it hard for people like herself, people with true illnesses, to get the help they needed. Plus, to take someone's money, basically stealing it from them! It was ridiculous! She always tried to look for the good in everyone, but Jason was right about his ex. She was despicable!

"Take it from me," Maddy said, "getting disability is hard, so if she isn't really sick, she had to have some help. Were any of the men she tricked with her schemes doctors?"

Jason smiled. "Yes, and this is where it gets really interesting. Seems like her latest con game from what Maria can figure out is none other than a doctor. He retired about eight months ago under some mysterious circumstances. Maria is doing more probing today. We're thinking he's the one that helped Andrea get disability, so she might still be with him. But then she found out about two weeks ago that she and I weren't divorced. So now she has decided to go after my money for herself and maybe this friend of hers. We aren't sure about that just yet. She hasn't said anything about the disability money, and she doesn't know I know about the scams. When I talked to Dave, he said that as far as my divorce goes, that point is moot. We are divorced, and the fact that there was an accident clears up that part of this farce. She thinks we will have to go through the whole court process again and that she is entitled to half my money and assets since the papers were never filed, but she's in for a rude awakening."

"Jason, can I ask you a question?" Maddy asked nervously.

"Of course, love."

"This is kinda rude and personal, but how much money do you have that would have her beating down your door again?"

Jason hesitated and looked toward the ocean. It wasn't that he didn't want to tell Maddy, but usually when women found out, they underwent a personality change. Basically they didn't want him anymore. They wanted what he could give them.

"Maddy, I'm a multimillionaire. I've put my energy into my work because I love it so much. The money I made, I in turn invested. Those investments have grown, and I live a minimal lifestyle. I don't need anything fancy...except I *do* like a big, flat-screen TV," he said, laughing. "I also want to make sure that my parents want for nothing," he continued. "I move so much and that is why my mom and dad live in my house in Las Vegas. I do have a motorhome that I use on the job most of the time. Anyway, I just reinvest the money I make, and it has grown to the point that if I didn't really love what I do, I wouldn't have to work anymore."

Maddy didn't know what to say. She hadn't thought he was poor or anything, but she'd never imagined that someone his age would be in a position to retire so extremely comfortably and not have to work another day in his life! And he was so humble and genuine. Not once had he ever flaunted his wealth the way so many people did. She looked at him with different eyes now, not because of the money, but because in spite of it he was so genuine and kind. His priorities were the passion he felt for his work and, above that, the care of his family. Her pride in him swelled as she looked at him and marveled at how she had gotten so lucky to have this man fall in love with her.

"I don't care about your money. I care about you and the fact that some insane woman wants to take advantage of your hard work and dedication to your family. But I do have a question. Why didn't you tell me about your money before now? Did you not trust me?" Maddy wasn't hurt by his secret; she just wanted to understand why.

"My past experiences have always turned out bad once a woman found out I was wealthy. Then it became sort of a game in the relationship, to see if she could marry for money. I've been burned a few times, discovering some women just wanted to be kept in luxury, not a relationship. That's why I usually just keep to myself and don't form close friendships or relationships in the places I work. But, like I told you before, from the moment I met you, I knew in my gut you were different. I just couldn't explain how. I hope you can understand where I'm coming from. I had planned to tell you when we got back from Key West, but that went south quick with the arrival of my ex." Jason's eyes pleaded with her to understand.

Maddy turned in her chair to face him and rested her hands on his thighs. "I do understand. I can imagine what you've been through. My family has never had that much material wealth, but having a successful family business always made us targets for idiots who were greedy and lazy. Like I said, I don't care about the money. *You* are the one I'm concerned about, and I want to be with you no matter what you have in the bank."

Jason was relieved by Maddy's words. She actually loved *him*, not the money, and he could tell she was speaking from the heart. This was a first for him, and he didn't know quite what to say or how to handle what he was feeling for this amazing woman sitting across from him.

"But you *are* divorced, right?"

"I am single—well, almost, in the eyes of the court. And I'm all yours if you still want me."

She leaned over and kissed him. "I definitely still want you, Mr. Burnett, more than you know."

"Well, there's more." Even though he would rather keep kissing Maddy to the point of joining her in one chair, he needed to tell her everything.

"More?"

"We think that Andrea and this doctor are both here in the Keys to make sure she gets another divorce hearing so that they can maybe split any money she thinks she might receive. This is all just speculation. We think it might be a payment of some sort for his helping her get disability. My attorney wants to nail her on that, because he handles disability cases too, and he is mad as hell about what she has done. Like you said a minute ago, too many people take advantage of the system, causing problems for others, so for now, we aren't going to mention the fact that I know the divorce is not an issue. Dave wants me to play along with her game for a few more days so he can gather the information he needs on her and her doctor so that he can report both of them to the disability board. As crazy as this might sound, I really feel sorry for her. She has no direction in her life, and I would have thought that by now she would have grown up. She's still the spoiled brat I married and divorced so long ago. So for now, we play the part. Maria is checking on the offshore accounts, because Dave said this will actually go to court, and they will both be charged with fraud and who knows what else at this point. Andrea really didn't know who she was messing with when she decided to come after me. I'm not vengeful, and I've left her alone even after what she did to me. But for once I can see what people have told me for so long. What goes around, comes around, and her little game is just about up!"

Maddy sat there trying to take it all in. Jason was free, but they had to give Dave and Maria time to gather information. Even though this was all part of the bigger picture that needed to be dealt with, she reasoned that Jason's time was going to be so preoccupied with Andrea and her friend that little time would be left for the two of them during her last week here in the Keys. Again, this was not what she'd hope for this week before she left to go back home. But then she remembered her resolve to be more flexible, and this was the perfect time to try out her new train of thought. Hopefully they would be able to fit some time in to talk about their relationship going forward, but that could only happen after Andrea and her possible coconspirator were wrapped up and handed over to the proper authorities.

"We have to be very careful, because if Andrea finds out we know what she's up to, things could get ugly, especially if her doctor friend is truly here with her. When people get backed into a corner, they get desperate," Maddy said cautiously.

"That had crossed my mind, so that's one of the reasons I'm here. When I went to the house and saw you were gone, I had to find you so I could tell you all this. Also to make sure you were ok. You said you talked to an older man this morning here on the beach?"

"When I got here, he was by himself, lying on a towel right over there." She pointed a little way down the beach. "I doubt seriously that's who we're looking for. He told me about how he moved here twenty years ago, what he did for a living, and about his wife and children. Plus, it was too early in the morning…and how would he know I'd be here?"

"I'm not saying that it was Andrea's friend, but we have to imagine that every stranger we come in contact with could be working with Andrea. I don't know if this man is dangerous, if he's forcing Andrea to scam me, or if they're working together.

So many unanswered questions, lots of variables to this situation, and we need to keep on our toes. I think it's time to let Riley help. Do you think she and Carter might be up for having dinner at her place tonight? I'm sure we're possibly being watched at our houses, and I don't want to meet in a restaurant. We wouldn't be able to talk openly. Tell them we'll bring dinner." Jason looked at her with concern and expectancy.

"Riley will love every minute of this. She knows everyone here, even at the grocery store. She seems to know every person on the island as well as their life history." And Maddy meant every word. "I'll call her in a bit. She's probably already expecting my call, since you showed up and I told her I just wanted a day to myself."

"I can go now that you know all the details of what I know so far about this mess. I understand if you want some time to yourself." Jason's eyes had a faraway look as he scanned the ocean's horizon.

"No, I want you to stay. Between my talk with that man this morning and the news you just gave me, I'm feeling better about all this *mess*, as you put it. So right now, I want to go swimming with you, like we did at the state park a few days ago."

Before long they were wading out into the waters of the Atlantic. A good one hundred yards out and the water level had just reached their thighs, another reason this beach was one of Maddy's favorites. She could just come here, sit and soak in the shallow water, and watch the little fish swim around her, the occasional sea grass waving back and forth. Now in the waist-deep water, they swam, or rather they held each other,

her arms and legs wrapped around him for support. The water was nice and warm, very relaxing, and just what both of them needed—a way to be with each other and release some stress but that didn't involve a bed, because at that moment, swimming together like this, she knew those thoughts were going through both of their minds.

As they made their way back to shore, splashing hand in hand through the shallows, Jason broke the silence.

"I guess I'd better get back to the house. I need to make a few calls, and I have a client that wants to have an online meeting through FaceTime. Nothing urgent, so that's why I didn't hurry, plus..." he said, planting a kiss on her forehead, "you make it very difficult to leave."

"I do my best," she smiled as she put her arms around his waist. "I'll call Riley in a minute and text you about dinner. No, I'll call you. Forgot about the no-texting rule."

"Just to be on the safe side." He gave her another exquisite kiss, and then she watched him stride off the beach to his car without putting his shirt back on. He was so fit and toned that his muscles rippled as he walked, almost hypnotizing her. She felt truly blessed that he had chosen her and felt comfortable enough to share his life's story with her. The sexy body that came with this caring man was just a sweet bonus.

As she sat back in the chair by herself, she now had double the number of things to think about, but for some reason she felt lighter. She couldn't quite explain what she was feeling. She knew that Jason was basically a free man and that he still wanted her to be a part of his life. But she'd had no idea this whole time that he was extremely wealthy. That took her completely by surprise. She had figured he must have some money to be able to travel and work like he did, but nothing like what he'd described. Although his not divulging this fact to her before now was a bit of a sting, she could understand his reasoning. She could just imagine what he had been through with money-hungry people and how careful he had to be, now more than ever.

34

As she dialed Riley's number, she began wondering what crazy phone greeting her friend would answer with this time—they were beginning to amuse her.

"He coerced me, I promise" was what came through on the other end of the line after the third ring.

Maddy couldn't help but laugh. "I'll bet. He twisted your arm and threatened you? No, I was actually calling to thank you."

"Really? Thought you'd be mad as a hornet because this was supposed to be your alone-by-yourself day. But he said it was real important, and with everything going on, I caved."

"You are forgiven, and I have a way for you to make it up to me. Can Jason and I invite ourselves to dinner at your house tonight? We want to talk to you and Carter about helping with something."

"What? Tell me now! You know I can't wait like that. That's like taking kids to an amusement park and telling them they can't go on any rides," Riley whined on the other end.

"Sorry, but it will have to wait till tonight. Is six thirty ok?" Maddy asked hopefully.

"That's fine," Riley said, moping. "But this better be worth making me wait all day."

"Riley, it's already noon, so quit whining. By the way, we'll bring dinner so you don't have to cook, ok? The deli looked good the other day, so we'll just go by there before we come over."

"I'll take you up on that, since I'm still knee deep in this project that was only supposed to take two days and now I'm at the five-day mark. Just make sure to get some of their mac and cheese. I can taste it already! And bring all the latest gossip."

"No problem there," Maddy said before she hung up. Then she called Jason to let him know their dinner date was on.

Since her day was not turning out quite like she had planned— again—she went home to take a nap and get ready for the evening. She called ahead to the deli and placed a dinner order for tonight for a six fifteen pickup. That was one thing out of the way. She showered and fixed some lunch, making a bit extra to bring for her dinner tonight, and then she grabbed her computer. She had never been one to search for information on people using the Internet, but after Jason's stunning revelation about his business, she wanted to know just how big his company was. And what she uncovered amazed her. He had a small, extremely tasteful website that showcased his work with pertinent information about himself, examples of past projects, and client testimonials. He had even worked with a few celebrities! Why hadn't she thought of researching information about him on the Internet before? She suddenly wondered why Riley hadn't said anything. She was always online checking out information on people she met. She must have searched for him. Maddy would have to pull her aside tonight and ask Riley about this.

As she read all about this man featured on the web page before her, Maddy seemed to be learning about someone completely different than the Jason she knew. He was well recognized in the home remodeling world and listed as a top architect in the United States. Now she understood why Andrea was hell-bent on money. More than likely her con games were getting old, or she was running out of men to scam. Then a nice, fat loophole presented itself, and she latched on with both hands.

Even though Jason's resume was beyond impressive, she didn't really see him any differently. He was the man who had carried her groceries in the house when she first arrived in the Keys. He was the same man that had rescued her three weeks ago in the middle of the night. He was still the man who listened to her, shared stories with her, and had made her laugh more than she had in a very a long time. He was the man who kissed her with so much fervor and passion that she practically lost track of time and space every time his lips touched hers. He was the man she knew she wanted to be with from now on.

Jason was at Maddy's house by six o'clock so that they could go together to pick up their dinner from the deli. As they drove there, she brought up the subject of her Google search.

"So, you've designed and remodeled homes for celebrities?"

Jason smiled and shook his head. "Ah, I guess you found my website. That's all Maria's fault. She was having a fit, saying I needed a website because everyone has one. I think I've seen it once or twice. I let her handle it. So, you were snooping around the Internet about me?" Jason asked with a slight grin on his face.

"When the man I love drops an 'I'm-a-multimillionaire' bomb on me, it leaves me in a bit of shock. I mean, you don't look like that."

"Ok, now I feel hurt. Do I look like a bum or something?"

"No!" Maddy exclaimed. "I didn't mean that. It's just that you could live anywhere, drive any car, have any thing, yet you live such a simple life. It just took me by surprise, that's all."

"I'll admit that at one time, I wanted to live the high life, and I tried it. I bought a Ferrari and I owned three houses—one in Maine, another in Arizona, and a beautiful home in Jackson Hole, Wyoming. But I was always on the road. I lived in suitcases, rental cars, and motorhomes. To tell you the truth, I loved it. That was until three weeks ago when I met you."

Just then they pulled up to the deli, and as soon as they were parked, before Maddy could reach for the handle to let herself out, Jason took her hand and looked her in the eyes.

"Three weeks ago I saw this beautiful woman across the street that I knew I had to meet but was so hesitant. While our first 'date' in the ER wasn't the most fun, I got to meet you finally. I tried to convince myself that I didn't want to get involved with anyone. Then when I got to spend that afternoon with you the day after the hospital, I didn't want to go home. And I haven't wanted to leave your side since. Whether you realize it or not—and maybe I shouldn't say this—Maddy, you have me wrapped around your finger. You've made me want to have a house again, a real address. To buy an old pickup truck and fix it up so we can go riding. To live a life that because of my past I thought I would never have the desire for again. But I want that now, and after this thing with Andrea is finished, I want us to talk about a future together. If you don't want the same thing, I'll be ok with that, as long as I know that you're happy."

"But, Jason…" was all she could say before he kissed her sweetly.

"Don't say anything right now. Just think about it. I know I've said a lot, but I had to tell you how I feel. Now, we'd better hurry or we're going to be late for dinner, and I'm sure Riley is chomping at the bit to hear what's going on." He opened the door before she could say another word.

Maddy was dumbfounded by his confession of how he felt for her. She'd wanted to tell him that she didn't care if he were rich or poor, that she just wanted him in her life. That she too wanted a future with him. When those words had come from him, her heart had swelled with joy, but he'd stopped her. Did he think she didn't have the same feelings as he did? Had she presented herself in a way that gave him doubts? She didn't think she had, but he had so much on his mind now, between his work project, the ex-wife, and herself. Maybe it would be better to wait until Andrea was out of the picture before they had a true discussion about their future together.

Riley opened the door before Maddy could even knock.

"You guys are late! You know you can't do that to me. I worry, plus—and I admit this—I'm too nosy! What's going on?"

"Let's get our dinner first and then we'll fill you in," Maddy said as she and Jason moved quickly into Riley's kitchen. Once they all had a plate of dinner and were seated at the table, Jason began. It was just the four of them—Jason, Maddy, Riley, and Carter—so they could speak openly about what was going on with Andrea, her con schemes, the fake disability, and the doctor who was not only helping her but was probably also a partner in this latest scheme to con Jason and take part of his wealth.

"Wow, when I said bring the gossip, you don't disappoint! Your ex is a piece of work," Riley said, looking at Jason with compassion. "Sorry you're having to go through such an ordeal with her. I think the word 'bitch' doesn't even begin to describe her."

"She certainly hasn't changed. But I never thought she would go this far. I guess she's learned a thing or two over the years. She was bad when we split, but this is at a professional level. That's why I'm here asking for help from you and Carter," Jason said. "You know the people of this island and the other towns around here. They might have heard some news, seen someone new in town who seems suspicious—you know, something out of the ordinary. I know this place is filled with tourists, but when someone new shows up who seems a bit shady, you know…most people who live here all the time, like you guys, know when something seems a bit odd."

"I'll ask around, discreetly, because I have a bunch of friends who own several of the local bars and restaurants in the town," Carter said. "They might have noticed a beautiful brunette attached to an old guy." Just then Riley punched him in the arm.

"She is not beautiful. She is a mean schemer and rotten to the core."

"I wasn't saying she was nice, just pretty. The men in the bars will notice a new girl in town," Carter said.

Maddy agreed. "He's right, Riley. You can't help but notice her, but I think that will work in Jason's favor. The problem is that she's probably claiming she's staying at one hotel for show while really staying in another. Maybe even on a different Key. Not too far away, but not too close. It's just a guess, and that's the hard part."

It was Carter to the rescue again.

"We know several people throughout the Keys, including some of the sheriffs. I'll ask Bill in Marathon if anyone suspicious has been around and if he's seen Andrea."

Jason perked up a little. "That would be incredible. I would love to catch both of them, because I'm sure she has an accomplice here. He's probably telling her what to do and say. I know the sheriff in Key West and I will call him tomorrow. I'll know more from my attorney, Dave, in the morning about what the next step is. He just advised me to stay low and not cause a scene but to record anything unusual and to watch if she's with anyone else. Hopefully, between Dave and Maria, we'll have more information in the morning. I'm just ready for all this to be over and done with."

Maddy reached over and stroked his arm, and he reached for her hand, kissing the back of it.

They got up to leave, and Carter filled Jason in about his friend in Marathon as they walked toward the door. At the same time, Maddy quickly pulled Riley aside.

"Did you do an Internet search on Jason when he moved here? I know you usually find out all you can, so don't deny it," Maddy said.

"I tried a search, but I didn't find anything. I Googled his name but nothing turned up. I figured he was just a guy drifting from job to job. Now I know I must have typed his name in wrong. Had *no* idea this man was a money magnet. And how come you didn't do a search? You had his real name!"

"I don't know. I just…I just didn't. I never Google anyone, even though my daughter constantly reminds me that I should, especially since I live basically alone now. And if I should go out on a date, which I wasn't really doing before I came here anyway. It never even crossed my mind once I started talking to Jason. But I did today, and I was blown away. I gotta go, but if you get a chance, look him up. He actually remodeled a home for one of your favorite actresses!"

"No way!" Riley said, just a bit too loud, making both men standing at the door look back at them.

"Is something wrong?" Jason asked as both women grinned back sheepishly.

"No, we're fine. Just girl talk," said Maddy. Looking back at Riley, she whispered, "We'll talk more tomorrow." And Riley quickly nodded her head.

35

They drove Jason's SUV to the end of the small street and parked in his driveway.

"I know it's late, but would you like to come over for a bit?" Maddy asked, hoping so much he would say yes.

"Maddy, you don't know how much I want to, but I can't. For one thing, it's past eleven, and I have to be on the job site at seven. And I also know you've had an exceptionally long day."

"Do you have to work on Saturday?" she asked.

"Unfortunately, yes. My client has asked if there's any way to move up the completion date by a few days. Promised the whole crew an extra bonus, so I couldn't say no. I'm really sorry. But we'll still have time together, I promise." He could see the disappointment on her face. He didn't want to tell her quite yet why he was trying to move faster on the project, and he especially didn't want to say anything more until after this scheme of Andrea's had been taken care of.

"I know you leave next Saturday, but I promise you we'll make time to be together. Remember what I told you earlier. I want to be with you always, Maddy. You have completely stolen my heart." He held her tighter than before as they stood at her front door, and the kiss he gave her left her feeling very loved. She wanted to take that next step with Jason, but she knew now wasn't the time. Not yet, her gut told her. But soon. Watching out her front window as he walked back to his little house across the street, she smiled, so happy inside. Yes, they may be going through a storm right now, but he had basically told her today that he wanted her now and always.

It had become such a habit now to look out the window each morning as soon as she got up to see if he had already gone to work. She kept hoping that one day she'd catch him before he left and maybe have a quick breakfast with him, but he was always gone. One of these days she would get up early enough for some time with him before work, but it probably wouldn't be before his current project was finished and Andrea was gone.

In the midst of this whirlwind of conflict and uncertainty, Maddy hadn't made any plans for the day. She'd been secretly hoping she and Jason could spend it together even if it meant working on the details of getting rid of Ms. A., as she now referred to Andrea, so she decided today would be a slow day, one to just putter around the house and enjoy the view from the lounger under the tiki hut. As she continued to muse, she realized that one thing she hadn't done since her arrival was to go out in the boat with Riley and Carter. They had been so busy that the subject had never come up. Suddenly though, she remembered something and instantly changed her plans. She wanted to go parasailing since she hadn't been able to in Key West. *That* was what she would do today. There had to be a place here locally that offered parasailing. She only wished she had someone to go with her.

"You are going parasailing with me today," Maddy told Riley when she answered her phone.

"Have you lost your mind? I'm not strapping myself to some parachute pulled by a boat, hoping it stays up in the air, operated by someone who probably doesn't know the first thing about it! Can't believe you want to do that! Anyway, why don't you take Jason with you?"

"Can't. He's working today and tomorrow," Maddy said. "So you're it."

"He's working on the weekend? You'll just have to wait for him. My butt isn't going up in the air like that. End of story."

"Ok, then at least help me find a place where I can go. You can stay in the boat. Please?" Maddy pleaded. "I've always wanted to go. The view has got to be breathtaking!"

Riley sighed. "Ok, I'll go, but this girl will be taking pictures of your ass up there while I sit in the boat and probably listen to you cry like a baby to come down."

"You are the best friend ever!" Maddy said excitedly.

"Yes, I am...and by the way, you are the luckiest girl ever. I did some snooping online last night about your island man. All I can say is wow! No wonder Miss Sleaze is suddenly making a reappearance in his life. The girl is nothing but greedy," Riley said.

"Carter and I talked about the two of you last night after you left. As corny as this sounds, you guys are made for each other. I wish I could have recorded you both last night. Doing things for each other, finishing the other's sentences—and his protectiveness over you is uncanny. Not the weird, controlling kind of protective, just actually wanting to do what's best for you. And girl, I've been around you when you were with your ex and the very few other men you've dated. Not once, even counting high school, have I ever seen you act like you do with this man. You guys just go together. Like I said before—two puzzle pieces that fit together perfectly."

Maddy blushed at her friend's remarks. "You know, Riley, that's how I've always seen you with Carter. I envied you every time we got together because my ex never treated me like that, and I wanted what you had. I honestly believe I was never truly in love with Hope's father. You and Carter had the relationship I always wanted, and now I think I've found it with Jason." Maddy concluded, feeling very content as she thought about her man.

"Do you ever hear from your ex anymore?" Riley asked.

"Only if it involves Hope, and now that she's married, she'll tell me bits and pieces of how her dad is doing. He finally found someone just right for him, and according to Hope, they're just right for each other. Then she'll start harping on me about getting back into the dating pool. But it's hard at my age, and when you have the complications that I have, most men can't handle it. I always felt like damaged goods, and I just didn't want to go through the rejection again. That's why I wanted to just concentrate on getting healthy and then maybe, possibly, consider dating again. Coming to the Keys was supposed to start my new and improved lifestyle. Doing things my way, physically and mentally. Since doctors tend to use me as a guinea pig, I'm more motivated to keep investigating this crazy illness than they are, and they admit it! When I get home I'll be making my first trip to the specialist…or, I have an appointment, I should say. At least all the required medical tests have been done already. But coming here was supposed to help me find a creative outlet to support my healing process and find a purpose. I also needed downtime. But meeting Jason has been worth every second I wasn't relaxing on the beach like I thought I would. Oh…sorry, I got way off track. Now I'm just rambling. I'm glad I have you to talk to," she said, wishing she could hug her friend through the phone.

"Well," Riley began, "looks like you're out of the dating pool now and getting dried off by one very fine man. And the bonus is he's stinking rich!"

"I know this is going to sound weird, but I never considered his wealth. I mean, I knew he had to have some money… but *really wealthy*? And I know everyone would say this, but I truly fell in love with this man before I knew any of that. Now I'm going home in a week, and his stupid ex-wife is determined to create chaos. I just hope this little plan of hers falls flat fast. Now, back to our adventure for today. Where is the nearest parasailing dock?" Maddy asked.

"There's someone right down the street, but when we're done we're going to do a little snooping at Steve's bar. I called him this morning, and he's had a customer that matches Andrea's description to a tee. He wasn't sure she was with anyone, but he did say she was flirting with just about every guy in the place. Even ruffled a few feathers among the wives and girlfriends."

"This woman is a piece of work," Maddy said, exasperated.

"What I figure is that if this scam with Jason doesn't pan out, she's thinking ahead, working the men to have someone waiting in the wings. Sounds like a whore to me. What a sad life!"

"Amen!"

36

Finding a place to parasail was much easier than Maddy had thought. There were plenty to choose from, including the one Riley mentioned, and they all had good reviews, so she just picked the closest and off they went. Her chosen place allowed people to launch off the boat, and that was what Maddy wanted. She had seen too many videos of people getting dragged through the sand on the beach when trying to parasail, and she definitely wanted to avoid that. She hoped to take her camera up with her, so she made sure to download all the pictures she'd taken so far in case the camera slipped out of her hands and into the ocean far below. Once again, she stowed her essentials in her backpack and headed over to pick up Riley, who happened to be waiting outside.

"You know I think you're crazy to do this," she remarked to Maddy as she climbed into her car.

"I can't believe you haven't done this before in all the time you've lived here! It will be fun, and I promise I won't coerce you if you decide not to do it. You can just go with me and enjoy the boat ride. If they make me pay for both, I will. It will just be nice having you there with me. We really haven't done a lot of fun things together since I got here," Maddy reminded her.

"I wonder why. Could it be that his name starts with a *J*? And personally, if I were in your shoes and found an unexpected gift across the street like that, I don't think you would have seen much of me either!" Riley said with a grin.

They were both laughing as they pulled up to the parasailing dock, and Maddy's excitement was over the top. She was so glad Riley was with her, even though she had still held onto the tiny hope that Jason would be able to come. She had called ahead to secure her eleven o'clock spot and had asked the girl several questions about the safety of her going out in the boat. She'd assured Maddy that the boat didn't go out too far from land and that help could be summoned if needed. She had stipulated, though, that four passengers were necessary to book the boat and that so far she and Riley were the only two who'd called. As a result, Maddy had decided ahead of time that if no one else showed up, she would pay for the whole boat. It was more than she'd intended on spending, but this was something she really wanted to do before she went back home.

Grabbing their bags, they made their way toward the curved walkway leading to the dock, and the scene that greeted them stopped both Maddy and Riley right in their tracks. You have *got* to be kidding me, Maddy thought. Andrea, in a revealing one-piece, black, netted bathing suit and a see-through skirt tied low around her hips, stood flirting with the man in the boat and two others who looked like they were preparing the boat for departure. She was so involved in her conversations that she hadn't yet noticed their arrival. As they got closer, Maddy, with a shock, immediately recognized the man in the boat—it was the mystery gentleman she'd met on the beach the other morning. They hadn't exchanged names at the time, but she knew he would remember her.

"Oh my! Well, look who it is. My husband's girl of the week!" Andrea chirped as she turned and spied the two women nearing the dock.

Maddy reached for Riley's arm before she could take a step toward Andrea. Causing a scene, or even hitting her—which she was sure was going through Riley's mind—wouldn't help their case, but Maddy couldn't say that aloud to remind her. At least now they had more people to ply for information about the little trollop and a possible guy she could be with.

"We're here for the eleven o'clock parasailing trip," Maddy told the older man, and she saw in his eyes that he instantly remembered her.

"I met you on the beach the other morning! So, how are you doing? Did you enjoy your beach time?"

"I'm fine, thanks, and it was wonderful. My favorite beach! You didn't tell me you owned a boat and offered parasailing trips."

"This is one of my hobbies. Remember that first trip I told you about when we came here on vacation? It was also the first time I parasailed, and I instantly loved it. At that time, though,

I had to start out from the water. That was a bit rough, but I loved it anyway. So, when I decided to do this, I made sure people could launch from the boat instead. By the way, my name is Robert, but everyone here calls me Bubba. These two guys here…" he said, pointing to the two younger men, "are my grandsons."

"Nice to meet you Bubba—again! This is my friend Riley. She's coming with me, but she isn't sure about the parasailing part." Maddy kept up the conversation, acutely aware of Andrea standing on the dock listening to everything that was said. Bubba had to have heard her snide comment, but for some reason he'd completely ignored it.

"We usually take four passengers, but if no one shows up in the next thirty minutes, I'll go ahead and take just the two of you."

"Oh, I would love to go! I've never been parasailing before!" Andrea piped in sweetly as she walked toward the boat. Maddy wanted to throw up.

"No way," Maddy said angrily. "She is not getting on this boat with me and my friend. Bubba, I'll pay for the other two spots myself. As long as she isn't on the boat with us."

Bubba watched the nonverbal exchange between the two women as they stood face to face on the dock near the boat. It definitely wasn't a friendly encounter.

"Well, seeing that Maddy and her friend actually booked the boat in advance, and you, young lady…" he said, looking at Andrea," just now decided to go, I think Maddy has the say-so in this case."

Maddy reached for wallet. "Here, Bubba, I'll pay for all four spots."

Bubba turned to look at Andrea standing on the dock.

"Sorry, but it looks like this boat is full. You'll have to wait for the next group to come. I think there are some openings in a few hours." He turned to his grandsons, giving them directions for boat preparations, and then helped both women on board. Soon they'd cast off the lines and were on their way toward the open ocean. Maddy looked back to the dock, and Andrea's expression was priceless! To say she was angry would be a complete understatement.

"So, I take it that wasn't a friend of yours on the dock," Bubba remarked as they made their way slowly out to sea.

Maddy laughed. "Not even close. If you only knew. I do have the money for the other spots. I can give it to you here or when we get back."

"No, this one is on me. Personally, I didn't want her on the boat either. She was making a play for my grandsons back there. She even made a pass at me, an old geezer!" he laughed. "Not sure what's going on with her, but clearly you do. Let's forget about all that now. Have you ever parasailed before?"

"No, but I've always wanted to. I admit I'm a bit nervous, though. That's why I called ahead to make sure we didn't go too far out. And I'm not sure my friend is going to go up, but I'll pay for her anyway."

"Susan told me I had a passenger with a medical condition this morning. Is that you?" he asked.

"Yes, but I'm doing ok. I just always scope things out before I do anything or go anywhere," Maddy said, speaking louder now over the motor as they moved faster toward open waters.

"Don't mean to be nosy, but whatcha got wrong with ya?" Bubba asked, his Tennessee drawl more pronounced as he raised his voice.

"I have a rare chronic illness whose symptoms resemble a severe allergic reaction. I've brought my medications with me, though, and I'm feeling ok today, I promise!" she said.

"I'll take care of you and your friend. Just when you're in the parasail, if you start feeling bad, show the hand signal to come down and we'll head back to the dock. Ok?" He smiled her and then went back to maneuvering the boat to a beautiful spot of clear, aqua water.

"Maddy, I really don't think I can do this. I mean, I know I might act like nothing bothers me, but I've got a thing about heights. I was going to try, really I was, but…do you mind if I just watch?"

"Riley, it's perfectly fine…on one condition. Will you video me so I can show everyone back home that I actually did it?" She quickly showed Riley how to use the video feature of her phone, because just then Bubba announced that it was showtime.

"Can I take my camera with me?"

"I usually tell people no, because even though you're strapped in, we like for you to hold on to both side straps. Promise me you'll hold the side strap with one hand and take pics with the other, ok? And if the camera falls into the ocean, there's nothing I can do about it. Ready to go?"

Maddy's heart beat quickly, and in her excitement she felt it flutter for a moment. They got her all strapped into the harness, and now she was ready to take flight. She gave Bubba the thumbs-up sign, and the boat started to move, the heavy cable she was attached to beginning to stretch out over the water.

As the line attached to her from the boat got longer and longer, she rose so high in the air that the many beautiful islands in the surrounding waters spread out beneath her like a cool tapestry. It was breathtaking! She made sure the wrist strap to her camera was nice and tight and began taking pictures, as many as she could. She had no words to describe what she was seeing. She wasn't sure how high up she was, but she seemed to be able to see for miles and miles in every direction. The water was spectacular—so many different hues of blue, turquoise, and aqua, interspersed with the islands' white beaches and their dark green mangrove trees. After taking what seemed like hundreds of pictures, she stopped and decided to just sit back and enjoy the experience. She did look straight down once, but this made her a bit panicky, so she focused back on the view in front of her. Being up here was like being in a whole other world.

She was so lost in her thoughts that before she knew it, her line had started drawing her closer and closer to the water and the boat. Her parasailing adventure had come to an end, and she felt exhilarated. She had done it! And it was everything she'd thought it would be and more. Plus, she had conquered a small fear and stepped out of her comfort zone. One thing she definitely could say about this month-long trip: her reluctance to leave the safety of what was familiar was being stripped away little by little, and she was beginning to feel this was the best thing for her.

"Bubba, that was absolutely fabulous! The view is simply beyond words. Riley, you really should go up. You will love it!" Maddy couldn't contain her excitement.

"Slow down there, girl," Riley told her. "I know it's probably something just peachy, but this girl likes her feet in the boat, not dangling from a harness in the air. Sorry!"

"You don't know what you're missing out on. I guess you'll just have to savor the moment through my pictures," Maddy said with a huge smile.

They made their way back to the dock, Maddy riding under the shelter of the canopy beside Bubba since she didn't want to risk too much sun exposure and trigger a possible reaction. She would have preferred to ride in the seats along the side of the boat where the water splashed up every now and then, enjoying the wind blowing through her hair while watching the scenery of the islands.

"Thanks, Bubba, for taking us, just me and Riley. That woman back there is bad news, and I want to stay away from her as much as possible. I hope for my sake she won't be at the dock when we get back."

"I doubt she will. She was just out flirting with the boys back there. Saw her walking from the restaurant next door, and then she started asking questions like she was interested in snorkeling. But I knew she wasn't interested in anything but those boys and maybe the owner of this boat. I can tell a gold digger a mile away." Bubba kept his eyes straight ahead as they neared the dock, but he had a huge smile on his face.

Back on land without the wind in their faces, both girls could tell it was getting a bit warmer today than it had been. And Maddy could feel the exhaustion coming on, so taking a nap sounded like a wonderful idea. Her adrenaline rush was over, but it had been incredible. She thanked Bubba again for understanding and for not charging them for the extra spots. And Riley had had her own good time on the boat while Maddy was flying through the air.

"Guess what? I found out some interesting information about Andrea from Bubba's grandsons," she said as soon as they were sitting in the air-conditioned car.

"You did?"

"Seems little Miss Bitchy Pants has been her flirty self at a bunch of local bars here. Last night she was at the one where our two boat guys happened to be. Apparently the man she was talking to was intent on getting her drunk and having his way with her, and she was doing some heavy duty flirting. Little slut!" Riley said before she could help herself.

"Anyway, she kept telling the guy sitting with her at the bar that she couldn't go anywhere with him even if she wanted to because she had someone waiting for her in Key West. She told him she was here in Islamorada just for show. She'd definitely had too much to drink and just started talking."

"You're serious?" Maddy said with a smile. "This is fantastic. If this is true, then her partner in all this is staying away from the scene just like Jason thought. Maybe, just maybe, her flirting and drinking has done her in. Now we just need to find this guy, but how?"

"We follow her there. You know, to Key West. The problem is we don't know when she'll head back," Riley said thoughtfully. "But maybe we could find out who's waiting for her, get some pictures, and do some research. With the Internet, you can't hide very well anymore."

"I'm not sure how, but once we tell Jason what you found out, I'm sure we can come up with some kind of plan. This is great! I know he's going to be excited that we finally have something on his ex. Right now, though, I think I'd better go home. The sun has me breaking out in a rash, and I'm really tired. But this has been a terrific morning in more ways than one," Maddy said with a smile.

37

As soon as she walked into the house, Maddy called Jason, only to be put through to voice mail. He'd said the weekend would be busy on the job site, but he also had his hands full trying to gather what clues he could about Andrea's devious scheme. Hopefully he would call soon so that she could give him the details they'd found out this morning on the boat ride. That might help put them a step in the right direction. She fixed herself a quick lunch and then went to lie down in her second-favorite spot in the house: the comfy couch.

A buzzing noise came from somewhere near her head. She woke up very groggy and realized the buzz was coming from her cell phone. How long had she slept, and where was that phone? She looked around and finally found it under her pillow, the tone set to silent. Ugh! She had forgotten to turn it back on after her boat ride. By the time she could answer, the caller had hung up. She looked at the number and saw that it had been Jason returning her call. Great! She hoped she could catch him if she called right back, but then the time on her phone caught her eye. It was six o'clock already! She had slept for four hours! Then she looked at her missed calls and saw that he had tried to call her three times in the last thirty minutes. Now he would be worried. And she was right—all of a sudden she heard a knock at the door. It took her a minute to get there, but when she swung it open, she saw Riley standing there, worried.

"Why aren't you answering your phone?"

"I'm sorry. Jason must have called you," Maddy said sleepily.

"Yes, and he was going a little nutty on the phone because he couldn't reach you. He called me, and then *I* got concerned, but then I remembered your saying how tired you were after our little adventure today. Still, all we could imagine was you passed out somewhere."

"I'm really sorry, but you guys know I try to call if I start feeling bad. You have to stop worrying like that. I called Jason when we got back but couldn't reach him. I didn't realize how tired I was, and then I broke out in a rash from the sun. The Benadryl I took knocked me out."

"He'll be here in a minute. I told him I would come and check on you, because I had dropped you off around lunch."

Just as Riley finished her sentence, Jason's car pulled up, and he came running up the stairs.

"I'm sorry, I'm sorry," she said as he hugged her up. "I had put my phone on silent when we went for the boat ride this morning and forgot to turn it back on."

"Man, you scared me," Jason said, not letting her go. "I got your message earlier, but I wasn't able to call. Then when you didn't answer your phone, I was concerned." He turned to Riley. "Sorry I panicked, but thanks for coming up here."

"Glad you called," she said as she turned to Maddy. "I know we probably seem like a pain in the ass right now, but at least you know we care about you."

"I'm just sorry I put so much stress on both of you. You don't deserve it, and I am truly grateful. But..." she began as she turned to Jason, "we—well, Riley—found out some interesting news about your wife today, and we need to come up with a plan."

"Please do not call her my wife, because as of today, she and I are *officially* divorced," he said emphatically. "It actually happened yesterday, but I found out this morning when I heard from Dave." Maddy was so excited at this that she reached up and gave him a long, passionate kiss, wrapping her arms around him and not caring that Riley was standing right there beside them.

"That's wonderful," she said when she finally allowed Jason to breathe.

"It certainly feels good to know she's finally part of my history," Jason said with a smile on his face.

"So, what happened?" Maddy asked as the three of them went in and sat together in the family room.

"Dave got in touch with the court clerk and relayed the news of my divorce problem. And Maria, my assistant, had already overnighted the original papers to Dave the day before. He talked to the original attorney, who had no idea what had happened. His office went to the courthouse with their information and refiled everything. Since it wasn't through their negligence but rather by accident that the papers were not officially filed the first time, there's no waiting period and no court case. I'm officially a free man. Andrea cannot come back and try to take anything from me that she didn't get in the original settlement."

Maddy leaned into him, and he hugged her, bestowing a kiss on the top of her head. It felt so good to know that part of this nightmare was finished and that Andrea wasn't his problem anymore.

"I'm happy she's out of the picture, but we have some news that might help us find that mystery person you were talking about last night," Riley told him as she took a drink from her water bottle.

"What news? Is this what you were calling me about earlier?" he asked, looking at Maddy.

"Yes. We found out a thing or two about your lovely Andrea." She looked at him meaningfully, and he rolled his eyes.

Riley filled Jason in on all the details they'd picked up during their boat ride and Maddy's parasailing adventure.

"So, you *did* go parasailing! Did you love it as much as you thought you would? I wish I could have been there," he said lovingly to Maddy.

"Ah, let's focus here, people, ok?" Riley admonished.

"Sorry, you're right. So, she *does* have someone here with her in the Keys. Dave mentioned that he still wants our help if possible. He did some more digging, and between what he found out and Maria's online investigating, seems like Andrea is in a lot of trouble. The men she's conned over the years recently found out about each other, so they're joining together to find her. Also, the IRS wants to talk to her about her income. To top this all off, the doctor that helped her get this supposed disability income is being investigated for fraud, but he skipped town and hasn't been seen. My guess is that he is probably the person with Andrea."

"If we just had a way to track her to Key West, we could probably find both of them and alert the authorities," Riley said. "How do we get her to leave town?"

"Oh, I think I can manage that. I have to work tomorrow, but if you two don't mind a little road trip, I have a plan," Jason said with a sly smile.

38

Everything was set. The strategy Jason had put together sounded good, and as long as things went as planned, they would hopefully be on their way to obtaining the much-needed information on Andrea and her accomplice. They'd gone over all the details one more time at Maddy's house, making sure they had covered everything. Maddy had to admit she was a bit nervous—she had never been involved in anything like this before. Snooping, car stakeouts, and sneaking around were a bit strange for her, but Riley was loving every minute of it, as if she were living out one of her favorite detective shows. Maddy just wanted to be done with the whole thing. Her nerves were slightly frayed.

"I would love to be a fly on the wall when you tell her the good news of your divorce!" Riley laughed, and Maddy had to agree with her. She didn't wish any harm to anyone, but there were some people who deserved a taste of their own medicine, and this woman was at the top of that list. And if all went as planned, she was about to get a big dose of it.

"If I know Andrea, she will throw a fit. That's why I'm meeting her at Ma's Fish Camp on Palm Avenue. If she does get a bit too loud, I'll have eyes and ears as witnesses. Bubba's idea was great, and I'm glad he'll be there," Jason said, looking at Maddy.

It was she who'd suggested calling Bubba, asking if he knew a nice restaurant that was pretty busy on Sundays and also if he minded taking his wife out for lunch there to be a witness if needed. She didn't tell him all the circumstances, only that the "gold digger," as he had called Andrea that morning on the boat, was trying to scam Jason. As soon as he'd heard that, Bubba had been more than happy to help, even offering to pay for his own meal so he could watch the potential show. But Jason had insisted that the meal would be on him for the help.

"And we'll be in the parking lot, ready to follow," said Riley the super sleuth. Even though this was serious, Riley was having trouble controlling her excitement at being involved in the plan.

"Both of you have to promise that you'll be careful. This isn't some game...and definitely not a TV show," Jason said, looking directly at Riley. "And as soon as I can break away from the job site, I will be right there. We'll keep in touch with phone calls only, so make sure your cell phones are set to ring." This time he looked at Maddy, and she smirked at him.

"This is so exciting!" Riley exclaimed.

"Gosh, Riley," Carter said. "Remember that you're not a detective and that what you're about to do is serious. This woman is a professional con, and there's no telling what she's capable of. And the man she's with? People like that can be dangerous. Like Jason said, this isn't one of your shows."

"Carter's right, and I honestly don't feel good about just the two of you following her, but we don't have a choice," Jason said, looking to Maddy and then to Riley. His original idea was that Carter would join them, but he unfortunately had a business meeting Monday in Miami, and he had to be there Sunday to prepare and set up for his company. Jason would have felt much better about this entire plan if Carter were accompanying the ladies.

"Jason, we will be ok. I promise we'll be careful—we'll stay far away but close enough to watch. And we won't do anything till you arrive. As for me, I'll make sure I take all my stuff with me: food, medication, water," Maddy assured him, making a check mark in the air as if she were marking off a list.

"I'll call you in the morning," Riley said as she and Carter stood up to leave. "Get some rest…and we'll take my car tomorrow. She knows yours," she said as she looked at Maddy.

"It sounds like everything is in place." She hugged her friends good night and shut the door.

"Maddy, are you sure you are up to doing this?" Jason asked as they went back to the family room.

"Most definitely. She is manipulative and cunning, and she's trying to interfere where she doesn't belong," she said. They both sat down on the couch, sitting as close together as possible. "She is mean, not only to you but to other men as well. Plus, she's the kind of person who makes it hard for deserving people to get the help they need. This woman is bad on so many levels. As far as this doctor goes, he's a real piece of work too. Do we know his name yet?"

"Damn, I forgot to tell everyone. His real name is Martin Cansty, but I'm sure if he's helping Andrea, as we suspect he is, he's probably using an alias. But don't ask around till I get there. Hopefully we won't have to. If things go as I think they will, she'll lead us right to him. Then we call the police and let them take it from there. Dave has talked to the authorities, and they're on alert for her here in the Keys. I just hope we can follow through with our plan before they find her. If the police get to her first, Cansty will probably leave town as quickly as possible and they won't find him. I want both of them behind bars where they can't do any of this in the future. But now that we have all the details in place, let's talk about something else."

"Like what?" Maddy said.

Instead of answering her question, he began kissing her. Her started with her lips, moved across her cheek, and then found the hollows of her neck. Soon he was back to her lips, causing her heart to beat faster with each passing moment. They were soon laying on the couch together, kissing, intertwined in each other. The house was silent except for their heavy breathing. It would be so easy right now to make love to this man, she thought. The closeness, the way he smelled, the muscles she could feel under his shirt all made her want him. As he kissed her and caressed her face, her arms, her back, Maddy's willpower was just about spent. It was Jason who broke the spell.

"I think it might be best for me to go home," he said breathlessly.

"It's still a little early. Is something wrong?" she asked, kissing him on the neck.

"No, actually everything is just right, and that's the problem. Maddy, it would be wonderful if I could just scoop you up in my arms, carry you to the bedroom, and make love to you. I've dreamed about that more times than you can imagine. But this relationship is so very special to me, and I want us both to be 100 percent sure of where we're heading. I also want this cloud of stress my ex has caused to be over and done with before we make our plans for the future." Jason could see the slight hurt of rejection in Maddy's eyes, but a smile also played on her lips.

"I promise, you have no idea how much I want to be with you. Just know that I'm probably going across the street to a very cold shower!"

This made Maddy chuckle slightly.

"Jason, I dream of being held in your arms, in the closest way that two people can be…but you're right. When that time comes, I want it to be perfect. Not rushed. Because you can never take back that first time. I guess we're on the same page where this is concerned, but it's so hard when I'm lying with you like this. Or when you kiss me. Or when you touch me. I swear, your kisses put me in some sort of trance—everything else goes away, leaving just me and you." Maddy propped herself up on her elbow and stared at him as she traced his lips with her finger, and soon her lips were on his again and she was pulling him closer, until there was nothing between them except the clothes they wore.

"I love you, Maddy. You are my everything."

"And you are mine."

39

The next morning arrived quickly. Maddy had slept a bit brokenly, the anticipation of the coming day interfering with her rest. Her usual quick look out the front window showed that Jason had left for the job site, so now she just needed to wait for his phone call confirming the luncheon. She got dressed quickly, ate breakfast, and packed what she needed for a quick trip to Key West. If things played out the way they hoped, they wouldn't be there very long. Then the phone rang. It was Jason.

"Hi there. How did it go?" she asked apprehensively.

"So far, so good. She's meeting me at the restaurant, but she protested at first, wanting to meet at some little bar. But I stuck to our spot, saying I wanted to meet in a more public place. I think she finally agreed because I acted like my news was something she would be happy to hear. If everything goes as planned, remind me to take some acting lessons. I might have a new career!"

He just laughed. "I know. Just joking with you. So, Bubba is going to be there, and no matter where we sit, he should be able to see what's going on. I talked to him this morning, and he's going to come in after us. His wife isn't going to be able to go, but his son wanted to be there instead, especially when he found out what his dad was up to. You'll never believe this— his son is a lawyer!"

"Then he'll probably love all this intrigue. If they only knew everything that was going on...wow." Maddy wondered what Bubba and his son would think.

"So, Riley and I will be waiting outside. I'm sure the drama queen will storm off once she gets the bad news, so you'll have to call us when she's walking out of the restaurant. We'll be ready to follow her."

"We're meeting at twelve thirty, perfect for a lunchtime crowd on a Sunday. I'll see you then...and, Maddy—I love you!" Jason's voice brought back their time on the couch together last night.

"I love you too," she said softly and clicked disconnect on her phone, sweet memories on her mind.

Riley picked her up at noon so they could get to the restaurant and find a spot toward the back of the parking lot before Jason or Andrea showed up. And she had packed for this trip—a cooler, blanket, pillow, binoculars, camera, and notebook were all neatly piled in the backseat.

"Well," she said, "we're on a stakeout. Isn't this so cool!" She still couldn't contain her excitement, acting like it was a great adventure.

"Riley, you have to remember this is really serious. We have to be careful."

"Yes, I got the speech from Carter *again* this morning. We will be, but this is so exciting! As weird as it sounds, I've always dreamed about doing something like this. I wonder sometimes if I should have become a detective." Her eyes could not hide the thrill she was feeling. But for Maddy it was just the opposite. She was very nervous, just praying that things went as planned. She knew they couldn't control everything, but they would do their best.

In another few minutes, Jason pulled up to the front of the restaurant and walked into the establishment. That is my man, looking so good, Maddy thought to herself. Then Andrea pulled up, parking two cars down from his. She was dressed in a black, skin-tight mini-dress and wore black stiletto heels. Her brown curls hung down around her shoulders. No way were men *not* going to be looking at her, which was of course what she wanted. Except this time she didn't know that the attention she received could be her downfall. She also wore a smile of smugness, like she was going in to catch her big prize. If she only knew what news was waiting for her inside, she would have never come. At least that was what Jason, Maddy, Riley, and Carter had anticipated when they'd hatched the scheme to catch her and her friend.

Inside, Jason was already seated at a table by the window overlooking the beach. He had just ordered a drink when Andrea made her entrance, flirting with the host as she walked over to the table.

"Well, it's about time we had this little meeting, don't you think? Was wondering when you were going to come to your senses," she said as she adjusted her seat and took a sip of the water already on the table.

"Yes, I finally realized that we needed to talk. I just had to absorb all the information you told me about. I also wanted some time to think about a few things and to check with my lawyer," Jason said as he looked around at the other patrons in the restaurant and then back at Andrea. She still had that smirk on her face.

"I hope he told you what my lawyer has already said. That way we can get through this nice and quick. We are still married, have been this whole time, so if you want to get rid of me, it means a trip back to court. But this time, I think alimony and 50 percent of your assets and cash will seal the deal. My lawyer is already drawing up the documents. I was just waiting for you to let me know where to have them sent…unless you want our lawyers to meet." She smiled sweetly, but the words coming out of her mouth sounded so self-assured that Jason couldn't wait to drop the bomb on her.

Just then, he saw Bubba and his son being seated one table over. Perfect. If fireworks were about to fly, they would be in a great spot to watch the show.

"I did talk to my attorney, Dave, and he did some investigating into our divorce. He is very knowledgeable of the law, including civil and criminal." He watched as her expression started to lose a little of its smugness.

"Yes, we had a few interesting phone calls. I told him what you revealed to me about our divorce not being finalized, and he did mention the possibility of another court date. But then he found out the circumstances around why the papers were never filed. He was able to obtain my original documents, thanks to Maria, and talk to Mr. Thornhill, my previous attorney. They were able to legally, legitimately, and irrevocably file the papers again this past Friday. Since it was almost ten years ago, our divorce became effective immediately, because the clerk that was delivering our papers to the courthouse that day had a car accident. Since that was something out of the lawyers' control, the papers were filed as though it was ten years ago. You will be receiving your copies shortly, or at least your attorney will. Where would you like them to be sent?" Jason's face wore a slight smile as he watched her cheeks become blood red.

"How dare you! I don't believe it. My lawyer would have called me if any of this were true, I'm sure of it!" She was angry, and her voice rose slightly with each word she spoke.

"It seems you have one incompetent lawyer, feeding you bullshit about this divorce not being legal. All he had to do was to check the circumstances surrounding why the papers were never filed, and the problem would have been fixed. You probably told him to hold off, thinking there was a loophole you could have me jump through to take my money. Sorry, sweetheart, but you aren't getting a thing from me." With that, Jason sat back in his chair and took a sip of his water.

"Oh, yes, I am! I deserve it! We have been married all these years according to the law, and I'm entitled to half of everything!" Now she was loud enough to draw the attention of most of the people in the restaurant, but she wasn't even aware of them—her full attention, and anger, was focused on Jason.

"You are so heartless, Jason! I've been fending on my own now for so long, just barely making it. You have more than enough, so helping me wouldn't make a dent in your lifestyle. I deserve that money!"

"Barely fending for yourself? You've got to be kidding! I've done more research than you think, and a few men out there are more than a little frustrated with a woman that calls herself Summer, Ally, Bailey—shall I go on?" he asked, knowing now that he'd pulled this off. Her face was now turning white as she realized he knew about her con games.

"You can't prove anything. You have nothing on me!"

Jason shrugged his shoulders. "Right now, the thing I know for sure is this: *We. Are. Not. Married.*" His words were so forceful and the look he gave her so intense that Andrea was forced to back down. "And if you should ever try to scam me again, you will regret it more than you can imagine." Jason's voice was like ice, and Andrea's resolve was broken. He could see in her eyes that she was scared now. She knew Jason was aware of her past.

"I'll wait till I hear from my lawyer, and then we will see," she said, but her voice was low and trembling, her confidence all but totally faded.

"Well, I've lost my appetite...unless you still want to order something. Shall I call for the waiter?" Jason asked, giving her a sarcastic smile.

She glared at him but said nothing, picked up her handbag, and stormed through the restaurant, practically pushing people out of the way as she headed toward the door. Jason picked up the phone and dialed Maddy's number.

"And here she comes."

"Did it work?" Maddy asked quickly.

"Like a charm. Be careful, sweetheart. I'll see you in a few hours. I love you."

"I love you too," Maddy said as she hung up. Just then Andrea emerged from the restaurant, her body language radiating volumes of fury.

"I guess that's our signal that the show has begun," Riley said as she glanced at Maddy. She turned and started the car.

"Don't follow too close, and—" was all Maddy could say before Riley cut her off.

"I got this. Promise. Just watch."

Both women did watch as the angry brunette threw her handbag in the car, got in, and slammed the door. With a rev of the engine, she backed out of the parking space and peeled out of the lot, tires squealing.

"That is one pissed-off bitch," Riley said as she eased her car out of their hiding spot. When Andrea turned south on Highway 1, Riley sped up and got on the road a few cars behind her.

"I'll keep her in sight while you drive. Thank goodness she's in a red car, which makes no sense to me if you're running or hiding. But she does seem to be a little on the flashy side," Maddy said, the small talk somewhat easing her nerves, which were at this moment trying to get the best of her.

"You think? Little drama queen with her too-tight clothes and flirting like a floozy?"

"Wow—I do think you just described her to a tee!" Maddy said, and even though Riley was right, she felt sorry for the woman, wondering how she had let her life get so messed up.

Andrea sped along the highway, not really entertaining the idea of a speed limit. Riley was keeping up, staying a few cars behind her, but the speeding was putting Maddy even more on edge. The cops in the Keys were more than happy to give out tickets, and that was the last thing they needed. But just enough cars kept getting in Andrea's way along the stretch of highway before them, and that helped in their quest to stay as close to her as they could.

Finally they arrived in Key West, and with the heavier traffic of the city, Riley and Maddy could more easily watch the small red car like a hawk. At one point they thought they'd lost her, but a traffic light brought them back behind her with only one car separating them. Since they were in Riley's car and wore hats and sunglasses, they were sure she wouldn't recognize them. Andrea followed Highway 1 until it turned into Truman Avenue. Then she made a left onto Georgia Street, where she parked her car in front of a small house, which actually looked very quaint and cute from the outside. Under different circumstances, Maddy would have loved to see the inside of the little house. Andrea opened the door to her car and got out much more slowly, showing a lot less energy than what they'd witnessed at the restaurant on Islamorada. She almost looked defeated, acting like she was dreading going into the house, as if she were getting ready to face angry parents.

She stood by the car and leaned against it, putting her hand to her head. They could see her reluctance to go in, but in a few minutes she seemed to pull herself together and stepped inside the door. They were parked far enough away for her not to see them but close enough to keep watch on the tiny place.

"That was a little weird. Felt like I was watching myself when I used to come home after curfew," Riley said. Maddy was puzzled too. Something didn't feel quite right, but the first part of their mission was now complete. Andrea was staying here in Key West, and judging by the presence of the second car parked in the front of the house, she wasn't alone.

40

"We're here at her house," Maddy told Jason. She had quickly dialed him once they were settled in and watching the house. They actually had a great vantage point and could see most of it, including the front windows and door. Now they waited.

"I'm already on my way there. I know I said don't do this, but text me the house address if you can see it, or the address of a home nearby. That way I can put it in my GPS. But I'll have to meet you somewhere. We can't have two cars sitting there. That would be too suspicious."

"But if we leave, we might miss something." Maddy was worried. One wrong move and they would have done all of this for nothing.

"Only for a few minutes, but I'll let you know where when I get there, ok?"

"Gotta go. Someone's coming out of the house. Bye!" And she quickly tapped End Call on the screen of her phone.

Andrea walked out, now dressed in a T-shirt and cut-off shorts, her hair pulled back in a ponytail. She looked almost like a young, innocent girl instead of the horrible woman they had come to know over the past few days. Both Riley and Maddy noticed that she was holding one side of her face and wiping tears.

"Good Lord, she looks like a completely different person. I don't think I would have recognized her!" Riley said quickly.

"Something isn't right, Riley. I most definitely don't like the woman, but this situation feels very strange."

Riley began taking pictures as Andrea took a seat in the swing at the side of the house. Using the binoculars they had brought with them, Maddy looked closer. She was right. Andrea was crying, and she had a huge red mark on the side of her face.

"Riley, she looks like she's been hit. Use your zoom lens. You'll see the mark on her face. Take a picture!"

Riley zoomed in with her camera. Andrea indeed had a huge red welt on her cheek, and tears flowed out of her eyes.

"What do we do? She's been hit. This whole thing is getting more complicated. Never thought it was something like this. Maybe she's being forced to do these things," Maddy said softly.

"Hey, I know this isn't what we thought, but don't go getting soft. She has scammed people, and I agree she doesn't deserve to be abused, but we're here to get to the bottom of this whole situation."

Before Maddy could say anything else, a man walked out of the house and sat by Andrea on the swing. She scooted away and he moved closer, acting like he was apologizing.

"Finally, we have him. This has to be Cansty. Take pictures! I pulled up his information online and put it on my iPad so we could compare the photos to make sure it's him." But they kept watching the exchange between the two people on the swing. It wasn't long before Andrea stood up and the man grabbed her wrist, but then he let it go and followed her back into the house.

They were so mesmerized by the unfolding scene that when Maddy's phone rang, they both jumped. Jason was calling.

"Hi, I'm here. I'm parked at Sandy's Cafe around the corner on Virginia Street. Can you come and get me? If not, I could probably walk—just didn't want to take a chance on her seeing me." Jason said quickly.

"We'll be there in a minute, and the situation is different than we expected, Jason," Maddy said softly.

"What do you mean?"

"I'll tell you when we get there."

It took them only two minutes to arrive at the cafe where Jason had parked his car. He quickly jumped into the backseat, and they hurried back to their secluded spot. They'd been gone only about five minutes, but when they arrived back at the house, the red car was gone.

"Jason, I think she's being abused by this guy. We think it's Cansty, but we haven't checked the pictures yet," Maddy told him as she pulled out her iPad and Riley searched for the best picture she had taken of the man. It was hard to tell by comparing the photos but it look like Cansty although they couldn't be sure.

"What do you mean abused? She looked perfectly fine to me, and she certainly didn't act it."

They proceeded to tell him everything they had seen during the past hour. Jason didn't say anything. He just listened as he tried to digest everything they were telling him.

"You know I can't stand the woman, but no one deserves to be hit. The pictures we have aren't really enough proof, but it was pretty obvious to both of us of what was going on," Riley said.

"But why?" Jason asked. "This doesn't add up. How do we find out what's really happening?"

"Well," Maddy said, "I've been thinking, and I know this will sound crazy...but I think we need to confront her."

"Yes, I agree. You are crazy! She might just haul off and hit you, especially after Jason dumped the divorce news on her!" Riley cracked.

"Listen, she knows she isn't getting any of Jason's money now. She hasn't gotten anything from her lawyer, but she must have thought this might possibly happen or she wouldn't have stormed down here. But I also don't think she anticipated getting hit or beaten by this guy she's with. He's part of this whole thing, but a piece of this puzzle is still missing. If we talk to her, tell her what we know—the scamming, her offshore account, the fake disability money—she'll likely feel cornered, but just maybe she'll tell us the real story."

Jason didn't say a word. He just wanted to be rid of the woman, but Maddy was right. They needed to find out the real reason behind Andrea's sudden reappearance in his life.

"We can't do anything right now, because she's gone. We'll have to wait till she gets back, but right now I have to find a bathroom," Riley said, squirming in her seat.

"I need to go too. Forgot that we hadn't even stopped till now. We've been running on adrenaline. My medicine!" Maddy suddenly exclaimed. She found her meds quickly and swallowed them down. "I promised I wouldn't forget them, and of course I did with all this excitement. And I hate to bother everyone, but I need to eat too."

"Let's go get some food to go and come back here. We can try to figure out what to do while we eat, and hopefully she'll show back up," Jason said. "And you," he said with his hand on Maddy's shoulder, "you need to come back here and rest. Looks like Riley packed for a camping trip."

"Hey, don't knock it. I wasn't sure what we'd need for this little stakeout we got going on. I was a little excited, ok?"

"You're forgiven, and to tell you the truth, I'm glad you went overboard. Jason is right. I am tired, but I think that's from forgetting my medicine. Let's go get you two something to eat. I already have mine in the backpack." Maddy was so hungry, and the medicine was making her tired.

"And find a restroom, pronto!"

They found a Wendy's close by, quickly used the bathroom, and then ordered some food to go. Maddy switched places in the car with Jason so she could stretch out in the backseat for a quick nap. She placed her ball cap on Jason's head at the same time, giving him a kiss on the neck.

"You have to wear the hat just in case. Less likely she'll recognize you," Maddy said as he rolled his eyes. "Besides, if you don't, Riley will get upset because you aren't playing by her detective rules." At this, Maddy laughed. Both looked at her as if she'd lost her mind.

"It's part of our detective outfits," Riley said seriously. She was really in her element with this cloak-and-dagger stuff. Jason couldn't help but laugh, too.

"Yes, go ahead and make fun of me, but you never know. If these two people are as smart as we think they may be, a disguise will help," she said as she drove back to the little yellow house.

The red sports car was still gone when they resumed their sheltered parking spot.

"All we can do now is sit and wait," Riley said. All three ate their food, excitement and anticipation having escalated their hunger. As soon as Maddy was finished, she spread a blanket against the stacks of tote bags along the right side of the seat and grabbed one of the pillows Riley had packed, laying her head against it and instantly relaxing in the warm air coming through the open windows of the car. She told them both not to let her sleep more than an hour, but the look on Jason's face told her he probably wouldn't wake her unless something happened. And before she knew it, she was asleep.

"So, what do you think about Maddy's suggestion?" Riley asked Jason as they sat eating their sandwiches and french fries.

Jason looked back to see Maddy sleeping soundly, looking so beautiful. She was doing so much for him that he could never repay. Is this what true love really was? It had to be, he thought as he continued to watch her.

"Hey! Did you hear me? Or do you need a nap too?"

"Sorry. Maddy does have a point. Maybe if we let Andrea know we're on to her and that we might be able to help, she might give us the truth. Especially since it appears that this guy has hit her. I just don't know what she'll do. She's so sneaky that this could all be just a ruse. Will she warn him? Will she run away? What? This is a tricky situation, because we're now down in her territory. At this point I'm not sure what she's capable of. She could even have a gun, for all I know. It might even be time to call in the police but we aren't completely sure that is Cansty."

"I never thought about that," Riley said. "Well, hopefully she will show back up. Then we'll find a safe way to talk to her."

41

Maddy awoke to the sound of bickering from the front seat. She knew that more than an hour had passed by because the sunlight was no longer as bright—it was definitely later in the day. In the front seat, Riley and Jason were talking about a new science-fiction movie, and apparently they had different opinions about a particular scene.

"You are so wrong! You just wait till it's out on Blu-ray. Then I can prove it to you," came Riley's very animated voice.

"Hey, sleepy head," Jason said, realizing that Maddy was awake. He turned around and reached into the backseat to give her a quick kiss.

"Sounds like you two were having quite a heated discussion," she said through a yawn.

"A movie we both love, but she is so wrong about her interpretations," he said, laughing as he glanced back at Riley.

"You just wait! I'll be able to show you how wrong you are!"

Maddy sat up and stretched. "I can tell that you let me sleep longer than an hour. What time is it?"

"About five thirty. Andrea still hasn't come back," Jason said with disappointment in his voice. Just as he finished the sentence, though, the red car came around the corner and pulled up in front of the house. Andrea got out, pulling out loads of shopping bags. Her hands full, she bumped the car door shut with her hip and walked into the house.

"At least we know why she's been gone so long," Riley remarked.

Watching Andrea walk into the house, Jason looked surprised.

"That didn't even look like the same person I talked to earlier today! I've never seen her in shorts, T-shirt...and flip-flops? A ponytail?" Jason sounded confused.

"We noticed that today ourselves," Maddy said.

"I sure hope she's going somewhere tonight. I don't relish the thought of camping out in the car all night," Riley said as they continued to watch the house.

"You two are going to stay at my friend's bed and breakfast. I already called him, and he has a room ready for the both of you. Maddy, do you remember how to get there?" he asked as he turned to look at her.

Maddy definitely remembered the little inn tucked away among the trees of Key West. It brought back very fond memories of their trip. It had been only days ago, but it seemed like weeks had gone by since then. She had hoped to go back there one day, but not under these circumstances.

"The little love nest, huh?" Riley kidded both of them.

"We don't have to go yet. It's still early, and hopefully they have plans tonight. We can follow them to wherever they go. Maybe Riley and I can try to talk to her." Maddy was hoping to act on this as quickly as possible.

Jason sighed. "I still have reservations about confronting her. She'll realize that she's going to have to deal with the authorities because of the number of men who have come forward, but then she might cooperate if this man really hit her. We just don't know all the facts, so it's hard to say. Maybe we should call the police and let them handle it—we know she's wanted for questioning on the scams. We don't even have to be involved except for turning her in.

"The problem is," Jason continued, "they don't have a warrant out for her yet. It's still being processed. They could question her, but last I heard they don't have anything in writing to hold her in jail. As for Cansty, they have a warrant out for him, so he will run. You both saw that Andrea had been hit, so he could become violent, and we don't want to confront him."

Just then, the man they'd seen earlier with Andrea walked out of the house, got in a black car, and sped off down the street. With him now out of the house, this was the perfect opportunity to talk to Andrea, but it would have to be quick, because the man who just left could return at any time. If Andrea didn't want to see them or talk, they could simply call the cops and be done with it. Or if something was amiss, as Maddy suspected, they could try to help.

Before they could make a joint decision, Maddy jumped out of the car and walked quickly toward the house. Jason and Riley sat stunned at first, not moving. What the hell was she doing? Jason thought. She was walking so quickly she was almost jogging. He and Riley simultaneously opened their doors and chased after her, but by the time they reached her Maddy was already knocking on the front door.

"What possessed you to do that?" he whispered in her ear.

From behind the closed door came Andrea's raised voice. "I told you to give me an hour and I'll be ready. Go ahead and I'll just meet you there."

Maddy looked at Jason and Riley, shrugged her shoulders, and knocked again. This time they heard footsteps heading toward them. When the door opened, the look on Andrea's face was utter shock.

"What in the hell are you doing here!" she yelled as she looked at Jason. "And brought the girlfriend too? And who are you?" she asked, looking at Riley.

"Andrea, we know something else is going on besides trying to scam Jason about the divorce. We know about the cons you pulled on other men, that you have an offshore account where you keep your money, and that you're collecting a fraudulent disability check each month. And don't think about running off anywhere, because we have the police on speed dial and Jason knows the sheriff." Maddy said everything so fast she was shaking.

Andrea stood rooted, still in shock but now with dread beginning to creep into her facial expression.

"We also followed you here this afternoon because we know that someone else is involved with your scheme, and we originally wanted to find out who and turn you both in. But Riley and I saw you get hurt this afternoon."

"First of all, you don't have anything on me, and I have no idea what you are talking about. I've never scammed anyone! You are crazy! As for getting hurt this afternoon, I don't know what you saw. If you're going to call the police, go ahead. You don't have anything on me!" she cried, but the tone of her voice said otherwise.

This time Jason talked. "Andrea, the men you have conned these past few years have just recently found out about each other and the fact that you swindled them out of their money. They know your real name, they are looking for you, and it won't be long before the police are involved. Some investigators have been called in, and they found your offshore account on Grand Cayman. But what also has them intrigued is how you got permanent disability for an illness you don't have. So there will be fraud charges too. The reason we came to talk to you before calling the police is because Maddy and Riley saw you come out of the house with a huge red mark on your face—we can still see it. You've just tried to cover it up with makeup. Rest assured, I'm all for turning you in, but both of these women want to make sure you get help if you're being abused...or if you're being coerced into this charade of taking people's money."

Andrea was now becoming unglued, and tears were welling up in her eyes.

"He made me do it. And he was the one who planned this whole scheme to come to the Keys and demand money when he found out about the divorce issue. He wanted the money. He said we would split whatever I got in half and then go our separate ways once and for all. He said I owed him after he helped me get disability. He even threatened me. I never asked for him to get me disability money, but he said it was an easy way for me to make a little extra cash each month. All I had to do was give him 30 percent of my check when it came in. It would be extra income for both of us."

"Can we come in?" Maddy asked.

Andrea moved away from the door and turned and walked to the little couch in the room. The house was nicely decorated; either someone lived here full-time or it was an upscale rental home.

"When you say *he*, is that the man that just left? Martin Cansty?"

"You know his name?" The look of shock returned to her face.

"He's being investigated too for fraud charges against the government. We know that, but it seems he may need to be charged with domestic violence too," Maddy said softly as she pointed to Andrea's cheek.

"He knew I was meeting you today," she began as she looked at Jason. "He was so sure you would just go ahead and give me some kind of settlement rather than going through another divorce hearing. We didn't know the circumstances of why the papers weren't delivered and filed. My lawyer never investigated further as to the cause. He just figured it was a clerical error, and usually there's some type of court case when something like this happens. Martin told me I wouldn't get 50 percent of your assets but that I should tell you that, hoping you would just write me a large check to get me out of your life. He also told me that if I didn't do this, he would have me arrested on scamming him out of $80,000. I didn't know he was being charged with fraud. As you can see," she said as she raised her hand to her cheek, "he wasn't too happy when he found out lunch didn't go as planned. As soon as I told him that you had already fixed the divorce papers, he hit me across the face. That was when I went outside to the swing. He followed and tried to apologize, but that was just a fake gesture. He is mean, and I regret ever getting involved with him. He's the type of person who gets violent when things don't go his way. And since things fizzled today, I'm expected to go to some club on Duval Street tonight that caters to the wealthy. He's hoping I can snag some single gentleman to play my con on one more time—we split the money, and then he promised to leave me alone. At least he says he will, but he's too controlling…and apparently, according to you, all my games have caught up with me. Right now, I don't care. I'm tired of this whole thing. Even though I haven't made all the right choices, I'm tired of being the abuse and running. But if I take off, he'll find me. And if the Feds are looking for me too, I might as well give up."

"I can't speak for the police or the government, because you really have screwed up," Maddy said as matter-of-factly as she could," but if you help to bring in Cansty, the investigators might go easier on you. I don't know the law, but if you help them, they'll likely take that into consideration. Also, you can bring him up on abuse charges, especially now with the welt on your face. You just have to make the choice."

Andrea sat there looking totally defeated. "Well, if I'm going to jail, so is his ass." That was all they needed to hear.

"I'm going to contact Mike, the local sheriff, and let him know what's going on. We'll tell him what club you both will be at tonight, and he can make a public arrest so Cansty doesn't run. But Andrea, for your sake, you'd better be telling us the truth, and you'd better not leave. We'll be watching, and if you make one wrong move, I promise you will regret it. We have your license plate number, your description, everything. You understand? And if you cooperate, this might be a little easier on you." Jason was looking at her like he could spit nails, but to Maddy's relief he was keeping his cool.

She nodded her head in agreement. "You'd better go. He'll be back any moment, and if he sees you here, there's no telling what he'll do. We'll probably be in his car tonight, the black jaguar. Since you're evidently already good at tailing people, you shouldn't have any trouble, but if you do, here's the nightclub we'll be at." She gave Jason a small slip of paper that had the name and address of where they would be.

As they walked out the door, Jason looked back at her.

"Remember what I said, Andrea. If you don't stick to this plan, you are screwed." Jason held her gaze, and she looked back at him defiantly.

"Looks like you will get your wish. To be rid of me." With that she slammed the door.

42

Just as they got into their car, the black Jaguar pulled up in front of the house.

"That was close. We timed that just right," Riley said, breathing a sigh of relief.

"I told you there was more to the story than we thought. And she's cooperating." Maddy was happy that after tonight—hopefully—this whole ordeal would be over with and finished.

"Honestly, I think she was a little too forthcoming. Agreeing to give herself to the authorities? That is not Andrea, and I don't buy it," Jason said skeptically. "We'll have to see what happens tonight. But I need to call Mike and give him the details—and hope he doesn't get pissed by our little sting operation."

Jason filled Mike in on the details of what had happened, starting at the beginning of the whole wretched situation.

Although Mike wasn't happy that they had taken it upon them-selves to do his work, he was glad they were safe and agreed to go along with their plan by having patrol cars close to the club. If it worked, Mike would have both felons in custody tonight. Now all that was left was to wait and watch for Andrea and Martin Cansty to make their move.

As they waited, hunger and thirst assailed them once again, but they didn't dare leave their spot. Maddy decided to switch spots with Riley, letting her in the back so she could find the food she'd packed. Soon they were munching on snacks as they waited and closely watched the little house down the street.

At around nine, both Andrea and Cansty walked out and got into the black Jaguar. She had her purse and a large tote bag that she put in the backseat, and they set off down the street. This time, instead of Riley behind the wheel, Jason drove, following as closely as he could. Maddy and Riley kept watch for the black car. It was much harder to keep track of the vehicle at night because of its color, but the traffic was light, and that helped them. At least they had the address of the bar should they get separated, but Jason still wasn't convinced that Andrea had turned this magical corner and wanted to help the authorities. That wasn't her, as much as Maddy wanted to believe it. He knew this game wasn't over, and when the black car sped through the light in front of them just as it turned red, Jason knew he was right. All three of them saw the sports car make a sudden left turn, heading in the opposite direction of the club Andrea had told them about.

"Dammit!" Jason yelled.

"What's going on?" Maddy asked anxiously.

"I knew she wasn't telling the truth," Jason said as he punched the gas pedal and weaved around cars trying to catch a glimpse of the Jaguar. "Get on my phone and call Mike—the number's in Recent Calls. Let him know what's happening. Give him the license plate number, and tell him that we're trying to keep up with them but that it's time for the police to get involved. They could be out of the city by now."

"Hello...Mike? This is Maddy Sumner, Jason Burnett's friend. He called you earlier about Andrea Novak and Martin Cansty. They've decided to flee town instead going through with the arrangement we made with Andrea earlier. They're driving a black Jaguar with a Pennsylvania license plate, number CX 582. We're trying to follow them, but they ran a red light and are heading out of the city."

Maddy was silent as Mike spoke on the other end. As she clicked the phone off, she relayed the sheriff's instructions.

"Mike has radioed the information to all available personnel and put out an APB for the apprehension of both of them. He's calling the stations along the Keys, hoping to catch them before they reach Florida City. He said for us to be careful, and if we do come in contact with them to stay away—just call 911 and wait for the police. He sounded a little upset and told us to stay out of the way."

"Right now I have no idea where they are," Jason said angrily. He couldn't believe they had slipped right out of their hands. All this work was mostly wasted, except for the fact that he wasn't married to this hateful woman anymore. And he was sure his sheriff friend was furious with him—and with himself for letting Jason talk him into helping with this. Andrea had played on Maddy's emotions and Jason had followed along, wanting to believe that Maddy might be right. Now he was regretting ever giving Andrea the benefit of the doubt. He also felt sorry for Maddy, because she had been thoroughly convinced that Andrea was telling the truth and wanted to turn over a new leaf. In the midst of all the turmoil around him, this one fact made him love Maddy even more— that she always chose to the see the good in others, even when they had hurt her, and this amazed him.

Now that they were leaving the lights of the city, it was darker and harder to look for the car that held the two fugitives. Fewer streetlights and businesses meant longer stretches of dark road. The Jaguar could be anywhere.

"I know it's hard, but keep looking. Riley, you take one side of the highway, and Maddy, you take the other. Look for anything." Jason was starting to sound desperate. To think they'd actually had them both this afternoon, and now they were gone! They should have called the police right then, but they'd thought they were helping Andrea after her "poor little me" act. They had to find them to make the situation right.

Before they knew it, they'd reached Marathon Key, which offered a plethora of places to hide. Jason knew that Mike had radioed the local police here about the situation, so hopefully Andrea and Cansty wouldn't make it back to the mainland of Florida. If they did, it would be like looking for a needle in a haystack. And it would be their fault.

"I hate to ask this, but I've really got to go to the bathroom again," Riley said. "I promise it will be the quickest stop ever!"

Maddy couldn't help but laugh, and Jason followed suit. They pulled into a McDonald's, and all three of them jumped out, Riley practically running for the restroom. True to her word, she was fast, and just as they were all getting back in the car, Jason looked up and saw the Jaguar driving past. He couldn't believe his eyes! They must have stopped somewhere, knowing that Jason, Maddy, and Riley were probably chasing them down. By taking their time, they also wouldn't be as noticeable to the police. Perfect! Now to just follow them and radio in to 911. Hopefully this nightmare would soon be over.

"Hurry, you two, they just went past us!" Jason urged.

"What? You got to be kidding! How?" Riley said as she slid into the backseat so Maddy could sit with Jason.

"They must have parked somewhere out of the way once they left the city. They probably knew we would be chasing them, along with the police, so they waited and let us pass by. Smart thinking. This whole time we've been in front of them, not behind. They were also probably doing the speed limit, drawing no attention to themselves."

Maddy thought for a moment.

"Riley, where are the binoculars?"

Fumbling through her tote bag, Riley at last handed them over, saying, "Here. Why do you want them?"

"Because when we get close to them, I want to check out the license plate. I wouldn't be surprised if they switched it somehow. That's why they're driving the speed limit and not rushing. And sitting somewhere, waiting for us to go by, they had plenty of time to change tags and who knows what else."

She's right, Jason thought. He kept driving, but they hadn't spotted the black car yet. He did manage to call and tell the Marathon police the latest about the car and its occupants. He knew they would in turn radio up to the next Key. It wasn't until they reached the Seven Mile Bridge that Jason realized Andrea and Cansty were only one car ahead of them.

"There they are. It's a black Jaguar. It has to be them. If this car in front would just move a little to the side, I could see the plates." But it was no use. Not until they were over the bridge could they even catch a glimpse of the license plate number.

"Riley, get ready to write down this number, ok?" Maddy said quickly as she continued to peer through the binoculars.

"Got it," Riley said, digging into her bag once again for paper and pen.

As they got off the bridge, the road widened enough for Maddy to finally see the license plate.

"They changed it, all right. It's a Florida plate now, and the number is C2B 90."

"Damn, you were right." Jason couldn't believe how much more complicated this was getting by the minute.

"Wait. I'm trying to see inside the vehicle." Maddy paused and was finally rewarded as the lights of oncoming cars illuminated the Jaguar's interior.

"It's a blond woman driving, and there's a man with a hat on in the passenger seat. What if it's not them?" Maddy was worried now. Were they following the wrong car?

"I'm still sure it's them," Jason said angrily. "They had plenty of time to switch plates. I wouldn't doubt if Andrea has a wig on and they switched drivers. That would throw the police off because they knew we would call. She was in on this all along." Jason quickly got on the phone to relay the new information to the police.

"So, this afternoon was nothing but a joke to her," Maddy said stoically. "And I played right into her hands."

"We all did, but now we know how good she is at what she does, and her Mr. Cansty has probably been helping her for quite a while, even if he is prone to violence. Andrea probably didn't care as long as she was getting some money." Jason reached over and squeezed Maddy's hand, reassuring her that it would be ok.

They had been keeping at least two cars between themselves and the Jaguar when suddenly the intervening cars veered into the left lane to go around, not wishing to be hampered by the speed limit through town, and they found themselves right behind them.

"I'm pulling up beside them. I have to know it's her," was all Jason said as he sped up and was suddenly side by side with the black car. But it was Maddy who caught the attention of the blond woman in the vehicle beside them. When Andrea realized who it was, she suddenly sped up the car, but it was no use. Blue lights from two police cars were behind her, and another was coming straight toward her from up ahead.

"She recognized me," Maddy said as Jason slowed down and pulled to the side to watch. The black car was surrounded, and Andrea had no choice but to pull over or risk being chased by police through the Keys. She pulled into the parking lot of a shopping center, slowly and innocently, but Jason now turned their car into the lot as well. He needed to see them in the back of a police car. Jason, Maddy, and Riley watched from a short distance away as the officers checked IDs and registration. Two more police cars arrived on the scene just as the officer had each of them step out of the vehicle. At that point, they were both handcuffed and placed in the back of two different police cars. Before Maddy or Riley knew what was happening, Jason had jumped out of the car and was heading toward the scene. Maddy wanted to stop him, but he was on a mission and nothing was getting in his way.

"Ralph!" Jason yelled across the parking lot. The officer turned around and immediately recognized him.

"Hey, what are you doing here? Haven't seen you in a while. Can't really talk right now—" but Jason cut him off.

"Are they going to jail?"

"Jason, you know I can't give you that kind of information."

"Ralph, I'm the one who gave Mike the details on these two in Key West. We've been following them," he said, pointing back to the car where Maddy and Riley sat. "We were the ones who found out they switched the plates on the car."

"You mean *this* is the ex-wife?"

"You know she's my ex?" Jason asked curiously.

"Of course. Little town, my friend, and news travels fast in the Keys. I heard about the scene at the restaurant earlier today too." Of course, Jason thought. That seemed like a lifetime ago.

"Seems these two have a pile of charges pending against them. And it looks like they messed with the wrong person," he said, giving Jason a mock punch in the arm. "Ever considered being a detective?" Ralph said with a laugh and Jason smiled.

"I'm just glad they're in your car going to jail, where they both belong."

"We will get in touch with you, probably tomorrow, when everything is sorted out. I think they might be transferred to Miami due to the extent of their crimes. Don't know all the details, but someone will let you know. Try to relax now. You guys put yourselves in a lot of danger today, but that was probably the only way to get her off your ass," Ralph said, smiling. "I probably would have done the same thing."

"You have no idea."

Back at the car, Maddy and Riley waited anxiously to find out what had happened. When Jason gave them all the details, Maddy sighed with relief, tears filling her eyes, and Riley gave out a loud, "Woohoo!"

It was finished. Andrea Novak and Martin Cansty were being put behind bars for what could be a very long time. Now she and Jason could breathe and concentrate on themselves, Maddy thought as she rode in the seat next to him on the drive home.

43

By the time they got home, it was close to one in the morning. Riley dropped Maddy and Jason off at Maddy's house and then headed home. It looked like Jason and Maddy would be making one more trip to Key West to get his car, which had been left behind when they'd suddenly had to leave that evening. Hopefully the parking lot owner hadn't had the car towed, but if it had been, Jason happened to know a few people there that could help him out.

"This has been a long day, and I'm so glad it's done. It worked," Maddy said happily as she wrapped her arms around his waist. He felt so good, and she just melted into him. They were both so very tired, but they were extremely glad that this fiasco was finally over. Maddy could never have imagined on her train ride here that her trip to the Keys would involve catching not one but two criminals. Wait until her mom heard *this* story! She just hoped she would be able to tell her before Riley did.

"Do you want to just stay the night?" Maddy asked. "It's so late, and we're going to have to go get your car in the morning." Jason leaned down and kissed her softly.

"I think I will take you up on that offer. But I'll sleep here on the couch." Maddy wanted to share her bed with him, but it wouldn't be tonight. They were both spent from such a long day.

"Let me get the spare blanket and pillow from the closet."

Once he was settled on the couch, she sat on the side and leaned over to kiss his forehead. He was already falling asleep.

"I love you, Jason," she said softly in his ear, giving him one more soft kiss.

"I love you back," he said before he started quietly snoring and she made her way to her room.

Someone was stroking her hair lightly, but she couldn't figure out if it was part of a dream or if there was someone really with her. She was groggy as she opened her eyes to see Jason, lying on the bed next to her. As soon as he saw that she was awake, he gave her a kiss on the cheek.

"Good morning, sleepyhead," he murmured as he stretched out beside of her, causing her to scoot over a bit. This made the blankets tight, but she didn't care. She snuggled right into him and smiled.

"Wanted to say good-bye instead of just dashing off this morning," he continued as he wrapped his arms around her, and she nestled even closer to him. "I can't thank you enough for helping me yesterday—and really over these last few days since we got home from our trip. You've been right there helping, not questioning me or getting upset that I was dealing with my ex."

"Why would I? Maddy asked him softly.

"For one thing, she was my ex-wife, officially now. She also took up some valuable time that was meant for the two of us. I can honestly say that I've never met a woman like you before, Maddy. I want to ask you something. I know you're supposed to leave this Saturday to go home, but would you consider staying another week? I know you have to give up this rental house, but you can come and stay with me. I have two extra bedrooms in the house. You can take your pick. I promise to be on my best behavior. Just give it some thought today. I'm not ready for you to go home."

Maddy wanted to say yes immediately, but she knew that her schedule was set. She told herself she would give it some thought, though, and see if things could be changed, because staying with him for another week sounded like utopia to her.

"I'll think about it. I have a few things scheduled back home, so I'm not sure, but you can't imagine how badly I would love to tell you yes right now."

"Please think about it...and as badly as I would love to stay here in bed with you, I've got to go to work. I'm already late, but that's one thing I can usually get away with, since I'm the boss—except for the fact that it sets a bad example for my employees. I did tell my foreman an abbreviated version of what was going on and our plan, just in case I wasn't here today or was late. I'm sure the police will have more questions too as more details surface. I'm calling Dave and Maria first thing this morning. I'll let you know what's happening as I find out."

By this time Maddy was sitting up in bed with Jason beside her. He was the other half of her that made everything feel complete. She loved the sound of that, and she wanted to stay with him. When he mentioned being questioned by the police, though, all that had happened the last few days came home to her. It made her a bit anxious, but she knew she could handle it.

"Let me know when you get any news, and I hope you have a good day at work now that this situation is mostly behind you," she said as she kissed him good-bye. Just then she heard the honk of a horn outside.

"That's George, my foreman. He is giving me a ride to the job site." He stole one more kiss from her, and then he was out the door.

When Maddy got up, even though she was feeling euphoric about Jason staying with her last night, her body was sending her signals of exhaustion once again. She had thought this might happen, but she had been determined to see everything through to completion yesterday. She hadn't eaten like normal. Her medications, though she had taken them, were off schedule, and she hadn't had nearly enough water because of their little stakeout adventure.

As she got out of bed, she noticed that her legs were very weak, she was starting to itch, and she had a rash on her arm. Her heart rate was elevated, and the brain fog was starting to set it. Even though she knew what was happening to her body and was a little frustrated at it, she had to admit that overall she still felt good. Yes, she had symptoms—somehow, though, something was different. As she thought about it, she realized how much she had accomplished over the last few days without a major mishap that could have led to a hospital visit. Yes, she was still taking medications, eating differently, and more, but she thought she could feel her body changing—or was it a mental shift? This feeling she was having right now was one of the reasons she'd come to the Keys—to have time to figure out a way to get better physically—but the changes were taking place in her mind also. She felt alive and was looking at her situation in an entirely different light.

Maybe it was the chances she had taken while she'd been here. Going to the beach by herself. Her parasailing adventure. Staying in a house by herself. Her trip to Key West with Jason. Or it was simply Jason himself? He had brought feelings back into her life that she had feared were gone forever.

She still needed to see the specialist in Chicago to check on the status of her condition and help her with this illness, and that would mean no extended stay with Jason. Everything was already scheduled and couldn't be changed. She would basically have just enough time to get home from this trip and turn around to make the long trip north. At least her parents were driving her there, so they could stop whenever they wanted to. And she would be able to cook her food in the little twelve-volt cooking oven she had. But she wanted to stay here with Jason so badly that it hurt to know she had to turn down his offer. Even with her current symptoms, she had never felt better. And it was because she had someone who loved her, to whom her past and her physical limitations didn't matter.

She also couldn't deny that the atmosphere and the weather here in Florida agreed with her. Yes, she'd had a few episodes during her stay, but she honestly felt better than she had in years. Her family would say it was just because she was on vacation or that she had met a man. She would agree with them about meeting the man of her dreams but not about the vacation. The Florida Keys and living on an island just agreed with her, body and soul. Maybe a permanent change of scenery would help her healing process.

Maddy resolved to spend the day resting and writing. Finally, after being here almost a month, she was ready to take the steps needed for her future. Had she not been through all that had happened over the last few weeks, she wouldn't have found out how strong she really was despite her condition, and she also wouldn't have found the strength to give in to her feelings of love for Jason. He believed in her and wanted to be with her no matter what her situation was. Such a beautiful gift she had been given! How glad she was that she had decided to be bold and take this trip.

Maddy finally got out of bed and dressed in her most comfy outfit. After enjoying a small meal and taking her medication on time for once, she grabbed her journal and water bottle and headed downstairs to the lounger under the tiki hut. It was beautiful outside once again—weather that was completely spoiling her. At first she just sat, taking in all the scenery and going over her discovery this morning about her feelings and her determination to make changes in her life. She found herself smiling, so happy to have a direction for herself but not one so rigid that she couldn't still live in the moment.

Just as she started to write out her morning thoughts, her cell phone rang, and she knew who it was without even looking.

"Whatcha doing?" Riley said before Maddy could say hello—again.

"I honestly don't know how you do it! I didn't even say a word and you were already talking!"

"It's a gift," she snickered on the other end. "So, I saw that Jason stayed at your place last night."

Maddy rolled her eyes. "Riley, you are definitely in the wrong career. You really do need to be a detective. Especially after seeing you in action yesterday—plus your love for cop shows and your fantastic ability to snoop."

"Yes, you're probably right, but Carter would flip a gasket. I had so many messages on my phone last night, because I didn't answer any of his calls all day yesterday. He was mad as a hornet when I got home!"

"You mean he called yesterday and you didn't answer?" Maddy asked incredulously.

"No. We were in the middle of getting this crazy situation taken care of. I know—bad decision, and he had every right to chew me out last night when I finally called him after I got home. I just got caught up in the excitement. Things like our little adventure yesterday just don't happen around here. Actually, it's pretty boring and too laid-back at times for this girl," Riley said wistfully.

"Give me boring and laid-back any day."

"So, give me the scoop. What happened?" she asked, and Maddy could just imagine the look on Riley's face.

"He swept me off my feet, carried me into the house while kissing me nonstop, and laid me on the bed—and then we made mad, passionate love."

"I knew it!" she squealed.

"You've got to be kidding me. You believed that?" Maddy couldn't believe her friend.

"I was hoping for you," Riley said in a flat tone. "Nah, I knew *that* wasn't happening. We were all too tired last night. What a day! Even though I was exhausted when I got home, I told Carter all the details, and he finally said he had to get up in three hours and could we talk more tomorrow. I guess I was rattling on too much. How are you feeling today?"

"Mentally, on top of the world. Physically, not as good. Yesterday's trip and the excitement have my system a bit out of whack, so I'm home for the day. But even though I'm not feeling my best, I feel better than I have in a long time. It's hard to explain, Riley, but it's like I'm healing in some ways. Being here in the Keys, meeting Jason, all the adventures—it has affected me in ways that are hard to explain. I wish so much that I could stay." Maddy's voice cracked a bit as she tried to talk.

"I know. I feel that same way. Time has flown by, and your trip has been filled with a lot more excitement than we planned, that's for sure. Maybe another reason you're feeling better is that you're allowing yourself to just enjoy. To do the things you love, like painting and drawing. Allowing yourself to feel again by letting Jason into your life. Sometimes it's not just medicine and pills that help heal." Riley's words were so true. She was right. It was time to start enjoying life instead of just doing life.

"You're right, Riley. So very right." Maddy paused, still contemplating her friend's wise words. "Well, I'm in the back of the house under the tiki hut, enjoying the scenery. I haven't spent as much time back here as I thought I would. Come down if you can."

"I have a ton of work to do, but if you need anything, I'm just down the street."

"Riley, thank you so much for being the best friend anyone could ever have. I had started clarifying some things this morning as I lay in bed thinking about everything that has been going on. Your words just now have made things even more clear," Maddy said, and a small tear ran down her cheek.

"Oh, I forgot. Jason said the police might be calling and questioning us about what happened yesterday. He told me that if he got any news, he would call. I'll let you know if I hear anything, ok?" she said.

"Please let me know the minute you find out anything. I'm wondering what will be the outcome for those two crazy idiots."

"Me too."

"And...Maddy? You're welcome. I just want you to be happy, and I think you're finally on the right path. I love you, girl," Riley said as the phone clicked off.

Maddy wrote out her new personal code for the life she wanted. Directions that would help her become who she truly wanted to be. When she was done, she smiled as she looked over the scenery. She had done what she came here to do. She was happy. She felt healthier, and she now had some sense of purpose. Most importantly, she had a man who wanted to be with her through it all. She suddenly felt very blessed. And as if on cue, another manatee came swimming by the dock, so close that Maddy could have reached out and touched it. An in the distance she saw a pair of dolphins break the surface of the water. She felt happy and content. The only thing that had her feeling a bit down was the fact that she had to leave this Saturday, but she was determined that until then, she was going to enjoy every single minute she could with Jason.

44

Jason couldn't help but be preoccupied with yesterday's events and Maddy's upcoming departure the coming weekend. He'd known from the beginning that she was only staying for a month, but he also hadn't expected to fall in love with her. And for her few remaining days on the island to be filled with con artists, an ex-wife, car chases, and police reports was driving him crazy. He had wanted their time together before she went back home to be special, and he was still working on a surprise for her. But nothing had been finalized yet, so he couldn't say anything. Hopefully he would know soon, though, and he was sure that she would love it because it would benefit their blossoming relationship. One piece of great news was that the remodel of the house he was managing was now far ahead of schedule because of some extra workers he'd hired, plus the fact that he'd worked the previous weekend. That would definitely help with what he was planning for himself and Maddy.

If she could just stay one more week…that was all he needed, and he hoped she would say yes to what he had asked her this morning before he left. He wanted and needed more time with her. He craved her now, and just the thought of her leaving left him unable to think straight. He wanted her with him.

As he'd predicted, the police contacted him later in the morning. Detective Spaulding wanted to talk to Jason, Maddy, and Riley separately to get their statements about the events of yesterday. But he wanted to speak to Jason first, since he'd been one of the main victims in this crime. Jason was able to find out that Andrea and Cansty were being held at the local police department in Marathon until all the details were sorted out, and that was where the three of them would have to go to give their statements. Jason told him that would be no problem and that he would get back to him as soon as possible.

He also had to figure out when he could go get his car in Key West. Maybe Maddy would be up for one more trip? That would certainly give them more time together, and at the same time they could stop and give their statements to the police. After that, hopefully they would be done with all of this, or least she wouldn't have to deal with it any more. He had a feeling that his involvement would last a bit longer, but he was ok with that. Just as long as both his ex and Cansty were convicted of the crimes they had inflicted on other people. They both deserved their punishment.

"Hey there," he said when Maddy answered her phone. "You sound like you were sleeping. I'm sorry if I woke you."

"Hi! No, I'm on the back porch under the tiki hut relaxing. Is everything ok?"

"Just wanted to give you the latest news." He gave her details about what the detective had said and how important their statements would be in this case.

"Seems like the evidence is stacking up against both of them, so I don't think they're going to be free for a very long time. Dave is faxing down copies of documents and statements from the men Andrea conned for their money along with the offshore bank account information that Maria found. As far as Cansty is concerned, the Feds already have plenty of evidence and warrants for his arrest. He is to be extradited back to his home state of Pennsylvania within the next few days. Looks like Andrea will be taken back to Nevada. That's where we were living when we got divorced, and she still lists it as her home state. Seems she played on wealthy men who'd come to Las Vegas for conventions. I can't say this enough—I just want it to be done and over." Maddy could hear the relief in Jason's voice even though a hint of anger still showed through.

"I was also calling to see if you might want to make another trip to Key West with me, maybe tomorrow? Need to get my car back since I'm without transportation. Plus we can give our statements to the police in Marathon. They asked if we could come as soon as possible, and it shouldn't take very long."

"We did make a quick getaway last night following those two, and I forgot all about leaving your car behind. I know this was a serious situation, but do admit I had a little fun. I've never done anything like that before. Now I know why Riley watches all those cop shows, but yesterday was enough for me," Maddy said with a sigh. "Today I'm feeling just a little bit tired but I'm doing ok."

"I'm sorry you had to go through all that. Feeling that bad?" Jason asked with concern.

"Actually, not as bad as I've experienced before, but I'm certainly feeling all the activity of yesterday. But in a way I feel better too. I know it sounds weird and complicated, but I'll explain better later. As for the trip tomorrow, I would love to go. Gives me some more time with you before I have to leave." Maddy suddenly remembered she wasn't going to mention that just yet.

"Have you thought about what I asked this morning?" he asked with hope in his voice.

"Jason, I have, but it's not a simple answer. I'll have to explain, but not now over the phone, ok?"

"No problem, I can wait. Dinner tonight at your house. How about takeout?"

"Sounds great. I'll call Riley to give her the latest update and let her know about giving her statement. Maybe she can go to the local police and talk to them so she doesn't have to make the trip to Marathon?" Maddy suggested.

"That will probably be fine, but I'll check to make sure. So I'll see you at dinner tonight."

"Yes, and I want some french fries from somewhere. I've been craving them!"

"Yes ma'am, I think I can handle that. I love you," he said in a very charming voice.

"I love you too, Jason." As she clicked to disconnect the call, she realized the talk with him about not staying would have to happen tonight. She didn't want their last few days to be out of sorts, but he didn't know about the doctors. Maybe once he found out all of what she was truly going through, he would change his mind about wanting to be with her at all. As she'd told him before, her dad referred to her as "high maintenance but worth every penny." She just hoped Jason would agree with her father's assessment.

Before she lay back down, she called Riley to give her the latest news, and she sounded mesmerized on the other end of the phone. She was more than willing to drive to Marathon to talk to the police, but the local station would be better because she did have more work to catch up on than she originally thought. She made Maddy promise to keep her in the loop with all the latest about Andrea and Cansty.

"Are you still feeling ok today?" she asked.

"I was actually getting ready to take a nap when Jason called. It's so relaxing out here, but a nap does sound good. Jason is coming for dinner, and we need to talk. Riley, before he left this morning, he asked me to consider staying another week with him at his house," Maddy told her hesitantly.

"And what did you say?"

"That I would have to think about it, because I have so much going on. He doesn't know about the specialist I'm going to see in Chicago when I get home. I'm afraid to tell him because I don't want to scare him away, but he deserves to know that if this relationship continues, it definitely will be out of the norm."

"Maddy, what is normal? There is no such thing! I don't care what anyone says. Like I keep telling you. When you two are together, I can tell you both belong with each other. He loves you, Maddy, I can see it—with every fiber of his being.

I have never seen a guy that smitten with a woman…except maybe me and Carter," she laughed. "But seriously, I think you need to give Jason just a little more credit. Go get your beauty sleep, and enjoy your evening, ok? Quit worrying!"

"Hey, Riley? One more thing. I might go with Jason tomorrow to get his car in Key West. It will give us some more time together. I'll let you know if we go."

"Might be good for you to take another little trip there. Just to get away before you do leave town. But I'm betting whether you leave town or stay, Jason is still going to be a part of your life somehow."

"We shall see," Maddy said as she clicked the phone off. She headed up the stairs and settled in on the sofa for a much-needed nap.

45

A tapping sound woke her up, and she immediately noticed that it was quite dark in the room. In the next moment, she realized she had practically slept away the entire afternoon! The brain fog that had decided to invade her head after lunch was still there, and at first she couldn't figure out where the tapping was coming from. Then it dawned on her—it was the front door, probably Jason. Great! Her hair was a mess, her face was devoid of makeup, and she still had on her "day" PJs, as she liked to call them at home. Definitely not how she wanted to appear at the door.

"Maddy, are you ok?" Jason said loudly from the other side of the door.

"Coming," she called as she quickly walked to the door, trying to tame her hair and make sure she looked somewhat presentable, quickly checking her reflection in the mirror by the door.

"Hi," she said sheepishly as she pulled it open. "I just woke up. Actually your knocks on the door acted as my alarm to get up. I can't believe I slept the whole afternoon."

"Then your body must have needed it," Jason said as he came in the door and gave her a big kiss. In his arms he held bags wafting delicious aromas.

"Wow, it all smells so good!" she said. She just hoped one of those bags had some french fries in it. "Let me go change into some different clothes. I'm still in my pajamas."

He deposited the bags on the table and turned to enfold her in a great big hug and give her a kiss, spinning her around gently. "You look perfect. And you certainly don't need to change clothes. Personally, I like your PJs."

"Wow, you're in a very good mood. Something I need to know?"

"Let's talk over dinner. I'm starved," he said. She went to get the plates and utensils while he emptied the bags onto the tiny table by the window. They would have water-view seating for their evening dinner, he said as he pulled her chair out for her. Something was surely going on for his mood to be this bright and cheerful. She couldn't wait to hear the details.

"So, I was able to get you the best fries on the island. I asked my foreman at work who had the best-unseasoned fries, and he called his friend. I tried them, and I must say they're pretty good." Her smiled widened as she saw the huge bag of fried potatoes he had for her. No way could she eat that many, but they would heat up just fine in the oven tomorrow for a snack.

"As for me, I'm having fried chicken, potato salad, and corn on the cob. Not island food, but some good southern food," Jason said as he conspicuously sniffed the food on his plate.

"You're in a terrific mood. What's going on?" Maddy asked.

"First, we don't have to go to Key West for my car. Some guys from work are going there tomorrow and they offered to pick it up for me. Second, I called the sheriff's department in Marathon, and we can all give our statements to the local police here on Islamorada instead of having to make another trip. Also, Cansty was moved today, and it looks like his case is pretty open and shut for federal fraud, domestic abuse, and blackmail. As for Andrea, she conned fifteen men for a total of over $1.2 million. They're filing a case against her, and it seems the evidence is pretty overwhelming, largely due to the offshore account on Grand Cayman that Maria found. Plus, the IRS is involved because of back taxes from several odd jobs where she received a 1099 as a contractor. I have no idea what she was doing. Also, federal fraud charges are being added for the fake disability that Cansty helped her obtain. She's being moved to a federal facility in Nevada tomorrow. According to Detective Spaulding, they pretty much screwed themselves royally when they tried to scam me." Jason seemed so happy that Maddy couldn't suppress a smile at how jubilant he was.

"So, that's all the police stuff. Now for some other news. The house I'm remodeling—it finished today! One-and-a-half weeks ahead of schedule! These are some hardworking people here, and they made it happen. So, we're all celebrating on a little boat cruise tomorrow night, and I want you to be my date, Miss Sumner, if you will accompany me," he asked, holding out his hand.

She laughed as she put her hand in his and said, "It would be my pleasure to be seen on the arm of the best-looking guy in the Keys." They grinned at each other over their plates.

"So, if your job is done, will you be leaving soon too?" Maddy asked as she continued to eat her french fries, not sure if she wanted to know his answer.

"Well, right now it means that after tomorrow, the next three days are totally just me and you. We can do whatever we want, whether it's going to the beach, cruising in a boat, watching a movie, taking a nap. I don't care. I just want to be with you. Did you have a chance to think about what I asked you this morning?" Jason asked thoughtfully as he looked into her eyes.

"Yes."

"And?"

"Jason, as much as I want to stay, I can't. I have to go back home, but believe me, if circumstances were different, I would stay here with you, because that is what I truly want."

"Why can't you stay?"

"Several months ago, between me and my local doctors, I finally found a physician who specializes in my disease. It took me two months to find someone to go see, and when I called for an appointment, there was a five-month waiting list. Next week when I get home, it will be just long enough to pay bills, wash clothes, and pack again. My parents are taking me to Chicago at the end of next week, because my appointment with the specialist is the following Monday. I'm not sure how long I'll be there or what tests they will do. It could be anything...or nothing at all." She saw Jason flinch, but he didn't say a word. "You don't know how much I would just love to stay here, but I've waited too long for this appointment. One of the reasons I came to the Keys when I did was that I needed a break from everything, including doctors, to just try to get some kind of order back in my life. At least I thought that I did. And then I met you."

She looked at him tenderly. "I realized today when I was outside looking around me, absorbing all the energy I could from this place, that I've lived my life constantly planning, never truly enjoying what was in front of me or what was going on in my life. My marriage was draining. My daughter, whom I love with all my heart, was a challenge with her diabetes. And then I got my own diagnosis. But today, as I was relaxing and thinking, it occurred to me that I should just go with the flow, live in the moment, and that everything doesn't always have to be planned out. Instead of making to-do lists and rigid plans, I'm making guidelines now. This new part of me wants to stay with you and say to hell with the specialist. But I've waited this long, and she might be able to help me reclaim more of my health, whether it's through traditional or alternative medicine. I want those closest to me not to have to worry so much. And I want to be able to do things again, if possible without so many restrictions. Things I had to give up...or at least that I thought I had to. But now, being here, I realize that if I can't get all those things back, it's ok, because I'm learning how to try new things. In other words, I wanted to be normal, but

Riley in all her wisdom today told me to ask myself: What is normal? And you know what? There is no such thing.

"Jason, I truly love you. I know it's been less than four weeks since we met, but there is something in your spirit, the way you treat me and others, your caring nature, that has stolen my heart, and I will never be the same. But I can't ask you to go on my roller-coaster ride with me. I don't know what this specialist will say or what I'll have to do. You've only known me a short time, and you've seen that I've had complications and needed to rest more than other people. I know I'm going to get better, but you deserve someone now who won't limit you. If you stay with me, I'm afraid I'll be like this heavy rock you constantly have to carry, and I don't want that to lead to resentment. I want more than anything for you to be happy. You deserve it."

By this time Maddy had tears in her eyes, because even though everything she'd said was true, she didn't want to let him go. He had become so much a part of her life, but she loved him too much to put him through the uncertainties she had to deal with.

"You sure are assuming a lot, Maddy. And yes, we have only known each other a short time, but I thought you could see more in me than just a shallow person."

"I never said you were shallow, and if I came across that way, I didn't mean it!"

"Maddy, you are the most wonderful woman I've had in my life…except for my mom, and she doesn't count in this situation. You are making decisions for me instead of letting me make my own choices. If I choose to be with you, that is my decision—and that's what I want, no matter what is going on. I don't care about the fact that you have an illness. What I care about is helping you get well, seeing your loving spirit, knowing that you choose to see the good in others no matter what they've done. That you stuck with me when an evil ex-wife showed up and threatened us. And you were even willing to help me find peace in that situation and put yourself at risk to do it. That's a special person in my book. You are kind, caring, considerate, helpful, and extremely beautiful to me. You are the kind of woman I've looked for my entire life, and just because there are some bumps in the road, I'm not running away. You might try to push me away, but I'm not that easily moved. I'm here with you for the long haul, Maddy. You might as well accept that.

"And as far as past is concerned, I have my own issues. You know that, because we've talked about it. And I need help to live in the present moment too. I get wrapped up in my plans, going from one job to another, barely taking a minute for myself. Maria has been on me for months to take a vacation, and I just keep working. Running away is probably an apt description of my life, although I don't want to admit it. But facing this thing with Andrea has taught me that it's time to slow down, and I don't think it's a coincidence that you happened to rent the house across the street from me at the same time. I personally think Someone intended for us to meet so that maybe we could help each other through this maze called life."

Maddy sat across from him, tears falling down her cheeks. Tears of happiness. He still wanted to be in her life, even with all the "bumps," as he referred to them. She already knew she didn't care about his so-called baggage. She just wanted this kind, loving man sitting across from her to be a part of her life from now on.

"So, what do we do next?" Maddy asked.

Jason reached over and wiped the tears from her cheeks.

"I say we relax this evening, have fun these next couple of days, and then enjoy a nice leisurely ride back to Charleston. My motorhome and driver will meet us here Saturday morning to drive *both* of us back to Charleston. I hear the city is pretty nice?" Jason asked, his eyes smiling.

"Your driver and motorhome? You want to go back to Charleston with me?" She was shocked, but she couldn't contain the happiness she was feeling inside.

"Yes. And wouldn't you know it? I have a job already lined up about forty-five minutes away from the city that's expected to take about a year. Remodeling a plantation home back to its former glory. You want to know something? That job came across my desk two months ago. The owner practically begged me to accept it, offering me an exorbitant amount of money. It became available to me before we'd even met. So you see? I was serious when I said Someone up there thinks we should be together." Jason finished his sentence as he was getting up from the chair and pulled her to her feet. He wrapped his arms around her slender waist as she reached up to cradle his face with her hands.

"So, can I officially call you my girlfriend now? I know that sounds kind of high school, but it has a nice ring to it, don't you think?"

"Girlfriend sounds good to me!" said Maddy, and she kissed him so passionately he almost fell over backward.

"And you told me you had a motorhome but a driver too! Are you sure about this?"

"Definitely! If I'm going to be working in Charleston, I might as well get the lay of the land and find a place to stay."

"Then let's enjoy these next few days in the Keys and have fun. I have to take you parasailing for sure!" Maddy said excitedly.

"That's something we will have to talk about," Jason said with a big smile.

He drew her into a kiss so deep and full of passion that they could hardly breathe, and their happiness spread through the room and gradually engulfed the little house by the sea. They were in love, and it didn't matter what they had to face. They would be together, and that was the best thing of all.

EPILOGUE

Riley was running around like a crazy person trying to make sure everything was just right. Even though the wedding planner was supposed to be doing the work, Riley was right behind her, making doubly sure everything was perfect. Her friend deserved the best wedding, and she was going to make sure it happened.

Maddy had gotten dressed at the hotel where her family was staying. Jason had flown her parents, Hope and Shawn, Hope's best friend Abbey, his own parents, and his assistant, Maria, and her husband in for the wedding. Riley was beside herself that Maddy and Jason had decided to come back to the Keys to get married.

Of course they would come back. This was where it had all started, and so they decided this is where they wanted to begin their married life. After all, Jason had proposed to her the very next night on the party boat cruise. Everyone was singing karaoke. He got up there and sang "Marry You", dancing over to sing just to Maddy as she sat stunned in her chair. When the song was over, he asked her properly, on one knee in front of everyone, presenting her with a gorgeous ring that took her breath away. Riley was in on the surprise and had helped with the ring selection at a well-known local jewelry shop. She still advised them to take it slow, but she knew they were meant for each other. They'd even used their last day there to look at possible houses for a vacation home, something Jason had always wanted to do but had never had anyone to share it with.

When she arrived home—not by train but by motorhome—her parents were a bit shocked. They were even more surprised when they saw the ring on their daughter's finger. It was the one the secret Riley had kept from Maddy's mom, and that made Maddy proud of her. Even though Jason and Maddy were above the age of asking parents' permission for marriage, Jason was respectful enough to spend time with them, telling of his intentions and how much Maddy meant to him. They had all made the trip to Chicago for Maddy's appointment and in the process had gotten to know each other better. The way her parents saw Jason treating Maddy during her appointments and testing really made the best impression on them. They could see that this man truly loved their daughter, and it meant the world to them.

And Jason was there to hold Maddy's hand every step of the way, even when she had to have another bone-marrow biopsy. He didn't flinch and stayed with her the whole time. Through all the appointments, he was there to take care of her. When the doctor told them that Maddy's illness hadn't progressed, they were all thankful, and she would coordinate Maddy's treatment with her doctors back home. Her illness was stable and hopefully would improve, mainly—the doctor said—because of Maddy's positive attitude and her willingness to look outside the box for treatments.

When they got back to Charleston, Jason found a house on Folly Beach that was one street back from the shore itself. It was perfect for him and Maddy if she wanted to stay with him.

Even though she did stay overnight, they decided they would wait for that magical moment when they got married, which was only two months away.

And the time had passed quickly, Maddy thought as she looked at herself in the mirror. She was wearing a crocheted white lace top with a matching crocheted white skirt that came down to the middle of her calves. Her earrings were made of seashells and silver, and she wore the little sea-turtle necklace Jason had bought for her on their first trip to Key West along with the dolphin bracelet around her wrist. They were getting married on Anne's Beach, in the water where they'd taken their first swim. It was their favorite spot, and they'd visited it each day right up to the time they left the Keys several months ago. It had been a whirlwind romance, but Maddy knew in her heart that this was the man God had sent into her life as her soul mate, and she thanked Him for giving her such a wonderful gift in this loving man.

As for Jason, he felt like the luckiest man alive. When he told his parents and then Maria about his and Maddy's engagement, everyone was over the moon with excitement.

"Son, you have made us so happy. We were worried that you had just decided love didn't exist anymore," said Jason's dad.

"I have to admit, I'd thought that once I'd finished a few more jobs, I was going to retire. Then I could live on my investments, and I would try something new to work on. And maybe date once more. But then I met Maddy in the Keys, and I knew it was meant to be. She showed me things I never thought I wanted."

"That, son," Jason's mom said, "is true love."

When it came to Maria, the first words out of her mouth were: "It's about damn time. I knew this girl was special."

"Maria, you haven't even met her."

"Yes, I have," Maria said more softly. "I met her through you. Every time you talked about her, Jason, you were like a different person. I've worked with you long enough and you've never talked about a woman like you did about Maddy. So yes, I haven't met her in person, but I know her pretty well. And she is one lucky lady to have snagged you!"

"That she is!" Jason agreed, laughing.

His hardest meeting had to have been with Maddy's daughter and her husband. Jason knew immediately that Hope was protective of her mom, and she had every right to be. But Jason had a talk, just himself and Hope, reassuring her that he loved her mom more than he could say. He told Hope he had every intention of making her mom the happiest woman ever and that he loved her more than anyone would ever know. Hope hugged him and sternly told him that if he did anything to hurt her momma, he would answer to her. Then she hugged him again tightly and gave him a kiss on the cheek.

"Are you ready, Momma?" Hope asked. "Riley just called and said they're heading to the beach and that the reception area on the boat is all ready. They just need a bride and groom."

Maddy took one more look in the mirror to make sure she looked her best for her husband-to-be. This had all happened so fast, but it was all so right. Although she'd thought she would never marry again, it was happening, and the happiness radiated through every part of her.

"Momma, you look beautiful. I don't think I've ever seen you this happy, and you deserve this more than anything. I love you, and I think—I know—there is a man waiting at the beach who loves you so much that words can't describe it. It's time to go find him and make him one very happy guy." At that moment, Maddy was very thankful for the waterproof mascara she was wearing, because tears of joy welled up in her eyes as she hugged her daughter.

The ride to Anne's Beach didn't take long, and when they arrived, Maddy saw that someone, probably Riley, had marked a special spot for the bride's car. As they pulled up, everyone was already there except her and Hope. All eyes turned to her as she stepped out of the car. Her nerves were about to get the best of her until she looked to the water and saw her groom standing ankle deep in the shallows with the minister. Jason was so handsome in his white, cotton, button-down shirt and khaki shorts. He looked so calm that she immediately felt the anxiety leave her body as she concentrated on him.

When he saw her, Jason felt like someone had just taken his breath away. She was gorgeous, and she was all his. He watched her lovingly as she discarded her sandals at the water's edge and began walking toward him through the water. Before he knew it, she was standing in front of him, looking more beautiful than ever.

"Are you ready for this life together?" Jason whispered to Maddy.

"I am. How about you?"

"More than you know."

ACKNOWLEDGMENTS

This novel would not have been possible without the love and support of so many special people in my life. To my wonderful husband, Jeff: you are my rock, and I love you with all of my being. Your support and belief in me means more than I can say. To my daughter, Holly: by watching you overcome hurdles that most of us will never experience in our lives, you have taught me how to persevere under trying circumstances. As I tell everyone – your are my "Energizer Bunny". To my parents, Sonny and Irene: I feel so blessed that I was chosen to be your daughter. Your love, kindness, caring, and generosity you show not only towards me and my family but also to others is a beacon for all to live by.

There are so many others along the way who also gave me encouragement, fostered my creativity, or just let me talk things out as they listened: Autumn Bennett - thanks for giving me pointers on writing and doing some proof reading; Jeanne Harstad - thank you for all the information, answering my questions and sharing your pictures of the Florida Keys; Laura Rivers – thanks for sharing your love of the Florida Keys with me and your wonderful photography; Kendi O'Neill – thank you for the information about living in Key West and sharing your wonderful blog with everyone; Ashley Townsend – had we not had that chance encounter several years ago, I would not have known that Mast Cell Disease existed so I thank you for sharing your story with me that help put my feet on a healing path; Amy Elizabeth Nelson – thank you for your support, the information you share on Mast Cell Disease every day through your Facebook group and for your friendship.

To my online friends – The ReLaunch Group at www.there launchshow.com, my wonderful friends at www.morningcoach. com and the great writer and artists groups I'm a part of: you all are absolutely amazing and have helped me more than I can put into words to make this transition into being an author. A very special thank you goes out to my friend and fellow author – Donna Lee Gauntlett. Our weekly and now daily chat sessions helped propelled me forward in this process of writing. Thanks for being my accountability partner, but even more now, a most wonderful and encouraging friend.

Love & Hugs!
Miki
PS – To learn more about the Florida Keys, please visit www. mikibennett.com. .

NOTE FROM THE AUTHOR

To all my readers:

This is a special note from me to you. I currently live with the same rare, chronic illness that Maddy has in this novel - Mastocytosis. It is very difficult at times to try to live life as normally as possible when you have a chronic illness and sometimes even tougher when that illness is "invisible". An "invisible illness" is one in which you look perfectly fine to everyone on the outside but you deal with physical and emotional symptoms daily that can make life challenging. Mast Cell Disease can sometimes be referred to as an "invisible illness" but there are many more: Lupus, Lyme Disease, Fibromyalgia, Diabetes and the list goes on. For more information on living with "invisible illnesses" and other chronic health issues, please visit my website: www. mikibennett.com.

With much love,
Miki

Other Novels by Miki Bennett:

"The Florida Keys Novels" series:

Forever in the Keys
Run Away to the Keys
Back to the Keys
A Wedding in the Keys

"Camping in High Heels" series:

Camping in High Heels
Camping in High Heels: Las Vegas
Camping in High Heels: California

ABOUT THE AUTHOR

Miki Bennett is an author whose passions include art, the newest trends in technology and visiting the beach as much as possible. Currently, she lives in Charleston, South Carolina, with her husband Jeff and her little dog, Emma.

Made in the USA
Columbia, SC
19 August 2018